CW00570830

The Raven Faction

by

Sam Montana

All RIGHTS RESERVED. This book contains material protected under International and Federal Copyright Laws and Treaties. Any unauthorized reprint or use of this material is prohibited. No part of this book may be reproduced or transmitted in any form or by any means, electronic or mechanical, including photocopying, recording, or by any information storage and retrieval system without express written permission from the author except for the use of brief quotations in a book review.

ISBN-13: 978-0-9894614-8-1
ISBN-10: 0-9894614-8-1

Copyright 2017 Sam Montana

Newgrange Publishing
Southwick, MA. 01077-9353
npbooks.montana@gmail.com

Library of Congress Control Number: 2018947238

Authors Statement

The Raven Faction is a work of fiction. The names, characters, businesses, places, events and incidents are either the products of the author's imagination or used in a fictitious manner. Any resemblance to actual persons, alive or dead is purely coincidental.

Cover Photograph
'Killarney Ravens'
Sam Montana

For Mic

‘Don’t spill blood until the raven
has flown over.’ - Thai

One

Boston

The movement was barely perceptible when she left the bed, a slight lift to the mattress, and he opened his eyes, watched her move towards the window where she stood naked with nothing between her and the morning rush of traffic except a sheer, white veil of curtain, and she would remain as such until every face that lingered on the sidewalk below was accounted for and only then move away.

Kris Shepard took long, hot showers and at times, he would drift back to sleep and awaken within a cascade of brown hair, and the soft touch of lips upon his. Sam Bordeaux loved his work, and the way of life it allowed him to pursue but would give it all up tomorrow for the woman who had left the bed warm and the scent of Amarige on the pillow beside his head.

Sam knew in no uncertain way that he enjoyed more than his share of everything that mattered or could ever matter, and perhaps for another man would have been cause for worry. But he was never one to question fate or stare too deeply into the dark abyss of the future, and this was a critical point, as six hours later and less than a mile from where he lingered, a bullet would enter his brain from a gun neither heard nor seen.

*****

Kris Shepard's first encounter with Sam occurred at the FBI Academy in Quantico, Virginia. As a recruit, Kris was required to complete the high intensity training program, which ranged from constitutional law and ethics to firearms, tactical vehicle operation and survival skills. Although, the training regimen designed for the young woman from South Dakota included a unique caveat.

Kris was exposed to a constant flow of people throughout the twenty one weeks of basic training, and unlike her fellow recruits would be expected to remember and indeed challenged to later identify individuals from these fleeting encounters by way of still shots, grainy videos and pixelated images of low resolution and closely cropped faces without visible hair or identifying marks of any type. Some would be in profile or wearing a hood, and others she had never laid eyes on, and this was when she noticed Sam for the second time.

Sam was the crew leader of a newly formed unit of FBI counter terrorism investigators working out of One Center Plaza in Boston. The crew consisted of eight members who were mainly digital media exploitation and forensics experts with foreign language skills including Russian, Arabic, French and Spanish. They reported directly to Jack O'Malley, the Special Agent in Charge.

After twenty-one weeks in Quantico, Kris proved beyond a doubt that she possessed the physical and mental capacity to go into the field as a Special Agent. The question of whether she belonged in the company of O'Malley's crew was another matter entirely. Scepticism was a fundamental commodity within a crew who poked and probed everyone and anything that entered their space whether in the flesh or bundled in metadata, and Kris fell way beyond their remit.

The woman was an artist with no background in mathematics or computer science, although the concept of her unique abilities was intriguing and the subject of intense curiosity when she reported for duty at One Center Plaza in Boston.

Following the customary round of introductions, Professor John Davis, a principal academic of Harvard's Department of Psychology sat down with Kris in an interrogation room and administered a test from his laptop. Her performance on the exam was transmitted live to Quantico for the benefit of the division chiefs while O'Malley's crew observed the proceedings from their conference room.

Kris's task was to identify or discount as many individuals as possible from those encountered during her basic training, including members of O'Malley's crew who made brief appearances at various points. If expectations were correct, she would do so without error in a timely fashion, which came down to a matter of seconds for each face flashed across the screen.

Without hesitation, Kris began to identify the crew members, and didn't matter the context or blatant attempts to disguise their identities. Her impromptu performance was flawless and exceeded even Professor Davis's expectations. In the immediate aftermath, there wasn't a sound to be heard out of Quantico or around the conference table until O'Malley broke the spell with a simple, 'Thanks John. That'll do.'

It was O'Malley who initially presented the idea at Quantico of a special unit built around what Professor Davis had come to term, a super recognizer, and the concept was immediately challenged and in equal parts denied relevance. If not for Davis's earlier work with a farsighted Scotland Yard, the proposal would have been dead on arrival.

Davis's research program at Harvard University probed the cause and effects of 'face-blindness,' or prosopagnosia. A condition marked by the inability to recognize even the most familiar of faces including the one staring back in the mirror.

Quite unexpectedly, the research revealed face blindness to be on a spectrum, which also ran in the opposite direction for a minute segment of the general population. For Davis, the existence of a subset of 'super recognizers', with exceptional abilities for facial recognition was a startling outcome and shifted the entire focus of his research.

After the results of his work were formally published the topic became a widely debated, but short lived source of interest within academia. Although, the practical implications of super recognizers didn't escape the attention of Harry Woodbridge, the technical guru and head of surveillance at Scotland Yard.

Woodbridge was charged with identifying the looters from the 2011 London riots and offered Professor Davis the opportunity to collaborate on the project. Davis quickly accepted and spent six weeks in London certifying a handful of super recognizers from within the ranks of Scotland Yard.

Out of two hundred thousand hours of CCTV footage of the riots, the computerized facial recognition systems only managed to identify one individual. At the end of the first week on duty, a single super recognizer from the team Davis's assembled had positively identified one hundred and ninety individuals from the sketchy footage of the riots. The cat had been thrown in with the pigeons and there would be no turning back.

It was during his sojourn at Scotland Yard that Davis made another interesting observation, which suggested that when artistic and facial recognition abilities were conjoined, the combination could lead to a high performing individual. His follow up research at Harvard confirmed the theory and sent him down the path towards Kris Shepard.

Two years later and nearly to the day Kris first laid eyes on Professor Davis in Cambridge, she heard the shot that took off the back of Sam's head and felt the pain and intense fear stab through her entire being, as they both tumbled to the floor.

Kris struggled to shake off the punch and burn of hot metal from the bullet that grazed her head on its way to Sam. The blood streaming down into her eyes, as she reached for him across the filthy floor of an abandoned building. Her voice mute then suddenly piercing when she called his name. A pool of blood spreading between them. The vague sound of gunfire and O'Malley lifting her away is all that remains of that moment.

Sam Bordeaux was buried in the family plot at Baton Rouge, Louisiana. Kris remained confined to Massachusetts General Hospital for three weeks following the shooting. Afterwards, she didn't have the slightest inclination to visit his grave, and perhaps never would.

Two

Boston

From the beginning, Professor John Davis was more than a psychologist in matters relating to Kris Shepard, and his interest went beyond the clinical or fascination he held for her unusual abilities. They genuinely enjoyed each other's company though separated by more than two decades.

Initially, it was mutual curiosity, which formed the basis of their relationship. Davis was scouring the Boston artistic community for participants in his expanded facial recognition research at Harvard, and Kris was a gift of the Boston Regional News by way of a two page article featuring her work as a stone sculptor. The lead in for the article immediately captured his attention with its bold lettered pronouncement, 'Human faces are carved in surprising ways into Shepard's work, suggesting the threads that connect myth, past and present, and even forces of nature.'

There was no way he was not going to interview the young, Ms. Shepard and thanks to the newspaper article, she wasn't hard to find. Kris worked out of a studio on the outskirts of Provincetown and lived in Cambridge for the balance of the year while pursuing a Master of Arts degree at Boston College.

At the time of their first meeting in early February of 2012, Kris was in the final year of the program at Boston College and teaching art classes a few evenings a week. She really didn't know what to make of Davis when he first approached her during one of her stone carving workshops at the Worcester Art Museum. For one thing, she had thirteen novice stone carvers all wanting and indeed needing her attention. She reluctantly agreed to speak to Davis following the workshop and hoped he would tire of the wait and simply disappear. Instead, he retreated to the balcony overlooking the multilevel sculpture studio and slowly became mesmerized by what transpired on the floor of the studio during the course of the evening.

Kris's manner of teaching was hands on, and she led by example with a hammer and chisel. Moving swiftly from student to student, she directed the creation of life sized faces emerging from within blocks of white marble.

The works held a striking realism and Davis noted that afterwards participants of the workshop assumed creative ownership of the work. Such was the beauty of Kris Shepard's approach coupled with the delicate and inherently narcissistic nature of the artistic ego, and he held little doubt they would all return for more of the same.

Kris was not what he expected given the black and white grainy image reproduced in the newspaper. She was tall and moved with the smooth, easy bearing of the Celtic women he had come to associate with South Boston. Her long, brown hair was tied in a ponytail that stretched halfway down her back accentuating a slender neck, which rose to the sharp undercut of her jawline and angular cheekbones set high and muted by striking blue eyes.

‘Sorry.’ Kris held out her hand and spoke with a raspy voice, which invariably followed an intense bout of stone carving.

‘No apologies necessary.’ Davis took her hand and was suddenly aware of the softness of his own. ‘I enjoyed watching you work.’

‘Thank you. You’re a very patient man. Perhaps you’d like to join us sometime?’

‘Actually, I’m among the few who truly possess no discernible talent for art.’

‘Better yet.’ Kris smiled. ‘What is it you’d like to speak to me about Professor?’

‘Please, call me John.’ Kris nodded, and he continued. ‘I’m conducting a research project that deals with prosopagnosia, a form of facc blindness, that prevents individuals from recognizing familiar faces, which includes close family members, and even their own image.’

‘That sounds horrible.’

‘It is, of course, and what brings me here is something I stumbled across in my early research, which is the existence of individuals with an exceptional ability to recall faces. It became obvious that the presence of artistic talent magnifies the facial recognition skills and is the current focus of my research.’

‘I see.’ Kris started to wipe down her stone carving tools. Placing each one carefully in a special cloth satchel.

‘I found the newspaper article about your work intriguing and took it upon myself to contact you. I’m hoping to gain your participation in the research program.’ Davis continued.

‘To be honest, I found the article embarrassing, and that the reporter took more than a few liberties with his descriptions of my work.’ Kris rolled the tool satchel and tied it together with a strip of worn leather then placed it in her backpack.

‘Perhaps it all comes down to interpretation, but it wasn’t the text that drew my attention, but rather the images of your work. They speak for themselves.’

‘And on that basis, you assume I’m a likely candidate for your research project?’

‘I suppose you could say that. I felt it at least warranted approaching you on the subject, and that was before I watched you bring about thirteen faces in stone over the course of three hours without the benefit of a model.’ Davis paused. ‘I’d like you to consider taking a series of tests that I created to sort out individuals with exceptional skills. It’s a worthy project, Kris.’

‘I’m sure it is, although, not something I care to be involved with at this time. But leave it with me for a while and I’ll get back to you, if I change my mind. Is that OK?’ Kris offered more as statement than question.

‘Certainly.’ An awkward silence followed Davis’s obvious disappointment, but he nodded agreement and turned back to the steep, metal staircase leading up to the main floor of the museum. ‘I hope to hear from you.’ He continued up the staircase, pausing at the top, and they held eye contact for a moment before he walked away.

For weeks afterwards, Kris did her best not to dwell on John Davis or his unusual request and for the most part succeeded. Daily life was absorbed by her work and studies at Boston College, and she intended to keep it that way. It was a matter of focus, which she guarded jealously and few managed to get past her defences.

At times, Kris was considered shy, reclusive or even anti-social. None of which applied. Her desire and need to be alone within the confines of her own space occurred on a subconscious level, void of premeditation, anxiety or a hint of animosity, and she had long since ceased apologising to those who took it upon themselves to be offended, and in spite of a lingering sense of trepidation, she decided to place the call to John Davis.

Kris was among the first group of artists to undertake the battery of tests Davis designed to evaluate the extent of individual powers of facial recognition and proceeded to take the results far beyond Davis's comfort level, and he worried the outcome represented a flaw within the testing protocol, and later that it didn't.

Funding for the research had increased dramatically in the wake of the unprecedented success of the Scotland Yard project, and it became obvious to Davis that his operating budget far exceeded what could be expected from the largess of the university alone, and it was safe to assume government involvement at some level.

Experience dictated that within reasonable and ethical parameters, the mechanics of how and from whom funding was appropriated was not something one questioned, as long as the monies continued to flow. Perhaps, if he had been less consumed by the accelerating pace of the project, things might have been different, and more attention paid when the projects computer system was upgraded by a generic group of technicians assigned by the university, who spoke little and worked quickly.

To be summoned to the Provost's office during the annual rounds of funding allocations was not unusual, to find the outer office void of staff offered a reason to pause. The door to the Provost's office was wide open, and Davis remained still trying to absorb the strange circumstances, a few moments later the sound of drapes being drawn moved him towards the open door. He entered the outsized office of the Provost cautiously, as in knowing he didn't belong there, and it was then he noticed a casually dressed man standing at the window.

O'Malley heard the Professor enter the room, but kept his back to him for a minute, which felt much longer from where Davis was standing. When he did turn, Davis, spoke first. 'Can I help you?' Delivered as though it was his space they occupied, which only served to deepen his level of discomfort with the odd situation.

'I certainly hope so, Professor Davis.'

'And you are?'

The man had closed the distance between them far quicker than Davis would have expected and offered his hand. 'Jack O'Malley.'

He passed on the handshake. 'I have a meeting in this office with the Provost. I don't suppose you would know where I might locate him, Mr. O'Malley?'

'The Provost has stepped out and generously allowed me the use of his office.'

'And he took his entire staff along?'

'One might say that, Professor Davis. But I won't insult your intelligence. Please, have a seat and I'll explain my reasons for being here.' O'Malley gestured towards the antique armchairs next to the fireplace, which was not an area Davis would normally expect to occupy.

'After you.' Davis could feel his confusion evaporating with each step and by the time they sat facing each other had just one question. 'CIA or FBI?'

O'Malley had removed his brown leather jacket and scarf. Placed both on the sofa near his chair and sat adjusting himself in a seat much softer than he was accustomed. 'FBI.' He finally answered.

'You have a badge, Mr. O'Malley?'

'I don't carry a badge, Professor.' O'Malley looked straight into Davis's eyes when he spoke. The direct, and steady tone of his words offered Davis more insight than if he had actually produced a badge, but still he persisted.

'I find that highly unusual, Mr. O'Malley.'

'And you should.' O'Malley smiled slightly. 'Call me, Jack, if you don't mind.'

'Tell me, Jack. Is that your real name?'

‘Yes.’

‘Perhaps now would be a good time to explain what this is all about.’

‘I’m here because the Agency has an interest in your research concerning super recognizers.’

‘I’d say you must, if you’re funding the program to a level that compels the Provost to relinquish his office. Or would that be programs?’

‘We do whatever we can to assist research that coincides with our national interests. The work you’re doing is compelling and obviously has wide implications.’

‘I’m honored. But tell me, what exactly is it you hope to gain from your investment, and why not simply knock on my office door, if you wanted to have a chat?’

‘Your cooperation obviously, and I know you’re not as naïve as that question suggests?’

‘You seem to know quite a bit about me.’

‘I know you spent five years in the army with two tours of Iraq served with distinction and then followed up with a PhD. in psychology.’

‘And yourself.’

‘Perhaps another time.’ O’Malley paused. ‘Right now, I’d like to hear your thoughts on collaborating with the FBI counter terrorism division here in Boston?’

‘Was that your crew who installed the upgrade on my computer system?’ Davis could feel his blood pressure starting to rise.

‘That’s right.’

‘And my phone, as well?’

‘One should assume that we are thorough, Professor.’

‘Call me, John, and to answer your question, I do have an interest in working with the FBI. For no reason beyond the fact that I can’t control your access to my work.’

‘There is a certain level of discretion that we feel obligated to pursue, but perhaps in your case this wasn’t the best approach. I appreciate your willingness to cooperate and we’ll do everything we can to make you comfortable with the arrangement.’

‘Fine, now I have work to do.’ Davis started to get up to leave.

‘Tell me about Kris Shepard.’

Davis sat back down. ‘You mean something you don’t already know?’

‘How comfortable are you with her test results?’

‘If you’re wondering if she’s for real. She is.’

‘I would like to meet her. Can you arrange it?’

‘I could. But I won’t’

‘Why would that be, John.’

'Because I don't intend to become a recruitment agent for you or anyone else, and I'm sure you know where to find her.'

'Alright, I'd say were done here.' O'Malley stood up, put on his scarf and threw the leather jacket over his shoulder. 'I won't keep you from your work any further. But I do want access to any written notes you've complied to date in relation to Kris Shepard.'

'I'll need some time.'

'Not a problem, John.' O'Malley placed his card on the table in front of Davis. 'By the end of the day will be fine.'

Three

Provincetown

Having completed her studies at Boston College, Kris was finally free to return to Provincetown and a long delayed body of work in progress, promised to a gallery on the Island of Nantucket, two years earlier.

Nantucket was a special place for Kris and before deciding on the move to Provincetown, she had toyed with the idea of setting up a studio on the wharf next to David Hostetler, who was one of the few sculptors she ever turned to for advice or inspiration. Provincetown was the easier commute, although with no longer being tethered to Boston College, the thought was intriguing once again.

It would take a few days to acclimate herself to being back in the studio. A sense of irretrievable loss always accompanied a prolonged absence from her work. Over the years, she had become acutely aware that each time she picked up the hammer and chisel became a one off encounter with the stone and what she created was unique to the day, to the hour and the moment itself. The work lived or died in the present, which was fine with Kris. It was the lost moments that hurt and knowing that whatever inner source moved the chisel across the stone, adhered to that same harsh reality.

She needed time to shake off the feelings of what could have been before revisiting the works in progress, which was purely a matter of immersion. Initially, more time was spent walking the beach at Race Point or along the Province Lands Trail with an occasional foray back to the studio. Slowly, the studio visits would intensify until remaining became the only option, and then nothing else mattered.

Two weeks after she arrived, Jack O'Malley spent his first evening in Provincetown at the Lobster Pot restaurant followed by a bottle of red in the Harbor Lounge. He would make his initial contact with the solitary and notably private young artist the following afternoon.

During the time that elapsed since she moved to the top of the list of potential super recognizers to recruit, O'Malley's team had investigated her background in South Dakota, Massachusetts and Ireland, where her mother was born in Galway on the Island of Inis Meain. They also ran checks on her immediate family, colleagues, professors and even some of her stone carving students were scrutinized. No close friends where known to exist.

Davis proved to be of little help filling in the blanks concerning the young woman and it was what he didn't say that worried O'Malley the most. Her routine of jogging at dawn and dusk each day was remotely monitored, along with the places she visited, the store where she bought her groceries and every click of the mouse or swipe across her iPad found an echo at One Center Plaza in Boston, a few doors down the hall from his office.

The primary decision of whether to pursue Kris required every member of O'Malley's crew to weigh in with their opinion, and only then did he take the Shepard dossier to New Hampshire for a weekend. The extensive fieldwork bestowed a heft upon the dossier, which defied the limited chronology of the young woman from South Dakota and certainly provided enough raw material to make a final assessment based on more than his gut instinct, although that would eventually prevail.

For nearly twenty years, O'Malley lived out of a suitcase as a roving, FBI Special Agent and the transient lifestyle agreed with the man. The only semblance of domestication he conceded was the small, wood framed cottage tucked into a cove on the western shore of Newfound Lake in Bristol, New Hampshire.

His parents had invested their life savings into a defunct, waterfront restaurant on the lake during the early nineteen eighties. They reopened it as a deli serving hot dogs and burgers along with sundaes heaped with whipped cream and nuts across an old fashioned ice cream bar lined with wooden backed stools. A small, rough-hewed waterfront cottage was part of the package.

His mother ran the deli from spring to fall while his father remained in South Boston delivering mail. Jack was barely old enough to help behind the counter, but too old to leave on the loose in the neighborhood over the long, hot summer vacations away from South Boston Catholic Academy.

Whether or not the summer diversions proved to be a financial success was a moot point, as far as his parents were concerned. A fact appreciated more in retrospect whenever he sat lakeside with his feet propped up on the porch railing or with a fire blazing in the woodstove, on a cold night in February.

The cottage was originally a three season affair with no insulation and an antiquated wood stove to push back against the perpetual chill of the White Mountains. Each evening at sunset, and even during the peak of summer, the scent of wood smoke hung in the air and held a special place in his earliest memories.

The kitchen was White Mountain functional and hot water wasn't included on the early list of amenities. Bathing took place either in the lake or out of the large, tin sink in the kitchen with uninterrupted views of a stand of old growth sugar maples through the back window of the cottage.

His parents spent six months a year living in the cottage after his father retired from the post office. At one point, Jack offered to have a contractor winterize the place, so they could get out of South Boston for longer periods, but his father would have none of it, and Jack never pushed the issue, nor expected a different reaction.

Sean O'Malley was never too long or far afield before a dash of melancholy would appear in his eyes. The shoulders would sag that little bit, which makes all the difference and Jack's mother would pack a bag, and even during the most sweat inducing heights of summer, the old boy would trek back to South Boston, like a trail weary beagle too long on a rabbit.

After his father passed away, Jack had the cottage insulated and updated for his mother with a new kitchen and indoor plumbing, although she found it difficult being there without his father and rarely spent more than a few days. Towards the end she lost interest altogether.

That first evening, Jack had barely settled into one of the chairs beside the fire when there was a familiar racket at the back door of the cottage. In a matter of seconds, Murphy O'Shea had placed his furry head on Jack's lap with his tail completely out of control. Murphy reverted to a puppy whenever he was around Jack and was always over the top with enthusiasm. A whine would be followed by a series of sharp barks and Murphy would shake and shiver until Jack pulled the dog up on his lap.

Murphy lived with the O'Shea's, a year round family who built a massive home on the opposite side of the cove. The tiny, English setter with one black ear had bonded with Jack over the years and shows up at the cottage whenever he senses Jack's presence.

Once the dog settled down Jack eased him from his lap and closed the back door. The lever action of the door was something Murphy learned to manipulate as soon as he was tall enough to reach the handle, and the door was always left unlocked for the little man.

His last visit with Murphy was the previous fall when he had stuffed a bottle of water into his backpack, and together they took a well-worn path leading away from the back door of the cottage and followed it through the stand of sugar maples to the trailhead for Nelson's Mountain.

The bald, granite peak of the mountain was their preferred destination since Murphy was old enough to make the trek. Jack enjoyed watching him run through the forest and invariably the dog wandered away on a scent trail only to come dashing past in a blur on his way to the peak.

For Murphy, the outings were a source of endless fascination with the sounds of the forest and a menagerie of scents to be discovered. An acute bout of indignation would kick in whenever he encountered the scent of another dog, the audacity of such an act beyond his comprehension. Jack brought along a lead for the rare occasions when they happened upon one of Murphy's nemesis on the trail.

Arriving at the summit that day, Jack spent the better part of an hour sitting on a large granite boulder in the shape of a bench. The eons old boulder had been tumbled, polished and deposited on top of the mountain by the same retreating glacier that had scoured the landscape and formed the lake below.

With the sun on his back and the crisp mountain air infused with the scent of pine he had sat looking down upon Newfound Lake shimmering in the afternoon sun. The White Mountains lay jagged and inviting on the horizon and he had promised himself to make another trek up Mount Washington, and no excuses this time around.

A text message brought him back to the moment. The three word message was hardly unwelcome. 'Dinner tomorrow tonight?'

'I'll bring the wine.' He responded.

'Of course, you will. How's seven thirty?'

'Perfect. Be nice to see you again.'

'Been missing you too and tell Murphy I said goodnight.'

'Will do.'

Marie O'Shea lost her husband, James, to cancer four years after they moved into the lake house. The youngest of her four sons had recently entered college, and Marie for the first time found herself alone within the rambling and isolated home.

Marie and Jack became close in the aftermath of the death of her husband. The basis of the relationship was purely platonic, a coincidence of time and place, as is often the way of such things. Jack had lost his seven year old son, Patrick, to a school bus accident, three years earlier and shortly thereafter he and his wife divorced.

The next morning, he was up early with Murphy and they took a walk onto the ice. The lake was dotted with bob houses, the small ice fishing shanties of various and often dubious construction. Most contain a single window allowing a view to the tip ups, and the spring loaded, sudden jolt of a tiny red flag, which brings the intrepid anglers out of the shanties in a rush to claim their prize in the form of legendary lake trout that inhabit the lake, and populate their fantasies throughout the summer. Murphy took every opportunity to piss on the odd structures.

After breakfast, he went out behind the cottage to the woodpile exposed by the recent thaw, an event that rarely lingered but a few days. The morning was bright, crisp and there was no place he would rather be with the axe in his hand and Murphy nearby watching his every move. If a perfect world existed, this was as close as he would come and having Murphy along made all things right

He split enough wood to satisfy the woodstove for a few days and grabbed an armful for the wood box. Murphy ran ahead and when he reached the back door flailed the door handle with both paws until it opened, and Jack followed him into the cottage. He loaded the wood box and put another log on the fire while Murphy enjoyed the treat sniffed out from under the rug in front of the woodstove. After a shower, Jack put on another pot of coffee and settled into the armchair beside the fire and opened the Shepard dossier. The initial background material concerned her birth father, Tom Shepard.

The man worked as a train engineer out of the rail yard at Selkirk, New York, and ran freight to and from Boston. Jack was not unfamiliar with the life of a railroad man, the per capita in South Boston was heavily weighted with men who either rode the rails or worked the switching yards that radiated from with the heart of South Station.

A few guys on his block had fathers who worked the road freight for years and they hardly knew the men. The hours were brutal, and the four man crews regularly spent up to twelve hours going one way with an eight hour layover waiting for them at the end of the track. The crews then stared down another twelve hours on the return trip followed by a night at home, and then back at it again.

Much of the time on the road was spent waiting somewhere along the main line for freight to be picked up or sorted by the yard crews or simply waiting for a train further down the track doing the same thing. The passenger trains also brought the entire works to a standstill. The swaying motion of moving boxcars too dangerous a risk in the passing and resulted in even more idle hours being added to an already slow and tedious journey.

The money was good, but the boredom weighed heavily and extracted a toll upon those with a natural proclivity towards drink and even those without were sorely tempted by the alcohol or the drugs embedded into the road trips.

More than a few of the men and they were all men, had one or more girlfriends in villages along the rail line from the Berkshires to Boston. The more industrious maintained shadow families on either end of the tracks, which became a study in perpetual motion.

Anne Joyce fit nicely into the away category, until Tom Shepard transferred to Boston and made their relationship official. Anne wouldn't be one to raise the question of his former existence in Selkirk and the need for answers never occurred to her until it was too late. Her grandfather, Padraig Joyce and three of her uncles worked at South Station in Boston, as train inspectors within a long held and hard fought Boston Irish tradition. Uncle Francie was the one who introduced her to the young Tom Shepard and regrets it to this very day.

The story line of the Joyce family in America was not unlike the scores who preceded them through Ellis Island. The Irish patriarch immigrates to work on the railroad or to join the police or fire brigade and imports as many willing family members, as possible. In 1959, there remained no shortage of the willing.

Jack could envision Padraig Joyce, a Galway man meeting Kris's grandmother, Maire Conneely of the Aran Islands at the Saturday night dance in the Irish Social Club of Roxbury. The attraction the Irish diaspora held for each other was the only remedy to overcoming their innate shyness. They revelled in the comfort that only the truly displaced can offer one another. Padraig and Marie were married May 3, 1962 and Anne Maire Joyce was born on November 15, 1963, a week before America had her heart fully and irreparably broken in Dallas, Texas.

Twenty two years later in the spring of 1985, Padraig Joyce dropped dead in Union Station of a massive heart attack. At the time, Anne was in her final semester at Boston College and after her daughter graduated, the heart sick Maire retreated to Inis Meain and remained on the island for the rest of her life.

The following June of 1986, Anne Marie Joyce and Thomas Anthony Shepard were married in the Church of Our Lady and St John at Inis Meain. The newlyweds spent a month wandering about Ireland with the last week in Dublin becoming the high water mark before Tom Shepard became a truly vicious work-in-progress.

Extended bouts of drinking accompanied by physical and mental abuse became more and more frequent. The only relief for Anne was when Tom left for a road trip, only to have him come back angrier than when he left. There was an element of hope when she became pregnant. Surely, a child would bring peace and joy back to their lives and expel the demons that had stolen her man.

Kris Shepard was born on August 12, 1987. In less than six months, the abuse started to turn towards the baby and Anne arrived at the tilting point. The last time Tom saw his daughter, Anne was carrying her down the front stairs of their apartment flanked by an uncle and two cousins. The rumor around South Boston was that the cousins honored Shepard with their presence again the following week, as soon as the wheels of the plane carrying Anne and Kris cleared the runway bound for Shannon Airport.

Anne brought the baby to Inis Meain beyond the reach of her soon to be ex-husband. She returned to Boston a few months later by herself and filed for divorce and the sole custody of Kris, which Tom Shepard didn't dare contest.

In the spring of 1988, Anne accepted a position with Mount Rushmore National Park in the Black Hills of South Dakota. The baby was to remain with Maire on Inis Meain until Anne had the opportunity to establish herself within the Park Service, as an Interpretive Ranger. Kris would take her first steps on Inis Meain.

In South Dakota, Anne rose quickly through the Mount Rushmore hierarchy on the strength of her teaching credentials and a laser like focus on her career. The first year she lived in staff housing on a cul-de-sac, halfway up Mount Rushmore from the village of Keystone, a narrow cluster of hotels, restaurants and tourist shops tucked into a gorge at the base of the mountain.

A year later, Anne remained the last person standing following an intense bout of infighting for the vacant position of Director of Education. She moved out of the one bedroom apartment into a cabin on the edge of Custer State Park.

In October of 1991, Anne married Dan Walker, a colleague and Chief of Interpretation at Mount Rushmore. Walker was born into the Blackfoot tribe of Northwest Montana and at six foot seven inches, the man was an imposing figure who became a gentle and stable presence in the lives of both Anne and the recently reunited, four year old Kris.

Three years later Tom Shepard died of complications brought on by unwavering devotion to the bottle and in May of 2001, Maire Conneely Joyce broke more than a few hearts by joining her beloved Padraig, in the cemetery on a knoll beside the sea at Inis Meain.

Jack spent the rest of that afternoon with the dossier on his lap, and finding no cause to remove Kris Shepard as his lead candidate for recruitment, loaded the woodstove and joined Marie O'Shea for dinner and an evening of conversation, which stretched further into the night than intended.

The following morning, he walked Murphy halfway across the cove where they parted company. He watched the dog run off across the ice towards home, pausing once to look back and Jack waved him off again. By noon he was back at One Center Place in Boston.

Four

Provincetown

Kris Shepard' studio in Provincetown was a large, open space connected on one end to a utility area containing an antiquated refrigerator that groaned more effectively than it chilled the few items consisting mainly of leftover pizza and bottled water.

A door on the other side of the utility room opened to another studio, which mirrored her own and belonged to Tyler Frank, a painter from Austin, Texas who spent his summers working in Provincetown and retreated to Austin with the first frost.

Tyler was seventy two years old and owned the building most of his adult life at the bequeath of Margaret Chang, a great aunt he met once, when she returned to Austin for the funeral of her beloved niece and Tyler's mother.

Margaret was a woman of mythical proportions within Provincetown society. A poet, who had commiserated with and encouraged a series of writers and artists including Eugene O'Neil, a struggling young writer at the time, living in a ramshackle, mice infested dune shack on the edge of Provincetown, harboring a trunk full of unproduced plays.

Margaret' husband owned a small fleet of fishing vessels, which never left Provincetown Harbor without him aboard one or the other. In his absence, Margaret devoted her time and ample resources to nurturing a generation of artists with legendary results, a legacy Tyler continues in his own limited way through the person of Kris Shepard.

Their adjoining studios form a horseshoe shaped compound, that in its day served as headquarters for the Chang Seafood Company. The gabled ends of both studios contain a bank of windows facing the harbor. A cluster of grey, weathered and barnacled wooden uprights stretch defiantly into the bay from the shoreline below the studios, the free standing skeletal remains of what was once Chang fishing piers, number three and four.

Kris lived above the studio in an apartment that overlooked Commercial Street and rambled the length of the building to the edge of the harbor. The furnishings were sparse and dated from the seventies when Tyler took possession of the property. He originally planned to live there himself, but chose instead to take up residence on the edge of town in the home formally occupied by Margaret Chang. The small, colorful Victorian held a view over Provincetown Harbor and Cape Cod Bay that Tyler found irresistible.

They met the summer following Kris' move from South Dakota to attend Boston College. Tyler attended a stone carving workshop she conducted at the Provincetown Art Association and they bonded almost immediately, which was not something either of them normally experienced. It wasn't long afterwards that Tyler took it upon himself to assume the role of mentor, although not in a purely artistic sense, but rather as a navigator of the rough and tumble competitive Boston artist community.

Tyler' family history in the oil fields of Texas combined with Margaret Chang' extensive real estate portfolio in Provincetown allowed him the financial independence to remain above the fray. As a well-known donor to art related causes, he was less than shy about exerting his influence or applying a not so subtle and thoroughly effective form of coercion on Kris' behalf. Tyler brought her work to the attention of critics, journalists and curators, which opened doors normally considered off limits to a young, blowin from the Midwest, regardless of talent.

Kris neither encouraged nor discouraged Tyler' efforts, which further convinced him of the need to do so. Her total lack of interest in self-promotion he found both frustrating and intriguing, although, his reticence to actively market his own work, was in his opinion another matter entirely. A point Kris was forced to raise when his efforts moved beyond her comfort zone.

Tyler defended his position as one of an established artist, and who didn't give a damn if his work ever sold, although the statement was mute, as his work was highly collectable and much anticipated well beyond the confines of Provincetown.

The thing about Tyler was she truly liked the man. They communicated in ways that defied their enormous age difference and the ease of being in his company was not something she experienced with many people. His irreverent sense of humor was refreshing and the intensity and focus he brought to the work she thoroughly understood.

They eventually arrived at a place where mutual interests and a deepening friendship replaced Tyler' overbearing attempts at patronage. Kris found herself drawn in by the live and let live atmosphere of Provincetown and the occasional weekends during semesters at Boston College started to run together in the summers, until leaving felt stranger than not. After graduation, Tyler reluctantly agreed to Kris' stipulations concerning a lease on the studio and apartment. He understood Kris' need to pay her own way, at least in theory and that worked for both of them.

In summer, the two artists occasionally worked together within the spacious alcove between the separate wings of the studios. Tyler installed a large cabana to provide shade, more for Kris's benefit than his own. She prefers to work in the open air, out of direct sunlight while Tyler ventures into the space only on the warmest of days, a Texan to the core.

It was not unusual that O'Malley's repeated knocks on the studio door went unanswered, but his persistence was, and broke the code of etiquette within the artist community that traditionally placed high value on the right to remain sequestered and undisturbed by outside influences within the confines of the studio.

Not to be deterred, O'Malley walked the length of the building along Commercial Street and turned down a narrow slipway leading out to the harbor. The back portion of the studio rested on wooden pillars and the high tide had ebbed under the building, forcing O'Malley to bend slightly and walk across the wet sands between barnacle encrusted pillars towards the secluded alcove.

Intensely focused on carving a block of white marble, Kris didn't notice his approach, and it wasn't until O'Malley was standing a few yards away and spoke her name that she looked up from the work. Perplexed by the intrusion, her first reaction was to stare at him for a moment before dismissing him as a tourist.

'Sorry. The studios are closed.' She returned her attention to the block of marble.

'Actually, I'm here to see you, Ms. Shepard.'

She looked up again. 'And you are?'

'Jack O'Malley, I'm with the counter terrorism unit of the FBI in Boston. Sorry for the intrusion.'

'Is there something I can do for you, Mr. O'Malley?'

'I certainly hope so. The Agency is collaborating with Professor John Davis in relation to his ongoing super recognizer research.'

'I didn't realize John worked with the government.'

'It's a recent development. May I get right to the point, Ms. Shepard.'

'Please do. And Kris is fine.' She put down the hammer and chisel, removed her safety glasses and took a drink from a bottle of water on the carving stand.

'The results of the super recognizer evaluation you participated in with Professor Davis were more than impressive.' Jack moved in a little closer. 'I've been assigned the job of forming an elite task force within the FBI based on exactly those abilities.' He paused. 'Our objective is to identify suspects before they have an opportunity to organize or initiate acts of terror. Professor Davis' work clearly demonstrates the impact of someone with your abilities in achieving that goal, and the reason I'm here today is that we need your help.'

Kris looked at O'Malley in silence long enough to make him wonder if she understood what he said then finally spoke. 'I don't know how much Professor Davis may have told you about me, as you see, I have a rather full life, one that I enjoy very much. And to be perfectly honest with you, I'm not someone you might consider a team player in the most basic sense of the word. It simply wouldn't work, even if I did have an interest, which I don't.' Kris picked up her safety glasses and slipped them over her head. 'I'm sorry Mr. O'Malley. Your time would be better served elsewhere.'

'Call me Jack.' He watched her pick up the hammer and chisel. 'In way of disclosure, Kris, you have already been vetted by my team.'

'You investigated me?' She put the hammer and chisel down again.

'I wouldn't be here otherwise.'

'I see.' She walked around the carving stand moving closer to him and spoke in a soft, even tone. 'In that case, I'll assume you're aware that my stepfather, Dan Walker, before becoming Chief of Interpretation at Mount Rushmore spent his early career in law enforcement for the Park Service.'

'Yes, we're fully aware of Dan's background.'

‘Of course.’ Kris continued. ‘I only mention this because having lived with Dan, allowed me to realize how much he and others like yourself are willing to relinquish to ensure that the rest of us can simply go about our lives in peace. I have nothing but respect for the work you do. But trust me, I would be of no value either to you or myself, if I accepted such an arrangement.’

‘You know Kris, when you’ve been at this for any length of time, one develops a gut feeling for the character of the person standing in front of you.’ Jack paused. ‘And one thing we both know beyond a doubt is that the unique skills you possess are found in few other people. Skills that could mean the difference between life and death.’

Kris held his gaze and after another long moment returned to her hammer and chisel. ‘I do appreciate your coming here today and it’s been nice meeting you, but the answer is still no.’

Jack’s impulse was to push it further, but instead he held back and opted to simply place his card on the carving stand. ‘Call me, if you change your mind or want to talk about anything.’

Kris looked up and smiled. Jack went back the way he came without knowing whether or not she picked up the card.

Less than a month after his visit to Provincetown, Jack was informed that Professor John Davis had jumped ship and relocated his research program to Paris, by invitation of the French government. The man was no stranger to France having lived and studied in Paris for many years. His mother and first wife were born there, and the issue of his dual

American and French citizenship had been a cause of concern for O'Malley, and there was little conciliation in knowing the professor walked away from Harvard with an empty briefcase.

The few certified super recognizers from the research program that Davis submitted to O'Malley had failed to meet the Agency's basic requirements for one reason or another that ranged from a history of drug abuse to domestic violence. An outcome, which in retrospect appeared to be a knowing and deliberate act by the professor. Kris Shepard was the only viable candidate that Davis involuntarily presented, and even with Kris there seemed to be a great deal withheld from the Agency.

The prospect of taping into Davis's research data in Paris was discussed at length and dismissed as too risky, at least initially. O'Malley was forced to place the operation on temporary hiatus, until an alternative source to Professor Davis could be identified and recruited, which wasn't happening anytime soon.

Five

Provincetown

The opening night of Kris' latest work at the gallery in Nantucket was a standing room only event and after twenty minutes became a sold out one as well. She returned to Provincetown a few days later with Tyler Frank, who flew up early from Texas for the opening.

Kris was physically and emotionally exhausted from a creative process that was obsessive and inescapable. She would need time to shake off the accumulated effects before she could begin to work again. The process was something that Tyler knew well, and he would walk the beach at Race Point with her in the evenings, and they would talk about the sea or the way the light played off the landscape or nothing at all.

Two weeks after the opening, on April 15, 2013 at 2:49 in the afternoon, her world changed in ways she couldn't have imagined, when two homemade bombs exploded twelve seconds apart at the finish line of the Boston Marathon.

The images coming out of Boston were chilling and horrific and it was impossible to turn away from the carnage inflicted on a place and people she knew so well. Kris left the studio that afternoon and walked the length of Commercial Street completely numb to her surroundings and with the same empty expression of every face encountered.

The Patriot's Day crowd along Commercial Street had dissipated and those remaining were gathered in small clusters trying to comprehend what happened or simply for reassurance. She walked past the town hall to Fisherman's Wharf and sat at the end, beyond the stacks of weary lobster traps with legs dangling over the edge of the wharf and her thoughts unable to move away from the finish line of the Boston Marathon.

That evening, the sound of her voice on the phone told Dan Walker something was amiss beyond their shared revulsion for the bloodshed unleashed in Boston. Two days later, Kris walked up the ramp at the arrivals gate of Rapid City Airport in South Dakota, and Dan was able to wrap his arm around her shoulder and take possession of her bag without the usual objection.

Dan was the only father Kris had ever known and hardly a decision was made without his advice being sought, and although her mother was a loving and supportive presence, Dan's uncomplicated approach to life went straight to the heart of whatever truly mattered to her.

Dan drove the Jeep towards Custer State Park for lunch at the State Game Lodge, a long standing tradition whenever Kris managed to return to the Black Hills. She hardly spoke a word, as the landscape rolled past and wildlife began to appear more frequently. Kris had always felt connected to the land and part of something bigger than herself in the Black Hills, and in some ways, she had never really left. Dan politely remained outside of her silence until they were sitting across from each other in the dining room of the State Game Lodge.

'Thanks for taking time away from work to meet me at the airport.' Kris was the first to speak.

'It's one of the few perks of being the Chief.' His smile made her feel warm and glad to be in his presence again.

'How is mother?'

'Anxious to get next to you.'

'I miss her too.' She reached across and rubbed his big hands that were folded together on the table between them.

'What's going on, Kris?'

'Mixed emotions.' She paused and looked across the table at Dan. 'I'm thinking about joining the FBI.' And for the first time experienced him with a loss for words and could feel the weight of her own, as Dan was trying to process what she had said to him.

A violent and convoluted history existed between Dan and the FBI. As a twelve year old boy, he was caught up in the 1973 standoff between the FBI, the United States Marshall Service and the American Indian Movement, which had occupied the town of Wounded Knee, less than a two hour drive from where they sat.

At the time, Dan was visiting his older brother Johnny who was married to an Oglala Sioux woman. They lived on the Pine Ridge Indian Reservation, where for seventy-one days the conflict ebbed and flowed with people dying and wounded on both sides of the conflict. When the siege ended, Dan wasn't the same carefree and innocent kid that returned to Montana.

His brother managed to survive the encounter, but a beating two months later was intended to kill, and left Johnny with a limp. He now lives alone, on the old family homestead in Montana and rarely leaves the reservation. For Dan and many others, all sense of justice for what transpired at Wounded Knee, remains in the wind.

After the bitter experience of Wounded Knee, Dan made a point of pushing back against discrimination and racism wherever encountered, and this included his present tenure with the National Park Service. His articulate and direct approach to these matters were something the Park Service found difficult to contain, and didn't quite know what to do with the big guy who was impossible to silence, and far too intelligent to ignore.

Mostly, they promoted him from park to park within the western territories, a futile attempt at diffusing their own communal anxiety, which allowed Dan to gain more traction with each move, and to work himself into the position of having the last word on whatever crossed his desk.

His career options often led to conflicted emotions, and the decision concerning whether to accept the position of Chief of Interpretation at Mount Rushmore was especially difficult. Dan felt compelled to return to his reservation in Montana and seek council from the tribal elders, as the reservation was his sanctuary, and the one place where the world according to the white man could not encroach upon his spirit. The deep, emotional connection to his tribal family and sheer physicality of the Montana landscape spoke directly to the man in ways that words never could.

The tribal elders responded by gathering for a sweat lodge ceremony to seek wisdom from the creator. Dan offered tobacco to the four directions and sat in the sweltering heat of the dark and sweetgrass scented lodge to pray for guidance. Afterwards, he spoke one on one with the elders and answered the questions they raised, but most of all he listened to their hopes, and the belief they expressed in Dan Walker, as a man and warrior fighting for the survival of the tribe on a new warpath.

Dan had left the reservation after graduating from high school and moved to Bozeman on a basketball scholarship with Montana State University. Six years later he left Bozeman with a Master of Business Administration degree and began his career by cleaning toilets and emptying trash bins, as a seasonal ranger for the Badlands National Park in South Dakota. His rise through the ranks of the Park Service, eventually led to Mount Rushmore, the iconic memorial and American, 'Shrine of Democracy', which stands proudly on the sacred and stolen lands of his ancestors.

When Dan first passed through the doors of the administration building at Mount Rushmore to claim his position as Chief of Interpretation, he did so as the sole Indian on the property, and when he convened the first full staff meeting the following day, the faces he encountered around the conference table were all white and as one proudly mentioned, owned a special connection to the mountain. A reference to members of staff who were the grandchildren, nieces or nephews of former officials and local supporters from the early years of Mount Rushmore.

Dan's subsequent directives, which placed emphasis on minority hiring practices would simmer beneath the surface, although the permanent employee population outwardly disowned the sly, albeit effective version of nepotism, a rash of transfer requests and early retirements followed, and a year later the interpretive staff held a thirty percent minority population. Yet, for Dan there could be no illusions, the challenges remained, but then again, he was a man built for the task, a true warrior.

'Talk to me.' Dan was back with her.

'It's the arrogance.' Kris started. 'I find impossible to ignore. The mindless slaughter by those who claim a self-anointed impunity for the atrocities they commit.'

'Atrocities are not a new phenomenon in America, Kris. Why now and why you?'

'This was too close. I feel it in here.' She held a hand to her chest.

'It's natural to experience intense feelings, at times like this. Is it truly from your heart, or is the anger speaking for you?'

'Both.'

'You can't have both.'

'I know.'

Dan sat in silence and held her gaze until she spoke again.

'It's more than just anger, Dan. I could live with anger.' Kris paused and looked away for a moment then continued. 'I can't live with knowing that I could prevent even one person from experiencing what happened in Boston.'

It suddenly occurred to Dan that the decision was formed before she ever stepped off the plane, whether she realized it or not, and he would make no attempt to walk her back. The best he could hope for was to diffuse the intensity of her anger. The one thing his experiences at Wounded Knee made clear was the heavy and enduring toll anger placed on the spirit.

He moved the conversation to common ground and shared experiences that carried throughout the meal and deep into Custer State Park, where they parked the Jeep and walked out into the prairie to sit within sight of a small herd of bison. It was there they cleansed their eyes, ears and hearts with the calming fragrance and purifying smoke of a bundle of sweetgrass.

Darkness settled by the time they arrived back in Keystone where Anne had the fireplace blazing in the great room. Kris spent another week hiking the Black Hills and spent the last day of her visit with Anne doing nothing but being together, and it was Anne who brought her back to Rapid City Airport.

The following day, Kris was in Jack O'Malley's office, and twenty one weeks later at Quantico, Virginia, the unlikely personage of Kris Shepard took possession of a badge and a mandate, which she swore to uphold. Dan Walker was there to shake her hand and to tell Kris he was honoured, to call her daughter. Her mother held her tight and long, and three hours later, Kris was on a flight back to Boston.

Six

Boston

The flight between Quantico and Boston was aboard the Cessna Encore that functioned as O'Malley' default center of operations whenever he ventured away from Boston, and both O'Malley and Sam Bordeaux, who was recently assigned as project coordinator for the team wasted no time in getting down to business.

This was the first opportunity for Kris to closely observe the men to which she was now inexorably linked and couldn't help but notice the white leather seats and bright wall panels reflected the light more favourably on Sam Bordeaux. At six two and one hundred eighty pounds, Sam was lean and muscular with a tight, angular face and he moved in the easy manner of an athlete. The sandy blond hair and brown eyes softened his look, but not enough to mistake him for someone not to be taken seriously.

Oddly enough the man seemed to be struggling with a streak of shyness, a bright flush started at the neckline of his shirt and worked its way up to his forehead whenever Kris maintained eye contact for any length of time, which was the last thing she normally sought.

Kris estimated O'Malley to be around five ten and one hundred sixty five pounds. His short brown hair speckled with grey, the blue eyes creased at the edges and the man appeared to be all legs. She placed his age around forty, but he showed the wear and tear of the sixteen years spent in service of the Agency.

O'Malley lifted a small table away from the wall panel to a raised position and opened his laptop. Sam shifted in his seat and waited for him to boot up. When he was ready to go, O'Malley pulled an iPad out of his briefcase and passed it to Kris. 'Set a password and when you get verification look at the camera and blink. The team's security system is encrypted with facial recognition and your already locked into the system, which you probably find amusing.'

With just the one click, Kris Shepard was officially on her first operation with the FBI. It felt better than she expected. Sam moved across the narrow aisle and sat with his hands folded waiting for Kris to get up and running. 'I'm good to go,' she finally announced to no one in particular.

'Go ahead and bring our new crew member up to speed, Sam.' Jack stood and hung up his jacket, loosened his tie and sat back down while Sam began the orientation.

'Open the first of the three folders, Kris.' Sam was no longer blushing when he spoke. 'This first folder contains incident reports from France and Germany. These reports were generated by our field agents in cooperation with their respective home teams and contain the times, locations and all relevant data that could be sourced electronically, digitally or by boots on the ground.' Sam allowed Kris a few minutes to conduct an overview of the documentation.

'The second folder contains a dossier and all available photographs of members of two terrorist cells before and after they were assassinated including the ballistics, autopsy and toxicology reports. The folder also includes photographs of immediate family members both male and female of each individual associated with the two cells.'

Sam gave her another minute. 'The third folder contains names and photographs of the known associates and suspects linked to the cells. The list is extensive and includes a segment of individuals we consider close to being operational ready, either as part of a cell or as lone wolves.' Sam looked over to O'Malley.

'Thanks Sam.' O'Malley turned to Kris. 'We'll get into the assassination aspect at the full staff meeting. For the moment, we need you to absorb the information and study the faces of everyone in the folders. We're launching the operation tomorrow after we introduce you to the rest of the team.' Jack looked up over his eyeglasses at Kris. 'How much time will you need?'

'I'll be ready in the morning.'

'With how many folders?'

'All of them.'

'I was hoping you were going to say that.' Jack shook his head slightly and smiled.

Two black Suburban's were waiting when the Cessna came to a standstill at Hanscom Air Force Base on the outskirts of Boston. O'Malley turned to Kris before climbing into the lead vehicle. 'Sam will be riding with you and they'll drop you at home.' With that O'Malley slid into the back seat then lowered the window. 'By the way, you moved.'

As the Suburban pulled away Kris turned to Sam. 'What is he talking about, I moved?'

'To a safe house. We need you close by.'

'Where are my things?'

'Some are at the new place. But for the most part still in Provincetown.' Sam put his hand on the door handle of the Suburban.

'And who chose what was to be moved?' Her voice was starting to tighten, which was never a good sign.

'I did.' Sam opened his door while Kris walked behind the Suburban and let herself into the back seat. The drive from Hanscom to downtown Boston passed in silence and when the Suburban finally stopped in front of a townhouse at Ridgeway Lane on Beacon Hill, they were both happy to be free of the close proximity.

They entered the townhouse and the SUV continued down to the end of Ridgeway Lane, turned right and merged into the flow of traffic on Cambridge Street. The new living arrangement was a furnished, two-bedroom townhouse spread over three floors with high ceilings, a formal dining room and private roof deck.

Sam coded her in and they proceeded room to room before ending the tour in the kitchen where a large, manila envelope was waiting for her attention. 'Everything you need to know is in the envelope and if you have any issues, I'll be happy to discuss them before the staff meeting in the morning.' With that Sam turned and was out the door.

The contents of the envelope included directions for the security system, the internet access code, a landline phone number and map of the surrounding area. Of greater interest was the combination to a lock and the receipt for her belongings, which remained sequestered in a special FBI storage facility and required an appointment to view.

Any items to be added or removed from the storage unit required approval from the FBI facility manager. The odd and disconcerting aspect was that every stitch of her clothing, shoes and personal belongings, including the items in the medicine cabinet, were in exactly the same position as when she left for Quantico nearly six months earlier. As though everything simply materialised within the closets, dressers and bookcases of the townhouse.

The refrigerator, kitchen cabinets and the walk-in pantry were fully stocked. In the oversized wine fridge she found a note under a bottle of Olga Raffault, Les Picasses 2007. 'Welcome to the crew.' Kris passed on the wine and headed for the shower and an evening of browsing faces late into the night.

The following morning, she went through her usual routine, a blend of yoga and tai chi, which normally would have been followed with a run, if she wasn't pressed for time. The images of the terror suspects from the folders on the iPad were committed to memory and she anticipated more to come after the initial staff meeting with her new colleagues.

Change never came easy for Kris and the abrupt, involuntary relocation didn't help matters. She was already apprehensive about reporting to FBI headquarters for the first time. Her only experience as an employee was limited to the sculpture workshops she conducted and maintained total control over, which for Kris was always a defining issue to be surmounted.

Even as a child, things needed to be a certain way to remain within her comfort zone, to the point that attending public schools wasn't an option. She wasn't a disruptive child in any manner, but simply refused to remain in a classroom with other children. Eventually, the effort of trying to keep her there became too labor intensive for all involved.

Dan and her mother assumed the sole responsibility for her education, as a temporary measure to allow Kris the chance to outgrow her issues with being part of a group. As it turned out they were exceptionally good at it and enjoyed the opportunity of being one on one with her.

They both adjusted their work schedules to allow for two days off each week and on the fifth day, Kris accompanied them to Mount Rushmore to spend her day in the company of park rangers or the curator, whose conversation and collection of artefacts she found especially fascinating.

Her education became increasingly eclectic over time and acted as a counterbalance to her natural tendency to focus on a single interest, which could and can still become all consuming. She learned how to cope and shake herself free of such entanglements, but there was nothing she could do to prevent them in the first place.

The walk to the office helped to take the edge off her concerns, and she appreciated O'Malley not making a promotion of introducing her to the rest of the crew. When he inquired about her level of comfort at the townhouse and apologized for the clandestine, but in his view necessary change of zip codes, she took the opportunity to express her displeasure.

'I need prior knowledge of these things in the future, Jack.'

'I know. I'll do what I can.' Wasn't the answer she wanted to hear, although believed he was sincere and chose to let it go, as best she could. Although, the ability to mute her natural inclinations, purely for the sake of getting along was not something she intended to cultivate.

O'Malley opened the staff meeting by requesting they sit down individually with Kris by the end of the day to bring her up to speed on their expertise and function within the crew, he then turned the meeting over to Sam.

Sam stood and moved to the end of the conference table, the lights in the room dimmed and a large wall monitor behind him displayed a map of Europe. 'We're going to open with visuals and then get into the surveillance data before moving into an open discussion. So please hold your questions for the short term.'

Sam focused the red dot of a laser on Lyon, France. 'Four months ago, our counterparts in France, the National Gendarmerie Intervention Group or NGIG, were conducting a long term surveillance operation of a suspected terrorist cell on the outskirts of Lyon. The operation disintegrated when an individual who was initially assumed to be a runner delivering either marching orders, money or information assassinated the entire cell.'

Sam created a sidebar with a cascading series of gruesome images. 'This is the aftermath of the runner' visit.' He allowed a few minutes for the images to sink in before removing the sidebar and directing the red dot to Germany. 'The GSG 9 Counter Terrorism Force in Germany experienced a similar event in Cologne two weeks ago. A single runner entered the premises under surveillance.' Another set of images appeared on the sidebar. 'This was obviously the work of a professional and both incidents appear to have been carried out by a single individual.'

The second set of images disappeared from the screen. Sam sat down and continued. 'We need to establish the identity of the assassin and what organization they represent, if any. The folders in front of you contain the surveillance reports and information that our Paris and Berlin teams gathered to date from the French and Germans. I want you to keep the folders shut for the moment, so we can get address any questions before we continue.'

Sarah O'Sullivan, one of the tech specialists on the crew posed the first question. 'How long have these sleeper cells been using runners?'

'At least two years we know about, but we suspect it was going on much longer. These are small cells of three to six individuals and they operate completely in the dark. No cell phones, computers or even a mode of transportation. They live quietly and move about only when necessary and remain essentially invisible or so they believed. The members of the cells you just witnessed were all professionals with military backgrounds and a range of specialties. Collectively, they were linked to prior attacks in Afghanistan, Belgium and Australia.

'How extensive was the surveillance? The question came from Will Jenkins, the second computer technician on the crew.

'Not enough apparently, but that information is in the folders.' Sam took a drink of water. 'Our focus at the moment is the lone gunman who took out these cells within days of their being apprehended. The lost opportunity for interrogation was a serious setback.'

'Is there a consensus on who the runner belongs to?' Jenkins followed up

'So far there have been no claims of responsibility and competing intelligence suggest the runner is associated with either ISIS or an al-Qaeda splinter group. Although, the sources are shaky, and the information received from the German and French surveillance crews is sparse, both digitally and forensically. The runner managed to get in and out leaving nothing, but images of his backside walking away.'

'Did the surveillance capture any partial images or profiles of the runner's face?' Kris asked.

'No. Not even close.'

'Thanks Sam, I'll take it from here.' O'Malley moved into the discussion. 'The collective theories in regard to the allegiance and motivation of the runner is clearly speculation, so let's keep an open mind.' He stood up and walked down to the wall monitor. 'Put the images of the Cologne cell back up, Sam.' O'Malley pointed towards an image of one of the dead terrorists. 'This guy was an explosives expert.' He moved the pointer. 'And these two led ragtag bands of roving fighters in Afghanistan and Syria that delivered serious hurt wherever they showed up.' He removed the red dot from the couch where the two men were sprawled out. 'They didn't make it to their feet and were dead within seconds of the runner entering the premises.'

O'Malley turned back to Sam. 'Put the Lyon cell up beside this group.' Five more images flowed down the sidebar and he placed the red dot on the forehead of one of the men killed on the couch in Cologne. 'This guy had a cousin killed in the Lyon cell and the corpse next to him is the younger brother of the assumed leader of a cell that recently surfaced in Springfield, right here in our backyard.'

O'Malley sat back down and continued. 'One thing I know with certainty, is that you don't kill one brother without killing the other. I believe the runner is headed to Western Massachusetts and for that reason we're about to take control of the surveillance operation in Springfield. Our objective is to shut down the cell and apprehend the runner, who is possibly more valuable from an intelligence perspective than these other cells combined.'

O'Malley paused and looked around the conference table. 'The runner is our pathway into whatever group is sponsoring these cells and could hold the answer to why they're being systematically eliminated.'

This brings me back to our newest crew member, Kris Shepard.' O'Malley looked over to Kris who made no attempt to acknowledge his reference. 'The working title for this operation is Raven, a name chosen based on the fact that ravens have a tremendous capacity to remember human faces and especially those who interfere with them.'

O'Malley sat back and looked around the room. 'Everyone here is aware of Professor John Davis' work with facial recognition and the possibilities it offers in our line of work. Unfortunately, Davis is no longer associated with our operation and has taken up residence in Paris.' He glanced over at Kris who gave no indication whether this was new information to her and then continued. 'Prior to his departure, Davis went to great lengths to separate the elite faction of super recognizers from the rest of the pack. Kris being the first person from his certification program to qualify for elite status and her presence on this crew is central to every aspect of the operation.'

O'Malley turned the meeting back over to Sam and after a short break for lunch, the crew spent the afternoon discussing the logistics of assuming control of the Springfield surveillance operation from their counterparts working out of Hartford, Connecticut.

Sam was thorough and precise with a broad range of technical knowledge and Kris could see why he was a natural choice as O'Malley' project coordinator. She also noticed that away from the conference table, he was self-contained and less forthcoming than the rest of the crew and she liked that about him. The staff meeting broke up late afternoon and Kris spent the balance of the day meeting with the individual crew members. The sun was setting by the time she walked back to Ridgeway Lane.

The proximity to so many people was mentally exhausting and her only impulse when reaching the townhouse was to put on her running shorts and sneakers, take a bottle of water from the fridge and go back out the door. A cool, steady breeze was coming off Boston Harbor and it felt good to move and focus on nothing except putting one foot in front of the other. She dearly missed running beside the sea at Race Point, and the solitude left behind in Provincetown weighed heavily on her equilibrium.

The sidewalks were nearly vacant, and she ran smooth and steady, as far as Cambridge Street with only the crossroads to slow her down. She circled around to Boston Common and back up to Beacon Hill, walking the last two blocks to Ridgeway Lane and found Sam standing in the alcove beside the front door of the townhouse.

'I'm glad that was you standing there, Sam.'

'Sorry.' He moved out to the sidewalk. Jack asked me to stop by to see if you needed anything.' He said with a voice much softer than the one she heard during the staff meeting.

'As in a pizza?' Her words slid out uncensored.

'That can be arranged.'

'C'mon in.' Kris opened the door to the townhouse. 'I'm cooling down too fast to continue this conversation out here.' She stepped back to allow Sam the space to enter. 'After you.' He hesitated, then went through the door ahead of her.

'I was kidding about the pizza.'

'It's not a problem. You must be hungry. It's been a long day.'

'Actually, I wasn't until we started talking about it.' She moved past Sam towards the kitchen. 'And you. have you had dinner?'

'Not yet.'

'Do you want to split one?'

'Sure.' Kris sensed the hesitation in his voice.

'Are you really?'

'Yeah, I am.' And suddenly he sounded it.

'I really have to shower.' She said while unlacing her running shoes. 'Would you mind ordering?'

'What would you like on it?'

'Your call.' Kris started down the hallway towards the bathroom and came back to kitchen. 'I'd offer you a glass of wine, if only I knew where to find the glasses.' She offered.

'Second cabinet from the window.' Sam replied. 'You want one?'

'Sounds lovely.' Kris kept the shower shorter than usual, but still by the time she returned to the kitchen an open box of steaming pizza sat atop the breakfast bar, along with two glasses of wine.

'You didn't have to wait for me.' He smiled for the first time she noticed all day. 'Really, I don't know how you could resist, it smells so delicious.'

'Came from Sorento's, a food truck that sets up every day at different locations around Beacon Hill.

They're parked just around the corner tonight. Behind the State House.'

'That was convenient.'

'I thought so. Help yourself.'

Kris was famished and tried to avoid embarrassing herself by wolfing the pizza down in her usual studio frame of mind, where hunger arrives suddenly in the form of a primordial mandate that demands immediate attention and once sated, disappears without ever breaking the rhythm of her work.

She was halfway through the second slice of pizza, before realizing how effortlessly the conversation was flowing between her and Sam, which was something she rarely experienced with a new acquaintance, if at all. Although, it was mainly questions on her part and they just kept coming.

'Someone mentioned you're from Louisiana.'

'And you can't remember who?' He smiled.

'Selective memory.'

'Of course.' He said while picking up another slice of pizza and added. 'Baton Rouge.'

'Tell me something about Baton Rouge.'

'It's hot.'

'Hot, like I should go there. Or just hot?'

'Both, at times.'

‘Do you miss it?’

‘I miss my dog?’

‘What kind of dog?’

‘An English Setter mix from the rescue center.

‘How old?’

‘Close to twelve they tell me.’

‘Name?’

‘Max.’

‘You see him often?’

‘Whenever I can. He lives with a friend now.’

‘You must have family there?’

‘Not anymore. My mother died of cancer when I was two and my father four years ago from a heart attack. He was a retired fire captain in Baton Rouge at the time. A neighbour saw him collapse in the backyard and called it in, but he was already dead when the emergency crew arrived. I was working undercover at the time.’ Sam paused. ‘I couldn’t make it back for the funeral.’

‘Sorry.’ She looked directly into his eyes for the first time. Sam looked away for a moment then returned her gaze and they held eye contact longer than either one of them expected, before her words broke it off again. ‘I can’t imagine how that feels.’

Her questions evaporated as quickly as they had started and after an uneasy silence, Sam picked up where she left off. 'Tell me something about the Black Hills.'

'I don't believe it's nearly as hot as Baton Rouge, by either definition.' She found her voice again.

'You miss it.'

'Every day.'

'Think you'll move back at some point?'

'At times, I think not, but I don't know. Part of me is still there.'

'And Ireland?'

'Ireland has always been a special place for me and I loved being there as a child.'

'Jack lived in Dublin for a few years. Were you aware of that?'

'No, he never mentioned it.'

'It's not something he talks about.'

'What was he doing in Dublin?'

'He went on a Fulbright scholarship to study literature at Trinity College and from what I understand, stayed another year working on a book. I don't know how that worked out, but his research brought him in contact with the FBI, and he ended up going through the academy. I believe he planned to work with Agency temporarily for the experience and never left.'

'Does he still write?'

'I don't know. He doesn't talk about it, and I don't bring it up.'

'That's interesting.' Kris took another sip of wine. 'Do you think Jack is correct about the runner showing up in Springfield?'

'He's usually right about these things.'

'You've worked with him often in past?'

'On and off for ten years. Mostly on.'

'He seems fair.'

'Fair enough. Thing with Jack is he always has your back, and not just in the field.'

'Good to know.'

'Better to reciprocate.'

'I'll remember that'.

'I'm sure you will. No offense intended'

'None taken.'

They finished the pizza and cleaned up together. An hour later they were still sitting at the breakfast bar, the conversation rambled light and easy and neither one of them noticed the time. Until finally Sam stood up. 'I should go.'

'Yeah.' Kris paused before answering.

Sam put on his jacket and she thanked him for the pizza and walked to him to the door. After he left, she locked the door and listened to his footsteps fading away along the cobblestones of Ridgeway lane.

The next morning the entire crew was on the way to Springfield. Sam drove the lead vehicle while Kris rode in the back seat of the second one, immersed in a fresh batch of images out of Quantico. It was day one of the operation and casual words were hard to come by.

Seven

Springfield

The Raven crew became operational on September 24, 2013 in Springfield, the weary and tattered birthplace of the Indian motorcycle, basketball and the Springfield rifle, a rambling study of urban decay clinging to the banks of the Connecticut River in Western Massachusetts.

The crew set up shop in a Victorian relic backed up to the edge of a polluted, foul smelling creek that reeked of rotten eggs and ran straight into the Connecticut River unabated. The house sat at the bottom of Mill Street, in the South End of the city across from a string of equally worn tenement blocks, recently transformed into a downhill run of crack houses.

A nursing home sat in the uphill shadow of the tenements, and feigned a semblance of normality with a fresh coat of baby blue paint to offset the contingent of elderly and pyjama clad residents, sequestered outside on a cluster of wooden benches. The only equal opportunity employer the residents of the neighborhood ever knew were the street gangs, drug dealers and pimps.

The Victorian was set back from the street, directly across from the tenements and projected a brooding, distinctly austere character, which in that neighborhood provided a layer of protection from unsolicited visitations. Built by one of the early manufacturing baron', the interior still retained the sheen of the glory days, before the tide ran out on the city.

O'Malley took possession of a spacious, oak panelled library on the second floor of the mansion overlooking the crack houses. One floor above, the crew worked out of a control room at the rear of the building, which spanned two adjoining bedrooms with ten-foot ceilings. A bank of wall mounted monitors dominated the space and were manned around the clock.

The ground floor of the mansion remained uninhabited by the crew and avoided with the exception of the marble tiled kitchen accessed by the former servant's staircase leading down from the upper floors. A doorway off the kitchen gave direct access to the old carriage house, which was converted into a six-car garage during the early fifties. The crew' vehicles were all pointed out towards Mill Street.

The kitchen was vast with natural light entering through a series of short, elongated windows set high in the outer wall. The floor contained an exquisite blend of black and white marble tiles, which complemented the white marble countertops and a series of elegant cabinets with cut glass fronts. The absence of visibility from the street allowed the kitchen to become functional and offered solace from the glare of monitors and computer screens and eased the tedium that eventually creeps into long term surveillance details.

The derelict mansion was acquired for the express use of the Alcohol, Tobacco and Firearms crew working out of Hartford, Connecticut. The crack factory across the street was at the crossroads of a burgeoning distribution network of crack and heroin throughout New England. The ATF found they gained more traction into the network by allowing the factory to remain up and running, gaining insight into the day to day transactions while following the wholesalers, transportation links and importers back to their source, where they could be dealt with separately.

ATF put forth a sustained and vigorous opposition to the takeover by O'Malley' crew, but never stood a chance against the counterterrorism task force and relinquished possession of the mansion with a veiled, catch you later threat, that O'Malley knew would be revisited. For the moment, he was happy enough working out of the library surrounded by empty bookshelves.

Homeland Security had held a monitoring operation of the two distinct elements of the Springfield cell in place until the crew settled into the site. The process took nearly a week and a thorough debriefing by Nolan St. James, head of the Homeland Security team gave O'Malley official ownership of the overall operation.

The first order of business was to get the technical gear up and running, followed by establishing a viable method for maintaining constant surveillance on both factions of the cell, which made the efforts labor intensive with a unique set of challenges.

Sarah O'Sullivan was assigned to head up the tech crew and was able to make short work of the first location, a narrow, two story home in the Hill McKnight district. The home, occupied by three war hardened cousins from Northern Afghanistan was located diagonally across the street from a fire station.

Sarah assumed control of the fire departments CCTV cameras then hijacked a private surveillance camera from an adjoining neighbors backyard to cover the rear of the house. The traffic camera' mounted at intersections on both ends of the street filled in the blind spots.

The Afghanistan cousins ventured out of the house one at a time, and only to gather food and supplies at the Stop and Shop Supermarket, a fifteen minute walk from the house. They may well have remained in the dark, if not for the one joint excursion they made to the cells second location, a week into the surveillance operation established by Homeland Security.

The second location, a rowhouse in the South End was four blocks from the mansion in an especially difficult position for surveillance. A distinct lack of CCTV coverage, along with the heightened awareness of the resident drug dealers made it impossible to conduct business as usual.

The neighborhood fronted Main Street and was divided into two matching halves, each a city block wide and separated by a solitary, dead end street running uphill past a series of narrow lanes before coming to an abrupt halt at the base of a twenty foot high, graffiti and gang tagged concrete wall.

Lane after lane of the interconnected rowhouses, sat vacant and boarded with only a few, isolated pockets of habitation consisting mainly of crack dealers, a colony of prostitutes and a contingent of truly desperate squatters. This second segment of the cell was wedged in between two vacant rowhouses on the last lane of the neighborhood, with their backs to the concrete wall and a heroin operation, three doors down.

The string of rowhouses across the lane from the embedded cell, sat derelict and cannibalized with all twenty one tenements stripped of their copper wiring, cast iron radiators, solid wood doors and anything else the salvage yards were willing to swap for cash in hand.

Every adjoining wall along the entire stretch of houses contained a hole punched in it big enough to push a wheel barrel through, allowing thieves to move from one end of the string of rowhouses to the other, without stepping out into the light of day.

Six weeks into the operation, a viable solution to the challenge of maintaining a constant vigil of the South End segment of the cell remained elusive. The heroin operation down the lane proved to be a substantial enterprise, which was impressively organized and shared some of the same personnel, as the crack factory across the street from the mansion.

The heroin operation was apparently and effectively part of a wider drug cartel and deployed a security team around the clock that provided blanket coverage of the close knit collection of rowhouses. The site was unapproachable by day and deadly by night. A no man' land, where nothing moved without notice and the gatekeepers maintained a one strike reputation. Nobody stumbled into the heroin compound twice without an invitation and made it out unscathed.

The cell had chosen their neighbors carefully and the fact they were allowed to exist within the cartels security zone was a development that raised a host of questions, including the possible business association between the heroin operation and the organization funding the cell. The answers to which required an immediate solution to the surveillance issues.

The satellite footage and thermal imaging acquired through Quantico, offered nothing of value for Kris, who needed more than the tops of heads and illuminated figures to establish an identity fix of individual members of the cell. Drones held similar limitations with the added attraction of being shot out of the air on previous attempts by the regional drug squad.

The scale of the operation and impunity under which it operated also concerned O'Malley. The fundamental hallmarks of corruption were blatantly obvious and the possibility of collusion within local law enforcement, posed a serious threat to the safety of the crew. They were on their own, a fact which left him with the one option he had been avoiding all along.

On Sunday, of the seventh week following the crew's arrival in Springfield, Sam left the mansion at 2:30 AM, by the back door of the garage. He slipped into the gully and followed the creek uphill, moving parallel to Maple Street, a two lane thoroughfare, which ran above the opposite bank of the creek. The occasional, unbroken street light, cast a faint glow down to the creek bed, littered with shopping carts, old tires and remnants of stolen bikes.

When he reached the Maple Street bridge, a quarter mile from the mansion, Sam pulled the hood up on his sweatshirt and scrambled up the bank, away from the creek. Once on the street, he walked quickly back in the direction he came from and turned up the hill at Pine Street, within view of the mansion, the crack factory and junkies perched on its doorstep. A pair of prostitutes worked the crossroads at the end of the block, while three more looked on from the curb.

Sam covered the uphill jaunt to Central Street in a matter of minutes and followed it back downhill towards Main Street. Close to the halfway point, he took an abrupt turn into an alleyway between two industrial garages with rear parking lots overlooking the collection of rowhouses.

From there, he slowly descended a heavily wooded slope and stood in the dark, behind the last derelict rowhouse in the string and directly across the lane from the cell. There he remained perfectly still, listening for any hint of sound emanating from within the rowhouse. Ten minutes later, he put on a pair of night vision goggles and entered the building through a partially boarded window.

'I'm in Sarah.' He spoke soft and direct.

'We're with you, Sam.' The interior of the rowhouse shimmered in a green tinted hue across the wall monitor in the control room. Sam crossed over what was previously the kitchen and stood at the edge of a hallway running between the living room, bathroom and two small bedrooms. A pair of rats scurried down the hallway to find cover.

The floor of the rowhouse was a minefield of hypodermic needles, broken beer bottles, bits of furniture and a pair of filthy mattresses. He followed the rats to the end of the hallway, pausing again before entering the adjoining rowhouse through the floor to ceiling breach in the wall created by the illicit salvage crew.

Sam repeated the pattern through four more rowhouses, reaching a point directly across from the heroin operation. He was barely in place when the voices of a pair of cartel guards on the lane outside passed unabated through the partially boarded windows, echoing within the empty chambers of the rowhouse, the beams from their flashlights slicing the darkness.

Sam waited until the voices faded down the lane and the lights disappeared before making a move towards the next rowhouse. He pressed forward through two more, finally arriving at his destination.

A shattered toilet from a bathroom on the second floor was on its side, straddling the last two steps of the stairway. Sam stepped over it to reach the landing, the bathroom lay straight ahead with bedrooms on either side. He entered the one on the left, overlooking the front door of the rowhouse occupied by the cell.

The remote camera was a grey, wafer thin two inches of high resolution, motion detecting set of eyes and ears. Sam held the barbed side of the unit tight against the weathered timber of the empty window frame. He gently rotated the camera with the palm of his hand until Sarah whispered, 'Perfect.' Then he pressed hard, setting it in place, turned away and made his way slowly down the staircase.

The plan was to place a second camera in another tenement on the way back, and Sam' journey was followed intently by the crew in the control room, who struggled not to second guess every sound or worry a presence to life within the black void of each doorway he passed along the way.

The second staircase to be negotiated was missing the first two treads and the third one squeaked loudly under his weight. Sam froze in place. The sound reverberating to the pit of his stomach. He waited in the dark. Nothing. The stair squeaked again when he moved off, and he waited longer the second time.

There wasn't much breathing going on back at the mansion, until Sam finally pressed the last camera in place and the front door of the drug cartel's rowhouse, assumed its central position on the wall of the control room.

Sam moved away from the window, crossed the bedroom and stopped at the doorway to peer down the staircase and immediately jerked his head back. The flicker of light in the room below shot through his consciousness and straight to his fingertips as they wrapped around the Glock.

His heart was beating in unison with the muffled voices rising from the floor below. He took a deep breath, let it out slowly and relaxed his grip on the Glock that was tight enough to regret. The voices ceased momentarily then returned in anger, the silence shattered by the sounds of a scuffle.

Two more voices echoed throughout the rowhouse, and the scuffle came to an abrupt halt. Sam carefully returned to the window, and down below he saw one of the cartel guards escorting a pair of young men away from the rowhouse. His body language suggested he was familiar with them and possibly junkies working as mules for the cartel that had engaged in a heroin related beef on company time.

Sam turned away from the window and began to move towards the staircase when he heard the first squeak from the staircase, a moment later, the second one placed the Glock front and center. He squatted. A harsh, erratic light flooded the landing, as the footsteps continued upwards and Sam let another deep breath slowly pass through his lips.

'Now where the fuck, are you?' Rang out from the lane outside.

'Right here!' The voice booming within the cavity of the staircase.

'Get your ass out here. We don't have time for this bullshit!' A long, eerie silence pursued, the light dancing around the landing and again, the voice from outside. 'I'm talking about right now, motherfucker!'

The light shifted off the landing, a squeak then another followed by grumbling that trailed outside. Sam stood and moved to the window once more. The two guards were walking away in single file. One ten yards ahead of the other. He holstered the Glock.

There wasn't a moment of the entire night that Kris didn't find brutally painful and exhausting to watch, and retreated to her room the moment she knew Sam was safe, and wrapped the darkness around herself like a cloak until he slid into bed beside her.

Eight

Springfield

Jack O'Malley sat alone in the dimly lit control room, the only source of light emanating from the wall monitors. He assigned himself the first watch of the rowhouse after Sam returned, and now he couldn't take his eyes off it. Beyond that front door lay his greatest fear, and one that would be impossible to reconcile, if allowed to move beyond the drug infested South End.

Earlier that day he requested and was granted the authority to shut down the operation and move on the cell at his sole discretion. Max Cooper, the Division Commander had offered no resistance and the nervous shutter that came out of Quantico was short lived. It was a relief knowing nothing stood between his gut instinct and the capacity for cold blooded murder that was waiting to be unleashed.

The risk of sending Sam into the derelict rowhouses had proved justified and brought the surveillance capabilities of the operation to a new level. But there was no escaping the fact that the cell was far too quiet and the runner long in coming. The questions he asked himself became more focused the longer he sat in the dark, and the answers clearly ominous. It was a possibility that rather than activating the cells, the runner had been assigned the task of shutting them down.

The female member of the Springfield cell was the wild card and had been inadvertently responsible for exposing her four male counterparts, all of whom were actively being sought by both German and French counter terrorism forces. The previously unknown woman had wandered into an apartment in the 19th arrondissement of Paris and straight into a French surveillance operation. She arrived with a young child in tow and left alone fifteen minutes later.

The Paris apartment belonged to the mother of one of the men killed the previous week by the runner in Cologne. The French had hoped to apprehend the surviving brother in the aftermath, but it was obvious by the mothers' demeanor that she didn't have the slightest idea that one of her sons was dead.

The French surveillance team followed the woman onto the Eurostar, which departed the Paris Gare du Nord bound for Heathrow, and they consequently alerted British authorities who took up the pursuit. A day later, she entered Canada on a British passport and immediately crossed over the border on a bus destined for Boston, Massachusetts. The Springfield transit terminal was a scheduled stop along the route.

A team from Homeland Security assumed the surveillance at the border, and later monitored the woman's progress from the Springfield bus terminal, as she walked the length of Main Street to the rowhouse in the South End. She was greeted by the much sought after second son of the woman from the 19th arrondissement of Paris, the suspected leader of the Springfield cell.

The exact nature of their relationship was unknown, but obviously important enough for the woman to relinquish the child, and board the Eurostar with a one-way ticket out of Paris. It appeared the father of the child was one of the brothers, and whether the woman was a widow or wife remained unclear.

Jack now believed the Springfield cell became activated the moment the woman crossed the threshold of the rowhouse, and if correct the only obstacles that remained between the terrorist cell and their dreams of paradise was the crew assembled in the mansion, and the runner.

'You must be exhausted?' Sarah's voice came from behind.

'No, I'm fine.' Jack's response sounding as distant as he felt.

'I couldn't sleep after watching that guard search the staircase, and Sam with no backup.' Sarah took a seat next to Jack at the control dcsk. 'It made me crazy not being able to do anything.' She looked up at the monitors and changed the subject. 'Have you decided what to do about the heroin operation?'

'Yeah. We're going to shut it down after we bring in the cell. The entire operation will be tagged a drug bust, which will draw less attention from the media and the possibility of another cell filling the gap before we have a chance at interrogation.'

'Swat?'

'Yeah. Max suggested we bring in two teams from Quantico to handle the drug cartel, and I intend to take him up on it.'

'Sounds ominous.' Will Jenkins stepped into the control room with another case of insomnia.

'We're getting close.' Jack turned to face him. 'And now that we have eyes on the drug operation, I want to know who we're up against.' He stood up to leave. 'We need still shots from various angles of anyone entering, leaving or moving about at either location, and I want you to hand them off to Kris, when she comes back on duty.'

"Get some sleep, Jack.' Sarah switched over to his empty seat. 'You look beat.'

He didn't argue but stopped on the way down to his bedroom and sat on the landing at the top of the staircase. He thought about the last few months and how the crew had handled the cohabitation and uncertainty surrounding the operation and was pleased by the amount of cohesion they maintained. With the exception of Sam and himself, the crew had never worked together, and no unwelcome surprises arose within the group from a personal perspective. The abundance of space, and laid back, bohemian atmosphere within the mansion had undoubtedly eased the sense of confinement.

The evolving relationship between Sam and Kris was something he didn't see coming, and doubted they did either. Having worked and lived with Sam on assignment for nearly ten years offered a level of insight, and the man simply didn't participate in romantic liaisons, and in relation to Kris most of what he knew about her came out of the dossier prepared by the agency. The abbreviated assessment by Professor Davis was less than forth coming, and nearly eliminated her as a candidate for the crew. Although, at this point he was glad that he took a chance on the unusual young woman from South Dakota.

‘Four days.’ Jack addressed the crew that afternoon when they reassembled in the control room. ‘I’ll establish the positioning and timing of the swat team’s incursion into the operation with Max Cooper.’ He continued. ‘Kris and I will be working with the South End team while Sam and Jenkins will handle the three cousins in Hill McKnight, with the second team. We need to have this cell in the back of the vans and on the way out of town before daylight.’

‘And the runner?’ Kris asked.

‘Max is assigning a crew to monitor both the South End and Hill McKnight locations after we conclude our business with the cell. It’s still possible the runner may show up on their doorstep, but we can’t risk leaving this cell being on the loose any longer.’

‘Who will be handling interrogation?’ Sarah asked.

‘We are. In the meantime, Sam will be coordinating the logistics with the swat teams while you handle the technical side of things.’ Jack answered. ‘Kris and Jenkins will be staying close to the monitors until we move on the cell.’ Jack paused and looked around the room. ‘Everyone good?’

‘Yeah.’ Sam gave the crew a second scan. ‘We’re good.’

Over the next two days, the atmosphere within the mansion shifted, as the operation moved to a new phase and pent up energies were finally released in a positive direction. Sam provided the swat teams with the layouts and background information they needed while Sarah worked to oversee the technical phase of the operation and ensure that all parties involved communicated effectively. Jack brought in another agent out of the Boston office, Craig Roberts, to serve as additional backup and second driver for transporting the cell out of Springfield.

By the third day, all that could be done to prepare was accomplished and the crew spent time either working out or resting while conversations strayed from what lay ahead. Jack spent that last morning in the library in conference calls with Quantico and Max Cooper. The swat teams were cleared and would be in place at Westover air base late that afternoon. He was in the process of gathering the few personal items he brought along two months earlier when Sarah called down from the control room.

'We need you upstairs right away, Jack.'

Kris received the same message and followed him up the staircase wearing her sweats and the headphones from a treadmill session around her neck. Sam and Craig Roberts were coming down the hallway when Jack entered the control room.

'What's going on?'

'It's what's not happening we're concerned with.' Jenkins gestured towards the monitors.

'In the last half hour, the cartel security in the South End has been noticeably absent.' Kris and Sam stood in the doorway. Roberts was a few steps into the control room and all eyes were on the monitors covering the South End. 'Even the guys working the choke points leading in from Main Street are no longer in place.' Sarah pointed out.

Less than thirty seconds later, the three cousins from Hill McKnight walked into the frame from the camera Sam installed on the rowhouse across from the cell. Nobody in the control room spoke or moved, and as they watched in stunned silence, the three cousins crossed the lane and the front door of the rowhouse opened for the first time. They entered without being greeted and the front door shut once again.

Jack looked at the camera's covering the house in Hill McKnight and back to Jenkins. 'I don't know, Jack.' He answered the unspoken question.

The entire crew had unconsciously been drawn closer to the monitors and stood shoulder to shoulder looking up when a fourth person appeared wearing a hooded sweatshirt and proceeded across the lane. Once again, the front door of the rowhouse was opened for the newcomer and before it closed again, the crew was in motion and it became all about the eight-minute journey from the mansion to the rowhouse. Sarah remained behind with eyes glued to the monitor, and at six minutes out she uttered the words Jack had feared. 'Shots fired.'

The two Suburban's careened off Main Street and drove unopposed, straight down the lane dividing the South End neighbourhood, the drug cartel's security remained nowhere in sight.

The runner had exited the rowhouse and was halfway across the lane with hood up and head down when the crew rounded the corner. The runner' arm rose in their direction without a turn of the head, and bullets randomly penetrated the lead Suburban, with Jack at the wheel and Jenkins lowering his window. The runner made it to the string of derelict rowhouses before Jenkins could get a shot off. Jack pulled up shy of where the runner entered the building and crouched with

Jenkins behind the open doors of the Suburban. Sam and Kris sped by towards the opposite end of the rowhouses with Craig Roberts at the wheel. Jack was the first to enter followed closely by Sam from the other end of the rowhouses. Jenkins and Kris were right behind them while Roberts drove the second Suburban back down the lane and positioned himself midway, facing the derelict buildings with a view of the entire block in both directions.

Jack cleared the entryway and moved into the building. His eyes struggling to adjust to the sudden darkness of the space. He went in deeper. Jenkins followed and they began clearing the ground floor, room by room. Jack climbed the staircase to the second floor while Jenkins remained below to secure the cleared area. Sam and Kris proceeded in the same fashion from the other end of the rowhouses.

Each section cleared brought them closer to each other with the runner being dangerously squeezed from both sides. The process of elimination was tedious and each rowhouse announced as it was cleared.

Jenkins took the lead into the second rowhouse and immediately stepped over blood droplets inside the doorway. The runner having paused to attend a wound. 'We have blood.' He spoke softly into the headset and signalled for Jack to hold up.

The sound of gunfire Sarah reported coming from the cell's rowhouse, suddenly made sense. The volume of noise was out of character with what they knew about the runner. A silencer being used during the previous executions and now it was apparent someone inside the rowhouse inflicted a serious wound on the runner before they were killed.

Jenkins followed the droplets to the edge of the gaping hole punched between the rowhouses with only three houses remaining between the crews. Jack joined him and peered into the opening. He could make out the familiar outline of Sam coming towards him from the other side of the makeshift tunnel connecting the hallways. The distance between them was punctuated by intense bands of sunlight pouring out of the windowless bedrooms and into the hallways, creating pockets of darkness between doorways. Jack moved through the opening towards Sam.

Having cleared the first bedroom leading away from the kitchen, Sam then waited in the dark shadows between the bedrooms, while Kris moved through the silt laden bands of sunlight from the doorway behind him. He waited for her eyes to adjust to the dark and then continued down the hallway towards the next bedroom, pausing before the doorway and listening for any sound that his presence may have attracted.

Sam went in quick, and exited a moment later to continue down the hallway towards the remaining bedroom. A few steps behind him, Kris passed through the patch of sunlight at the doorway and took the lead. Three steps later the image of the gun appeared suddenly at chest height along the door jamb of the final bedroom, less than fifteen feet away.

From Jack's position he watched the runner lean slightly into the hallway for what amounted to a fraction of a second before disappearing back into the room. Sam and Kris both went down, and he never heard a shot.

All sense of time and movement, as Jack knew it ceased to exist. The gap separating them imploding in on itself. He reached the doorway with Jenkins close behind. Kris was the only one moving in the hallway, and he lifted her away while Jenkins continued the pursuit into the sunlit, vacant bedroom at approximately the same moment Craig Roberts was being knocked backwards by a rapid succession of gunshots that landed him on his back, a final bullet placed between his eyes before the runner entered the Suburban.

Nine

Black Hills

Dan Walker stood at the far end of the secure zone at the arrivals gate of Rapid City Airport, South Dakota, and at six foot seven dominated the space. He wore shaded sunglasses, a brown, aviators leather jacket opened to the waist with a black river driver's shirt underneath. The braids flowing down to his chest framed and accented an expression, which was beginning to unsettle the TSA agents manning the exit.

Dan remained focused on the line of passengers making their way into building from the tarmac. Kris was the last to exit the plane and as the line began to dissipate, he moved closer to the exit.

'Hey.' Kris uttered the only word to pass between them before they walked away with Dan's arm across her shoulder. Nor did they speak while the Jeep moved across the barren, gravel roads towards the Black Hills, a billowing cloud of dust clinging to the back of the Wrangler.

The weather was unseasonably mild for the middle of December and they rode under a bright, cloudless sky all the way to Bluebird Butte. Dan parked at the base of the butte and they started up the trail leading to the crest, moving past a pair of bull bison resting in the grove of ponderosa pine.

At the crest they sat side by side on a weathered, wooden bench along the edge of the butte. Deep in the valley below, a solitary bull bison was crossing a high plains meadow, his huge head swinging back and forth with the slow, measured primordial grace only a bison can achieve. A handful of mountain bluebird fresh out of the Bighorns floated effortlessly at eye level, scouring the updraft amidst the bounty of insects cast from below.

The silent vigil continued with no regard to time or anything belonging to the world beyond the one they alone occupied. Dan eventually entered the silence. 'Do you feel a need to talk about it, Kris?'

'No.' She squeezed his hand. 'I'd like to see mother now.

In the weeks to follow, Kris wandered in and out of the vertigo, which had become part of her existence since the shooting. A scar ran across her temple and disappeared into the hair above her ear, a vivid trail of the bullet she had shared with Sam.

Neither Dan or her mother made an attempt to enter the grief Kris held close. There was no other way and even as a child she suffered loss on her own terms. The outward signs of turmoil would remain absent in spite of a hurt that went far deeper than all that came before and Dan feared the pain would push her towards a dark place, as he remained powerless to intervene.

The cold weather arrived a few days into the new year and retreated once more in the middle of February. The vertigo was starting to relax its grip on her equilibrium and a dry, snowless winter allowed Kris the opportunity to wander the open plains and along familiar trails through the Black Hills. Her physical strength waned during the extended periods of inactivity and was slowly returning, while each moment spent alone held the need for another.

Kris chose a clear, cold morning and Dan drove her to the Harney Peak trailhead near the edge of Sylvan Lake. The sun was barely up and the trailhead parking lot empty. Dan sat in the Jeep and watched her cross over a footbridge atop a dry creek, and then disappear as the trail rounded a mammoth granite outcropping. He could tell by the way she moved that the vertigo had flared and waited with eyes locked on the trail before slowly moving away.

The trail ascended through a narrow, uneven stretch before launching into a steep, extended climb that was difficult under normal circumstances. Kris pushed on, feeling the earth rise and fall under each weightless and nauseating step she took. Her vision struggled to remain focused with each turn of the head, and all that was close appeared distant, and whatever lay beyond swayed uncontrollably, as she struggled to remain upright with the aid of a hiking pole. A mule deer fearlessly watched her passage from beside the trail.

Slowly, she traversed the rises, plateaus and switchbacks at the same steady pace, wavering at times before regaining her balance and a semblance of control over her forward motion. Three hours into a two hour climb, she passed under a natural stone arch below the summit, and pulled herself up a winding metal staircase leading to a pathway cut step by step into the granite, the path rising further than she was able to lift her head.

A three story, stone tower dominates the nearly barren summit of Harney Peak. The door of the tower opens onto a landing with a staircase dropping down to the former living quarters of forest service personnel. A metal ladder fastened to the wall of the landing leads to a glass enclosed lookout station. Kris passed through the landing onto an open terrace enclosed by thick, stone walls and then continued to a pathway leading away from the tower. She followed the pathway to a point where the natural curvature of the summit obliterated the tower and sat beside a small scrub pine, which bore the weight of a brightly colored assortment of ribbons forming a large prayer bundle.

Kris looked down upon a sea of ponderosa pine flowing away from the summit, and relentlessly pierced by imposing spheres of granite. The Badlands stretched across the distant horizon in a shimmer of white. She laid down with her head on the backpack, the sun on her face and closed her eyes. A pair of hawks circled silently above, and later she awoke to a cold breeze and a darkening sky. The hawks were gone, and bands of rain were moving away from the Badlands towards the Black Hills.

She removed a hooded sweatshirt and rain gear from the backpack, slipped into both and shouldered the backpack, barely making it to the forest service tower, as the cold rain began to fall and quickly turned to sleet. Climbing up to the lookout station, she watched the cell approach, engulf the forest below, and quickly rise above the peak in a fury of wind driven hail that accumulated along the granite steps leading down from the summit.

After the storm cleared the mountain, she climbed down the ladder from the lookout platform and left the tower as another cell was bearing down in the distance, and suddenly realized the vertigo had lifted. This allowed her to follow the rough and unmarked Indian trail down the mountain, the way Dan had taken her since she was old enough to make the climb, and by the time the second cell passed over the mountain, she was halfway through the Black Elk Forest. The lower elevation brought only rain, and two hours later she was back in the Wrangler with both hands wrapped around a warm cup of coffee.

The following week a blizzard barrelled across the plains out of the Southwest, shutting off access to the hiking trails throughout the Black Hills. The wind driven bitter cold lingered long after the storm and became a catalyst for what was to follow.

Restless and housebound, Kris grew increasingly edgy. The waves of vertigo were occurring with less frequency, but more intense and she considered moving back into the studio at Provincetown for no other reason than to expel the anxiety before it spilled over.

Whether by chance or design, her mother was forced to cancel a scheduled return to Ireland. Anne made the journey to the Aran Islands annually to check on her mothers' cottage and arrange for whatever maintenance issues needed attention. The cottage and the Aran Islands were too isolated and removed from the mainland, for her to ever consider returning permanently, although she could never part with the cottage. She asked Kris to take her place.

Ten

Aran Islands

The ferry moved away from the docks at Rossaveal Harbor at six o'clock in the evening on the last run of the day to the sparsely populated and windswept Aran Islands of Galway, Ireland.

A slashing rain buffeted the ferry as it sailed out of the harbor and straight into the wind driven swell of the open sea. In better weather, the journey of ten nautical miles lasted roughly forty-five minutes before the ferry slipped through a narrow gap in the seawall at Inis Meain, a construction of rectangular and uniformly cut granite blocks stacked one upon the other, a tactile statement of defiance against the often hostile North Atlantic.

Kris had settled into one of the well-worn seats within the cool and damp of the passenger cabin of the ferry bound for the island of Inis Meain, and was joined by three other travellers, all residents of Inis Oirr, the second and final destination that evening. Kris soon realized her presence onboard constituted the only reason for the ferry to hazard the narrow passageway of the Inis Meain seawall under the fierce winds and rising sea.

Her journey began the previous day at Rapid City Airport in South Dakota with layovers in Minneapolis and Boston that lead eventually to a predawn arrival at Shannon Airport on the West Coast of Ireland.

Sleep was never an option for Kris on the overnight flight from Boston to Shannon. The best she could manage was to linger in a near state, which allowed for way too much contemplation and with eyes weary beyond all chance of reading, the inflight movies offered a reprieve from herself.

When the plane landed at Shannon, the Irish passport helped to avoid the long queue of Americans winding through customs, a perk of the dual citizenship acquired as a child. Once beyond the inbound checkpoint, she considered sleeping off the effects of the journey at the Park Inn Hotel, a short walk across the parking lot from the airport terminal.

The crackling in her ears signaled a pending bout of vertigo, and long periods of sleep remained the only way to maintain her equilibrium. Unfortunately, the Met Éireann weather advisory at the airport was warning of a status orange series of back to back gales bearing down on the entire western seaboard of Ireland. Her only chance of getting from Galway City Centre out to Inis Meain would be on the ferry that evening.

If weather conditions took a turn for the worse and prompted Met Éireann to elevate the warning to status red, she could become stranded in Galway, and it wasn't uncommon for winter gales to last a week or more.

Kris opted instead for breakfast at the Park Inn before the nausea took hold, as she knew it must. Afterwards, she waited out the hour and a half before the first bus bound for Galway arrived at the airport. It was ten o'clock before she finally walked bleary eyed across Eyre Square in Galway City Center.

The ferry office is located on the edge of the square, a few doors down from the Skeffington Arms Hotel or 'The Skeff', as locals refer to the popular hotel and pub. She purchased her ticket for the trip to Inis Meain and left her suitcase at the ferry office until the shuttle bus from Galway to Rossaveal boarded at five o'clock that evening.

The brisk sea air coming off Galway Bay felt good on her face. The calm and overcast morning offering only the slightest hint of the storms barreling towards the coast as she walked up through Eyre Square from the ferry office with a backpack over her shoulder.

Her energy levels started to return on the walk down the hill towards Tesco Supermarket. The timing was good, as she needed to stuff the backpack with whatever amount of food items she could manage to carry up the hill and back across Eyre Square to the ferry office. The winter shelves of the only shop on Inis Meain were stocked at the mercy of the sea and winds, and notoriously barren.

Kris was thirteen on her last visit to Inis Meain, the summer before her grandmother died in May of 2001, and some of the basic survival techniques had stayed with her. The foremost being the necessity of having enough food staples on hand to ride out the weather, regardless of whatever warnings Met Éireann was offering at the moment.

Her last shopping excursion in Galway had been in the company of her grandmother to gather items either unavailable or too expensive to claim shelf space at the island shop. Often, the quest for an exotic spice or a special knitting needle was known to span the length and breadth of Galway City

Center. A leisurely lunch always followed such quixotic pursuits, and they would sit across from each other and speak of things of little consequence to the world at large, and she missed her grandmother more at that moment than ever before.

After her grandmother died, the cottage on Inis Meain remained vacant and there was concern of the damp taking over if it remained uninhabited. The practical solution was to rent the cottage to one of the teachers, writers or artists who came to work on the island during the long, wet winters. The summers were left open in the event her mother wanted or needed to extend her annual visit.

With the gathering of a few necessities behind her and the backpack deposited at the Ferry office, Kris took a stroll to get reacquainted with the city centre and started at upper Shop Street where buskers still worked the usual places. Although, she has never felt compelled to add to their collection baskets, as much as her grandmother encouraged by pressing a few coins extracted from an old leather pouch into the palm of her hand saying, 'I'll wait here, love.'

The smells drifting out of the open doors of a French boulangerie were tempting, but she knew better than test the boundaries of the vertigo and wouldn't eat again until she reached the island. At the bottom of Shop Street, she continued past the Spanish Arch to Galway Museum, and spent time with the stone sculpture of poet, Padraic O'Conaire, the work as captivating as the first time she happened upon it years earlier in Eyre Square. Time and vandals prompted the move into the museum, and in the process stole the works true essence, the sculptor never intended the work to be sequestered from the light of day, and it matters.

Leaving the museum, Kris strolled 'The Long Walk', and sat on a bench beside Galway Bay. The fatigue getting harder to ignore the longer she remained still, and finally stood and made her way past the docklands to Queen Street and up to Eyre Square, settling into a booth at the back of 'The Skeff' with a pot of tea.

The booth was dark and littered with large, soft cushions, and she deleted all her unread email with one click, checked the latest weather report issued by Met Éireann, and immediately dozed off within the seductive warmth of the open peat fire. Two hours later, the old gentleman seated beside the fireplace whom she spoke with earlier was gently shaking her shoulder saying, 'Sorry lovely, you'll be after missing your ferry, so.'

She bolted upright in her seat with only fifteen minutes to get to the ferry office, gather her belongings and cover the two blocks between there and the shuttle to Rossaveal. She thanked the old man and slid a twenty Euro note across the bar on the way out for the tea and a few pints for her timekeeper. The next ten minutes were spent in a frenzied dash to the ferry office and ended in a cold sweat by the time she boarded the bus.

The ride out of the city towards Rossaveal took her mind off the near miss. So many things had changed in her absence and then again so much remained the same. The much anticipated storm was settling in by the time they reached the outskirts of Salthill and beginning to feel like a siege. Fierce winds were rocking the bus and the windshield wipers worked furiously trying to keep pace with the rain.

The driver appeared unfazed and continued along as though the evening was dry and clear. Nor was there a flicker of concern to be found on the faces of the other passengers, and Kris expected the stoic nature would remain unshaken beyond the relative tranquillity of the road winding through the Connemara darkness.

Mic Conner, the ferry captain and his entire crew were also unmistakably within their element, and never more obvious to Kris than on that night, as the ferry circled slow and wide amid the massive swells and torrential rain, a few hundred metres off the shores of Inis Meain.

Jehr Dan was doing his best to hold the ferry in position for a run at the narrow entrance of the harbor were the winds to slacken long enough to offer a window of opportunity. For Kris, the tumultuous voyage seemed endless, as halfway across Galway Bay the vertigo resurfaced and left her struggling to keep the nausea under control.

Jehr Dan was determined to get Kris onto the pier at Inis Meain, but eventually had to abandon the illusion of squeezing through the gap in the seawall, as winds were increasing the longer they hesitated. He made the decision to attempt a landing at the freight dock on the other end of the island with the hope of finding a semblance of shelter from the storm.

The ferry bucked and stammered along parallel to the sandy stretch of Trá Leichtreach beach that was lost to the darkness, and eventually they rounded the edge of the island past the knoll where Padraig and Maire Joyce were laid to rest within the walled compound of the cemetery.

Kris knew what lay ahead when the ferry arrived at the freight pier and started to gather herself both mentally and physically. There would be only one attempt to get her ashore and she desperately wanted and needed to be free of the ferry. The gale force winds smeared rivulets of rain and sea foam across the windows of the passenger cabin and offered no chance to gage how close they were to the dock. All she could do was stand and wedge herself between the last two rows of seats for a quick exit, if the opportunity presented itself.

The moment finally struck, and she was barely able to keep up with what ensued. The violence engulfing the ferry ceased without warning, and the instant tranquillity created its own brand of chaos, as in one swift move, the oldest member of the crew took possession of her backpack, unlatched the door leading out to the lower deck and disappeared.

By the time Kris dragged her suitcase out the door, the man was halfway up the metal ladder on his way to the upper deck. The ferry was still heaving on the storm driven swells and she grabbed onto the side rail, struggling to get her bearings, the entire ferry starkly illuminated by banks of floodlights running the length of the pier.

The ferry rose and fell precariously, barely inches from the seaweed infested wall of the pier, the platform looming far above the ferry and lost within the glare of the floodlights. Kris started up the metal ladder to the upper deck clutching her suitcase with one hand, the railing in the other and climbed as quickly as she could with the suitcase suspended in mid-air.

She reached the upper deck as the crew was setting the metal gangplank to breach the distance between the ferry and the platform of the pier, which was still a few feet above where they stood, and forced

Kris to pull herself up the rain slicked incline by using the metal handrail while the suitcase trailed behind. She was barely free of the gangplank when the crew dragged it aboard and looking back at the ferry, Mic Conner was standing in the open door of the bridge house, and momentarily held her gaze, turned and went back inside.

Standing on the edge of the pier, she found herself surrounded by a collection of boxes containing food and household items shucked off the ferry. From out of the darkness, a contingent of islanders in cars and tractors began arriving to collect the goods. A tall woman with a mass of blond hair whipping about her face took possession of Kris' backpack and mouthed something lost to the wind, gave up trying after the second attempt and motioned for Kris to follow her into an old, grey passenger van.

Kris placed the suitcase in the back of the van beside the backpack and looked back towards the ferry pulling away from the dock. The older crewman was moving down the metal ladder to the lower deck and back into the safety of the passenger cabin. Ten minutes later the pier would be dark and empty, as though the tumultuous episode never occurred.

Once inside the van the woman turned and spoke a few words in Irish to Kris, who was two rows back and surrounded by wet boxes.

'Sorry, I don't speak Irish.'

'No worries. Where are you staying?' The woman's brogue held a familiar cadence, and had a calming effect on Kris, as though returning home after a long journey.

‘The Conneely Cottage, please.’ Kris answered and the woman peered into the rear view mirror to get a better look at her but didn’t say anything, and they rode along in silence through a maze of narrow, stone walled lanes and Kris lost all bearings in relation to the pier, her grandmother’s cottage and the sea.

Exhaustion from the vertigo was seeping into her bones and she leaned back on the seat, realizing at that moment how close she was to the edge, and how desperate her need for solitude. A series of lightning flashes illuminated the cottage on a distant knoll, and she longed for more that never came.

Built on the highest point of the island the cottage overlooks the patchwork of small fields, ancient stone walls and traditional homes scattered across the landscape, and hardly a movement by man, woman or beast fails to escape notice, albeit by design or happenstance. In one direction, the mountains of Connemara appear close to the touch across the open waters of Galway Bay, and in another the shimmering coastline of Co. Clare from the Burren to O’Brien’s Tower.

When the van arrived at the cart road leading up to the cottage, the woman made an aggressive attempt to navigate the steep, rain slicked track only to have the van slide back down. Then without hesitation she got out of the van, placed the suitcase and backpack in the wet grass beside the muddy track, collected her five euro fee and disappeared back down the lane.

Suddenly alone in all consuming darkness, the cold wind howling above a deluge of rain, and the vague form of the cottage looming above, Kris placed the backpack on her shoulders, lifted the suitcase with both hands and proceeded to sidestep up the muddy track. At the top of the slope she passed between two stone outbuildings to find herself facing a towering set of wooden gates between her and the entrance to the cottage.

Her grandfather constructed the gates to prevent the cold winds of winter from scouring the gap between the cottage and limestone cliff that runs parallel, and Kris had never seen them closed before. The gates were bound by chains and secured with a lock, leaving no choice but to return between the outbuildings and venture across the soggy, rough patch of the front garden to the narrow gravel lane leading back towards the gates and entrance to the cottage.

Fifteen minutes later her cold, wet fingers were turning numb, as she fumbled around for a skeleton key that mercifully was still kept above the back door and allowed her to finally lurch into the vestibule and across the threshold of the cottage. The key for the lock holding the chains together was attached to a strip of leather hanging on the coat rack beside the door. She opened the gates and gathered her rain soaked suitcase.

The act of closing the cottage door behind her was empowering and for the first time in days she felt in control of the most basic elements of her life. This in spite of the bone chilling cold that gave the familiar surroundings a harshness she had never experienced, and the heavy drapes covering the doors and windows only contributed to the dark, moody atmosphere.

The backpack was saturated, and she spread the contents across the kitchen table, placed the cheese in refrigerator, hung the backpack in the vestibule leaving the rest to sort out in the morning. The most pressing need was to build a fire in the woodstove, and she set about trying to light a handful of damp kindling, which took repeated efforts to finally catch hold under a few chunks of peat.

Her grandfather inherited and renovated the cottage long before her mother was born and the woodstove was located in the sitting room, a tall, open space stretching to the rafters. Opposite the stove, a wooden staircase climbs alongside the wall to a landing that connects bedrooms at both ends of the cottage.

A short distance from the woodstove an alcove that her grandmother referred to as 'the cubby' was tucked below the landing and filled entirely by an oversized, red leather sofa and velvet cushions that became the center of her world during the long, dark days of winter. Evenings were spent by the fire with an open book, a ball of yarn and a hot toddy.

Kris thought about unpacking the suitcase but possessed neither the energy nor the will. A pair of sweats and hooded sweatshirt was all she really needed, and after changing out of the wet clothes went upstairs and took a comforter from one of the beds, came back down and shut off the lights then curled up on the sofa.

Sleep was immediate but short lived and she awoke with her heart racing and the room spinning, the dreams and night sweats becoming more frequent and intense, and she sat there in the dark with knees drawn to her chest, the comforter held tight and took slow, deep breaths until her heartbeat began to settle and the image of Sam lying beside her in a pool of blood began to fade.

How long she remained upright or when the roaring fire became a faint glow in the dark escaped with the wind itself, and it was the silence that caused her eyes to open again, and she didn't move or want to move, and when she awoke the second time the drapes were edged in sunlight and the sound of a passing tractor made everything real again. There was enough life remaining in the embers to stoke and tease with kindling topped by two long, slender bits of peat, and drawing back the drapes brought a burst of sunlight into the sitting room.

She opened the upper half of the wooden door leading onto the narrow patch of front garden enclosed by a stonewall teetering on the edge of the bluff, and beyond only a brilliant expanse of sky, a plethora of stonewalls flowing towards the sea, and in the far distance a man with a dog at his side moving slowly towards the pier along the rise and fall of a slender lane.

The air was cold, and it was a different, sharper cold on Inis Meain than she left behind in Co. Kerry, and she slipped back into her road weary jeans and pulled a pair of dry sneakers out of the suitcase. The jacket worn the previous night remained soaked, and she laid it across the back of her grandmothers' rocking chair and placed it close to the woodstove. Then she went about the ground floor pulling back drapes and opening windows to chase out the damp, and with the light of day had the first real look at the cottage, which remained utterly unchanged, as she had hoped.

The white porcelain wood stove was still as attractive as the day it was installed, the year her grandmother returned from Boston for good. The stove became the centrepiece of a kitchen update long in the coming and many a rainy afternoon was spent chatting over a pot of tea and a plate of fresh baked scones. Kris built another fire and then went straight for the coffee and brown bread from Tesco.

The heat from the porcelain stove rose through a vent in the ceiling and started the process of warming the bedroom above the kitchen, the one her grandmother had called her own, and Kris intended to do likewise. The coffee from Tesco was better than expected and she poured another mug from the French press and afterwards poked around the kitchen cabinets that still held the odd bits of condiments, crackers and a scary looking jar of instant coffee from various tenants to be thrown away and the cabinets cleaned, but the most pressing need was to unpack the hiking boots and get out into the landscape shouting at her through the open windows.

A half hour later the hiking boots were laced, the rain jacket stuffed into the backpack and she was passing through the open gates, side stepping the muddy footprints from the previous night to trek alongside the stone outbuilding where her grandmother hung flowers to dry, and then across a patch of rough ground to a narrow gap in the stonewall that runs along the top of the ridge.

The ground beneath her feet turned to stone, slab after slab weathered smooth and glistening in the sunlight with barely a space separating one from the other, the occasional tuft of grass or bold clutch of wildflowers rising up through a fissure to break the soft, grey stretch of limestone flowing to the edge of Gregory Sound, the storm swollen patch of sea that lay between the islands of Inis Meain and Inis Mor.

Kris wandered randomly through the maze of iconic stonewalls that dominate the windswept, barren landscape and silently embody the harsh realities of daily sustenance hauled from the sea or conjured from the stone clad earth, and she continued past pillars of odd shaped stones carefully stacked in a manner that resembled prayer bundles of a different order, naively created to appeal to whatever deity inspired the hands and backs of the impromptu artists.

At times, Kris remained still and listened to nothing at all, not the wind or birds or a solitary voice to pierce the moment, and watched in the distance to the rise and fall of an angry sea running headlong into the Cliffs of Moher, and shattering into mute bursts of white foam only to fall away into a cloud of mist, and then again and again.

The tide was out when she reached the edge of the sea and a dark limestone plateau stretched along the shoreline in both directions, and in places covered by a sheen of green moss exposed to the harsh light of day, the tattered remains of a seaweed colony and bowl shaped tidal pools tumbled smooth by boulders imprisoned within the ebb and flow of relentless storms.

Kris picked a small granite stone from a shallow pool, attracted by its dull, satin finish and held it in the palm of her hand as she followed the plateau along the shoreline, pausing only to avoid the surge of a gathering tide until finally being forced to climb above the plateau and return to a footpath worn tight to the fieldstone barrier facing the sea, the wall battered and breached by the violent storm surge that arrived in the dark of night and stole the precious grounds upon which it lay, bit by bit.

The weight of the stone felt good in her hand and she squeezed hard and tried to recall the last time she touched stone, felt the warmth of her hand slowly absorbed or knew the moment it would allow the finely honed edge of a chisel to penetrate its weathered, brittle shell without harm, one to the other.

The walkabout came to an end on a shelf of flat, grey limestone with her legs dangling over the edge, the wind rising and a harsh chill beginning to settle over the island. She brushed the hair from her eyes with fingertips tracing the raw edges of the tender scar above her ear and let the stone roll off her palm into the sea, watching it disappear without a sound and stood and made her way back to the cottage as rain began to fall.

Slipping into a heavy knit sweater she went about the cottage shutting windows, stoked and added more turf to the wood stoves then boiled a large pot of rice and opened a can of soup. By the time she sat down at the long, wooden table in the kitchen and looked out over the island, a steel grey shroud was clinging to the shoreline and offering the tantalizing suggestion that nothing lay beyond.

Gale force winds returned that evening and scoured the island for three days with storm surges creeping further and further inland beyond the already battered and tumbled stonewalls from the previous month, and hardly a soul ventured into the lanes unless driven there by the need to attend livestock or school or the pub, and the ferry remained sequestered and bound to the pier at Inis Oirr.

Kris spent the time unpacking and organizing the cottage as best she could and didn't mind the rain then or ever, and the sense of being cut off from the world was especially comforting, and she continued to sleep in the sitting room on the big, red sofa not far from the woodstove. It would take a week or more of the bedrooms upstairs being exposed to the warm and dry before she could claim the space, but the cubby remained inviting and the bookcases scattered about harbored Joyce, Beckett, Behan and the usual suspects along with a slew of unfamiliar European and American authors her grandmother felt the need to support and the choice of genres reliably eclectic and of little consequence to the process.

The first month on Inis Meain occurred in a haze of cleaning, organising and gathering the fundamentals of life, as one does on a tiny island in the North Atlantic. The basic necessities never come easy and priorities are watered down beyond a point hardly thought possible in another time and place and a sense of control slowly seeped back into her waking moments even as the nights continued to be littered by the nightmares that accompanied her to the island.

On the promise of a stretch of weather as calm and clear to be expected of late March, Kris ventured another ferry crossing and bus journey into Galway City. The list of items that she didn't want to live without was growing, and she also felt a need to spend a few days getting reacquainted with her new hometown.

She left the cottage in early morning darkness, the night clear and star studded with a full moon illuminating the lanes, and in the distance, between night sky and sea, the erratic shimmer of lights created a false horizon and traced the coastline from Connemara to Galway City, and offered the only indication of life beyond herself.

The air was cold and she walked quickly with the nearly empty suitcase in tow and arrived at the ferry pier early and stood at the edge of the seawall and watched the landscape slowly transformed by the rising sun, the first light making a failed attempt to pry a rainbow from the sea, and at half seven the ferry silently rounded the northern tip of the island from Inis Oirr.

The narrow channel between the seawall and pier was calm and the ferry made an effortless spin within the tight quarters of the tiny harbor and came to rest alongside the pier. Ropes were cast onto the platform of the dock and tied off by an elderly gentlemen in a swede cap who harvested cockles in the tidal flat that lay beyond the harbor, and to Kris the scene appeared choreographed with the island doctor, librarian, and a pair of part time teachers streaming across the short metal gangplank.

The outbound passengers boarded in the same rapid fashion while the swede capped gentleman handed off his freshly harvested batch of cockles bound for Galway, and the blond taxi driver passed along a pair of suitcases to the lower deck. At the last possible moment, the crew retrieved the gangplank and the ropes were unleashed from the pier by the youngest member of the crew who then jumped aboard with the ferry already in motion.

Kris had been the last passenger to board and no sooner across the upper deck and down the metal ladder to the passenger cabin when the ferry started through the channel towards Rossaveal. She deposited her suitcase and backpack inside the cabin and went back out to the lower deck and sat on a bench tucked in close to the passenger cabin and watched the island slowly fade into the distance and become a thin, grey speck suspended above the turbulent wake of the full throttled ferry. A sudden squall forced her back inside halfway to Rossaveal.

The islanders and crew spoke Irish amongst themselves and she found it easy to remain unencumbered by conversation, although the curiosity flowing in her direction was both palpable and aloof in a shy, self-conscious manner that she found attractive. The crew to a man were happy enough to settle into a chosen niche and close their eyes or sail along with yesterday newspaper only to come alive again as the ferry approached the berth at Rossaveal.

The exodus from the ferry was equally efficient with the entire roster of passengers disgorged onto the dock and guided swiftly up the ramp towards the waiting bus, the whistler once again at the wheel. One hour later Kris was checking into the Skeff for a two-night stay, which the manager extended a third night as a perk for living on the island, a lovely gesture that was politely declined.

The room was basic and clean with breakfast included and a decent internet connection, which she hadn't accessed in over a month. She unpacked the few clothing items brought for the occasion and headed down to the pub to check her email. The inbox contained a mountain of spam along with a few travel receipts and follow up surveys from the initial travel bookings for the trip to Ireland. Her mother sent a brief note to say she was thinking of her with no answer required, although, Kris promised herself to make the effort.

The simple act of eating a tomato and cheese sandwich with an order of chips and a pint of Guinness felt decadent. After lunch, she walked over to St. Augustine Street to join the Galway City

Library then cut across to Shop Street with buskers out in force on the clear and unusually warm day, the street filled with locals taking extended lunch breaks to bask in the sunshine.

The afternoon was spent propped against the wall of the Spanish Arch beside the River Corrib, which was mad with runoff from the storms, and she sat with the sun on her legs and a slightly worn copy of 'The Selected Letters of Vincent Van Gogh' in her lap, a used copy obtained from Charlie Byrne's Bookstore on Middle Street, and the only interruption all afternoon was a hungry gull in search of a handout. The language and lovely manner in which Van Gogh expressed himself was not something she expected to find and finished the book that evening in a booth next to the fireplace at the Skeff and was in bed by ten o'clock.

The first full day in Galway consisted of crossing items off a list that seemed to grow as she went along. Only so much could be wheeled in the suitcase or carried over her shoulder on a single outing that included hauling the entire collection up the ladder and off the ferry at Inis Meain. The upper deck of the ferry was wide open, and the rain and rough seas made the passenger cabin on the lower deck the only option for keeping items safe and dry.

On the final day Kris wandered into some of the smaller shops and hardware stores for future reference then split the afternoon between the library and museum. In the evening, she indulged the urge for a pizza and half a carafe of house red at Fat Freddy's on Quay Street and the next morning was happily aboard the ten thirty ferry pulling away from the dock at Rossaveal.

Eleven

Inis Meain

With daylight hours growing longer in April, the life Kris was living assumed a rhythm that continued to be dominated by bouts of vertigo and complicated a profound desire to simply get on with daily existence, as found on Inis Meain.

On good days, the afternoons were spent repairing anything to do with the cottage or outbuildings that was within her power to make right again and this included her grandmothers much loved and pampered bicycle found suspended by its frame from the ceiling of one of the outbuildings, and after topping off the air in the tires with the hand pump, tightening the chain and raising the seat, the bicycle was returned to its former resting place beside the back door of the cottage.

Evenings, with the exception of an occasional stroll to watch the sunset were all about books. The elderly librarian at the Inis Meain branch of the Galway Library had apparently taken Kris on as a personal project and not only kept her supplied with a steady flow of books from the mainland but also knitted her a hat and a pair of gloves and she suspected an unsolicited sweater was in the works.

Returning from a walk along the beach during the last week of May, she found a package waiting at the back door of the cottage. Inside she found two leather bundles smothered in loose straw. The first bundle contained a braided wand of sweet grass and a short hammer with a round head shaped like a cylinder. The second, a cloth pouch that held her stone carving tools, handmade at a foundry in France and a gift from Dan Walker two years earlier. She hadn't laid eyes on the tools since joining the FBI.

The contents of the box and its arrival not a totally unexpected reaction to her decision to remain on the island. Dan had once again offered a way forward and the braided sweet grass would be used three weeks later to purify both the cottage and studio space created within a stone outbuilding that lay halfway between the cottage and the pier.

Dan was the force behind her early introduction to stone carving when in the spring of the year Kris turned ten, a well-known sculptor from New England accepted the position of Sculptor-In-Residence at Mount Rushmore. The man was noted for his ability to carve faces in stone and along with his duties pertaining to the mountain, he conducted a series of stone carving class during the summer months for teachers and artists from South Dakota and Wyoming. Dan arranged to have Kris inserted into the class and not just for a week, but for the entire summer, if this pleased her, which it very much did.

Each morning of that first summer, Dan dropped her off at the sculptor's studio and Kris worked side by side with an array of art teachers. She was the only child allowed to participate and whenever her arms grew too tired to swing the hammer, she sat in the shade and read a book.

Dan worked a short walk away in the administration building and joined Kris each day for lunch. They often walked the Presidential Trial that runs along the base of the monument and at times, they departed the trail and climbed up towards the monument to share lunch in a grove of Ponderosa pine with a view towards the thin, white outline of the Badlands along the edge of the horizon. Dan returned to the studio after work and they would discuss her latest efforts and what she hoped to accomplish the next day and even at that tender age, carving the human face was her only interest.

There was no message of any type to accompany the package, nor was one required. The cleansing smoke of the braided sweet grass would remove all sources of negativity from the cottage and studio. While the hammer and chisels were intended to tame the darker forces of her spirit, as only Dan knew they would.

The morning after the package arrived Kris left the cottage before sunrise. The family field was located at the end of a short track that branched away from the lane leading down to the pier. The thatched roof outbuilding was built out of fieldstone with the windowless backside towards the lane. On the other side nothing stood between the outbuilding and the sea except a stonewall, meticulously built and rebuilt by the generations who came before her.

She sat outside on the bench her grandfather had built along the wall of the outbuilding facing the sea, and leaning back with eyes closed, listened to the sound of the breakers crashing against the rocky shoreline. The sea was running strong with a light wind rising from the west, and after a while came the sounds of footsteps accompanied by voices of outbound travelers winding their way down to the pier, and then nothing but the rhythms of the sea, the wind and the low, slow sounds of her heartbeat.

The outbuilding was a bare bones open space with a woodstove and two large windows facing the sea that were protected from the fierce winter storms by shutters in desperate need of a coat of paint. The windows were hinged to swing inwards while the shutters latched to the outside wall and allowed a fair amount of natural light to filter through and fortunately for Kris, the lack of electrical power suited her style of stone carving, which simply requires a hammer, chisel and decent stone. The latter in ample supply a few metres beyond the stonewall that separated the outbuilding from the sea.

The days to follow were spent removing farming tools, an old wheel barrel without handles and years' worth of rusted and obsolete clutter from the outbuilding. A ladder found lashed to the rafters was used to climb onto the roof and scrape down the inside of the flute pipe with a wire brush duct taped to a broom handle. Afterwards she cleaned the grate and scraped out the inside of the wood stove.

At the end of the second week the outbuilding was beginning to show promise as a studio, and she ordered a load of peat briquettes to be delivered from the island shop and then managed to turn the leftover timber used by her grandfather to construct the tall, wooden gates at the cottage into a set of stone carving stands that could accommodate her penchant for keeping two sculptures simultaneously in progress.

With the exception of the small patch that her grandfather had once cultivated for a garden, the field behind the outbuilding was a nearly continuous shelf of limestone, polished and scoured over the eons by unabated winds and driving rain.

Although, Kris had always found the barren and limestone encrusted landscape to be an attractive and soothing presence, not unlike the granite outcroppings that shape and define the Black Hills of South Dakota.

The thought of what her predecessors went through to simply exist on the island was daunting and the limestone a serious impediment to overcome. The meagre amounts of soil that existed to grow crops was created by mixing seaweed and sand collected on the shore and hauled to the field on the back of a donkey or more commonly, the islander became the beast of burden, and the relentless gales of winter assured the entire process would be revisited in the spring.

Kris dismantled a section of the stonewall bordering the lane to allow the load of peat briquettes to be delivered next to the outbuilding. Afterwards, she rebuilt the stonewall leaving a gap wide enough to accommodate the bicycle, and for the final aspect of the project she purified the space with the smoke of braided sweet grass at sunrise of the seventeenth day following Dan's silent intervention.

The morning routine remained the same after the studio was ready and started in the predawn with the scrawny figure of a small free roaming chicken running out of the semi-darkness in a mad dash from her night roost towards the back door of the cottage in search of vegetable scraps from the previous evening. She appeared to be gaining weight since Kris arrived at the cottage, although the aggressive nature of the rest of the free roaming brood made survival an ongoing challenge, and the tiny chicken hardly possessed an ounce of fight.

When the weather allowed, Kris wandered over to the remote and uninhabited west side of the island, and started to jog for short periods, which was tempting fate as far as the vertigo was concerned. Yet, it felt good to push back against the physical barrier holding her captive for so long and to regain even a small semblance of control. The early morning jaunt was usually followed by a couple hard boiled eggs and a bowl of steel cut oats that had been brought to a boil in a small pan and left to simmer while she changed into her carving jeans and a hooded sweatshirt.

After breakfast she gathered the stone carving tools and started down to the studio. More often than not the farmers dog would be waiting beside the bicycle when Kris came out of the cottage, which meant leaving the bike behind and making the trek with the old boy trailing alongside, and if she ventured too far out in front, the dog would stop walking and stand in the lane listening for her footsteps. This required her to stop and talk him over to where she was standing, and they would sit down next to a stonewall and wait until he recaptured his bearings, and the fact that a dog and chicken were becoming her closest friends on the island gave no pause.

The stones gathered from the edge of the sea were pale white and tumbled smooth by the constant pounding of the breakers, a tightly grained form of granite that resisted the chisel with each swing of the hammer, tough carving but the coloration was attractive and the shapes chosen to limit the amount of material to be removed.

Kris spent the better part of a day selecting and then physically transporting the stones that outweighed her from the shore to the outbuilding, and later felt good to finally stand in the doorway and see the

stones on the carving stands, knowing she was about to be consumed by the sculpting process, and drawn irresistibly to a place deep within herself that lay beyond reach for too long.
She would eventually choose to carve the face of a woman in one of the stones, a finely detailed portrait of no one in particular, and the other a primitive carving of a man captured within a hood, an expressively vacant work that somehow felt right for the time and place, a man besieged by the elements and powerless and acutely aware of his conditional status, the eyes dull and the jaw firmly set.

More stones would make their way to the carving stands over the course of the summer, including another run at carving a portrait of Samuel Beckett, the reclusive Irish born playwright who lived, worked and died in Paris, France. An attempt that continued to elude what attracted her most about the man, the unapologetic nature of his desire to be a solitary, anonymous being in a world perceived as not necessarily a cheerful place to wander and in some ways aligned with the man in the hood who preceded him on the carving stand.

As summer faded to autumn the trek back to the cottage was often in darkness, followed by a shower, dinner and falling asleep with an open book across her chest. The solitary lifestyle was easy on the senses and over the course of the summer she felt herself growing physically stronger day by day. The morning walkabout had been transformed into a steady run of an hour or more with the exception of a recurring bout of vertigo, and even then became a matter of a slow walk with only a few days totally lost.

The autumn rains began to linger for longer spells with the overcast skies and steady loss of natural light bringing the stone carving activity at the studio nearly to a halt, although there was consolation to be found in the long shadows and moody atmosphere of the evolving landscape, as the sun moved ever lower across the horizon. The dark afternoons were spent preparing the cottage and outbuildings for the winter storms that would arrive soon enough. Kris also made a few trips into Galway to gather items from a winter supply list that included dried and canned food, batteries, bottled water and candles. The essentials needed to maintain her independence during the extended bouts of isolation from the mainland that were a given.

In Galway, a taxi was enlisted to deliver supplies gathered from Tesco and Lidl's to the docklands, and then placed on a skid to be loaded onto the cargo ship that makes a weekly run to all three of the Aran Islands. The skid would be off loaded onto the freight pier at Inis Meain and hauled by tractor up to the cottage to be sorted. The amount of goods on the skid suggested she was over thinking what was truly needed but found that easier to live with than the prospect of a forced exodus.

At one point, the thought of returning to the Black Hills for the winter crossed her mind but was dismissed as quickly as it arrived and after a week of cleaning and organizing the weather was predicted to clear for a three day stretch and she took the opportunity to spend the time in the studio. It was there, as she was working in late afternoon that she felt a presence behind her and turned to find Jack O'Malley standing in the doorway.

They hadn't spoken since she departed Boston and for what seemed an endless moment, neither made an attempt to bridge the silence, their eyes both searching and knowing at once, and finally, 'I wouldn't be here Kris, if there was another choice.'

During the last conversation they shared, Kris made it clear that her desire to remain with the agency had died along with Sam on that dirty tenement floor and a return to active service would depend on more than simply being declared physically ready, and also knew with certainty that she wasn't the right person to seek justice for Sam, as badly as she wanted and needed it to happen. But this felt different and the expression on O'Malley's face such that she put down the hammer and chisel. 'What is it, Jack.'

'John Davis is dead.' He remained standing in the doorway, and for a moment, Kris struggled to process the words placed between them. 'He was shot three days ago in Paris while riding a bicycle through Luxembourg Gardens.'

'Robbery?'

'No.'

'Suspect?'

'Yes.' Jack walked into the studio. 'He was shot by the same gun that killed Sam.'

Kris searched O'Malley's eyes for any hint of something beyond the cold reality of his message and there was nothing to be found, and she moved past him, out into the wind and the gathering dusk and took a seat on the bench facing the sea. Jack gave her a few moments then sat down next to her and waited for Kris to speak.

'Why Davis? What's the connection?'

'You are.' His answer nearly as stunning as the news of John being killed and neither made any sense.

'What do you have?'

'Ballistics matched the gun to the assassinations in Europe.'

'CCTV?'

'Not in the area where John was gunned down'

'Witnesses?'

'The French authorities identified the members of a small group practicing yoga on a podium within view of the crime scene, but none of the participants heard a gunshot or witnessed the murder.'

'And how am I connected?'

'We believe the assassinations in France and Germany were conducted with the intention of drawing our crew into the surveillance loop for the express purpose of killing both you and John. The only reason he lived as long as he did was because the runner took a hit inside the house by someone in the Springfield cell.'

'How could the runner possibly know about me or John and especially the activities of our crew?'

‘We believe the group that the runner is connected to became aware of the interviews John gave to the Boston media during a six-month period in early 2012. He spoke at length about his research involving the facial recognition abilities of a select group of individuals recruited to work with a newly formed FBI counter terrorism unit.’

‘Why would he do that?’

‘John became excited whenever he spoke about the research program and the obvious implications for law enforcement. Afterwards, when we expressed our concerns over the release of the information he deeply regretted being so open, but of course it was too late.’

‘That still doesn’t explain why our crew was so important when Scotland Yard has a team doing the same work and more being trained in France. Why us?’

‘We discovered that John’s computer was hacked while he was still at Harvard and exposed the fact that your abilities far exceeded what Scotland Yard or anyone else has to offer. The leading theory suggests a substantial attack was in the planning stages and you were perceived as an obstacle, along with Davis and our crew.’

‘How close are you to sorting out which group the runner belongs to?’

‘We still have nothing on the runner or his possible connections. No image captures, fingerprints or DNA matches from the various crime scenes and the same holds true for our chain of informants in Europe.’

‘What makes you so sure it’s a guy?’ Kris stood up from the bench and was looking down at Jack.

‘No reason. Why do you ask?’

‘I dream a lot.’ Kris stopped talking for a moment and stood looking down at him and Jack remained silent, and she began again. ‘The dream is always the same. Sam is just behind me in the hallway.’ She paused again and gathered her thoughts. ‘In the split second before I’m hit, a dark figure leans out of the doorway and I try to warn Sam, but the words won’t come, and then I wake up soaked through with sweat and the image of the runner is always gone. I just realized as we spoke that the figure leaning into the hallway is a woman. The runner’s a woman, Jack.’

‘Alright.’ Jack held her gaze and repeated himself. ‘Alright.’ Then he looked away towards the sea and back up at Kris. ‘You’re sure.’

‘Yes.’

‘Do you have a face?’

‘No.’ She hesitated. ‘Just a vague image in the back of my mind, if the dream can be trusted.’

‘This could change everything’, Jack continued. ‘Our potential list of male candidates for the runner is enormous, but not for a woman working with either Isis or Al-Qaeda.’ He paused again. ‘Even without a face or a name this narrows the list of potential targets, and I think we should follow through with your gut instinct on this one.’

Jack stood up facing her. ‘There’s more, Kris. The hacker was able to gain access to your personal information from Davis's computer and we sent a team to the Black Hills to provide protection for your parents. The reason I'm here is to bring you back to where we can keep you safe. It's getting dark and we should move.'

Kris felt a searing jolt of panic course through her body, as she held his gaze. 'Tell me everything. I want to know exactly what you're doing for my parents.'

'That's all there is Kris. We have people with your parents to the extent they'll allow.' He paused. 'Dan is someone well acquainted with taking care of himself and his family. But we both know he's out of his element with this and you need to talk him.' Jack looked up at the cottage and back at Kris. 'I have a chopper waiting at the airport on the other side of the island, and the plane is being refueled at Galway Airport. Take whatever you need from the cottage and lock up.' His voice was clear and steady. 'We're leaving now.'

Kris closed the studio and pushed the bike through the narrow slot in the stone wall and they walked silently side by side up the lane towards the cottage. The handful of streetlights scattered about the island were beginning to hum and glow a dull shade of amber that would slowly turn a pale yellow and be nearly devoured by the purity of the ascending darkness.

Kris's thoughts ran rampant with the fear and confusion of what was happening with her parents and she did as O'Malley instructed and less than an hour later watched the lights of the cottages on Inis Meain fade into darkness, as the chopper crossed Galway Bay.

As soon as the jet was airborne and reached cruising altitude, Jack handed her a cell phone then walked up the aisle to the cockpit. Dan picked up on the first ring as though no one else could be on the other end. 'Where are you, Kris?'

'I'm on the way to Boston. You guys alright?'

'We're worried about you. They wouldn't let us contact you and your mothers beside herself.'

'I'm sorry, Dan.'

'It's OK. This is not your fault.'

'Dan.' Kris paused. 'I need you to do exactly as Jack O'Malley tells you to do.' There was silence on the other end of the line. 'You have to trust me on this. I've seen what this person is capable of and I need to know your safe.' And still nothing on the other end of the line, and she spoke as calmly as she could manage. 'Please, Dan.' And she waited and finally heard the sharp exhale of breath pass through his lips. 'Tell O'Malley we'll accept his offer, but I need to speak to him right now.'

She called Jack to the seat facing her and handed him the phone. Kris could only hear one side of the conversation but knew exactly what Dan was saying in no uncertain terms. Jack listened patiently and finally, 'I intend to do nothing less, Dan.' And after the call they sat for a moment looking across at each other. 'We need to get some rest, Kris, tomorrow is going to be a long day.' Jack stood and moved across the aisle. Kris reclined the seat and pulled a blanket up around her shoulders and closed her eyes, but there would be no sleeping.

Twelve

Boston

The jet landed at Hanscom Air Force Base in darkness and came to rest beside two vehicles waiting within a large, illuminated hanger. Jack remained locked in a three-way conversation with his French and German counterparts on the drive into Boston while Kris sat quietly looking out the window. The closer they moved towards Boston the more she felt torn from another place and time. It had been only a matter of hours since Jack showed up at her studio, and already her life on Inis Meain assumed a dream like quality, a way of being in the world that was slipping away moment by moment.

They followed a familiar route through the nearly deserted streets of Boston and upon arriving at Beacon Hill, made the turn into Ridgeway Lane and stopped in front of the townhouse. O'Malley held the phone away from his ear. 'The code is the same one you used last time only in reverse order. I'll see you at the office in a few hours.'

Kris stepped onto the cobblestone sidewalk in front of the townhouse and into the glow of soft light from the streetlamp in front of the townhouse, as the van bearing O'Malley continued down Ridgeway Lane and disappeared around the corner in the direction of One Center Plaza. Kris keyed in the code and one of the agents from the second vehicle opened the front door and together they entered into a space she never intended to occupy again.

Moving from room to room, the agent cleared the townhouse, a function that only served to further her growing sense of disconnect from the island. Afterwards the agent returned to the vehicle stationed near the front door, and Kris placed her suitcase in the bedroom, laid down on the bed with eyes open and thoughts struggling to make sense of all that had transpired. The most pressing concern was dealing with the impact this was having on her parents, and she felt the weight of the intrusion into their lives, while knowing too well the level of danger they were facing, and it was difficult not to feel responsible for placing them in jeopardy.

Later, she awoke with a start not knowing how long she had slept and sat up on the edge of the bed, staring into the darkness and the silence and took a deep breath, let it go slowly then forced herself to stand and take off her clothing still embedded with stone dust from the studio at Inis Meain, and indulged herself with a long, hot shower and felt the illusion of inner strength seep back into her bones and that would have to do for the moment.

When she finally arrived at headquarters escorted by the two agents assigned as bodyguards, the new team O'Malley put together was already gathered in the conference room. There was a hesitation to the proceedings when she walked into the meeting and although passing quickly didn't feel that way to Kris. The awkward moment broken by Sarah O'Sullivan, a tall, green eyed woman who was a late comer to the crew led by Sam Bordeaux and someone to whom Kris had felt a certain affinity, and now rose from her seat to wrap her arms around Kris. 'Sorry we had to bring you back, but it was the only option.'

Sarah proceeded to introduce Kris to the other members of the crew and ten minutes later, Jack walked through the door followed by Anthony Russo, the new crew chief chosen to replace Sam. It soon became obvious to Kris from the manner in which the crew communicated that they shared a history of working together, and the atmosphere was charged and positive and helped calm the uneasiness in the pit of her stomach. The mere fact of being thrust into the presence of so many people after months of leading a solitary existence was disconcerting and not a situation she ever willfully pursued but would adapt as best she could.

The newly established crew received an unexpected breakthrough just two days into the painstaking task of sorting through CCTV footage when an image was forwarded from Paris by the head of the counter terrorism unit assigned to investigate the assassination of John Davis. An American tourist who happened to be taking a picture of his new bride at Luxembourg Gardens had inadvertently captured an image of a person wearing a hooded sweatshirt in the vicinity of the location where John Davis was killed.

The couple were questioned on the day but hadn't noticed anything or anyone beside each other and were allowed to leave France with a request to contact the Gendarmerie Nationale in the event anything came to mind. The image was discovered after returning to the States and they immediately notified the French authorities. Russo brought the image up on the large screen in the conference room and the entire crew sat riveted to their seats while Kris walked up to the screen and stood within a foot of the individual who had killed Sam.

The runner was looking back over her shoulder and presumably to the point where John Davis lay dead. The runner' face was angled slightly when the shutter clicked with only a narrow profile visible within the hood clinging tight to her face. 'Crop the face and send the image over to me', she instructed Russo and with that returned to her seat.

'We need to narrow our search to the CCTV footage leading away from Luxembourg Gardens towards the nearest source of public transportation for one hour before and after Davis was killed.' O'Malley took over the conversation. 'And we also want to know if any of the cameras on the streets or in the Metro were malfunctioning or out of service during that same time period.' Then he turned back to Kris, 'What do you need from me?'

'An interrogation room to myself with a twenty-inch monitor and a steady stream of images.' She answered without hesitation. Although, three hours after receiving the image of the runner, the initial excitement began to wane, as no further sightings were discovered within Luxembourg Gardens. The chance encounter with the runner appeared to be a one-off event in spite of the French authorities granting the crew emergency access to the CCTV coverage of the entire 6th arrondissement of Paris.

The crew then began to scour the footage leading away from the murder scene, a tedious and labor intensive undertaking further complicated by the large volume of pedestrian traffic on the day, and the need to work street by street, and then increase the time factor by fifteen minutes increments with each additional scan. O'Malley continued to pressure his French counterparts and later that day obtained a report from the Métro de Paris, the organization responsible for the CCTV maintenance of the Paris Metro Region and immediately reconvened the crew in the conference room.

The report revealed that the Saint Sulpice Metro Station on the Rue de Rennes had been offline for twenty-six minutes at approximately eleven thirty-two, which was thirteen minutes after Davis was killed in Luxembourg Gardens, and the consensus immediately shifted from the lone wolf theory to one of complicity, as someone had intentionally knocked the Saint Sulpice Station offline, and it obviously wasn't the runner.

O'Malley redirected the search to focus on the point from where Davis was killed to the Saint Sulpice Metro Station, as well as whatever footage was available from metro stations that could be reached within thirty minutes of the Saint Sulpice platform in both directions.

'It was also brought to my attention that Davis had an encounter with a band of pickpockets at the Bastille metro station the day before he was killed.' O'Malley added. 'John had inadvertently found himself in the middle of a police operation directed at pickpocket activity within the metro and was subsequently interviewed on the station platform following the incident.'

'According to the report, the band of pickpockets consisted of a handful of young women and three older males who had surrounded a pair of American tourists in one of the metro cars. The unwitting couple were in the process of being relieved of their valuables when Davis stepped into the group and pulled out the female tourist then went back in for her husband who was too shell shocked to move and had to be torn away. Davis then sequestered the couple behind him and for whatever reason the males of the group backed off and when the car reached the Bastille station the undercover unit made the arrests on the platform.'

'This is the only known movement by Davis prior to his murder and offers an opportunity to determine whether he was being followed at the time. The CCTV footage from both the metro car and the station platform have been preserved and are in the process of being forwarded. When the footage arrives, I want the image of every passenger on the metro car isolated and sent over to Kris, and the crowd on the station platform scanned for anyone showing an interest in Davis.'

'Alright then.' O'Malley stood up. 'The couches in the anteroom beside my office are available if anyone needs to catch a few hours of sleep, but I want a rotation going with no more than two people off at a time until we get this sorted.' O'Malley then turned to Kris, 'We need to talk.'

Kris followed O'Malley out of the conference room and down the hallway to the kitchenette. He poured two black coffees and handed one to Kris. 'Not especially hot but has a kick to it.'

She took coffee in both hands. 'What's on your mind, Jack?'

'I noticed you were a bit unsteady when you came into the conference room. You all right?

'I'm fine.'

'You can't be replaced, Kris, and we need to keep you as healthy as possible. Perhaps some rest is in order.'

'Not right away. I need to get past the footage from the metro stations, and if we don't come up with anything by then I'll take some time off.' Kris moved to a table and O'Malley took a seat across from her. 'Tell me something.' She continued. 'The incident with the pickpockets on the metro. How much do you know about Davis's past?'

'Not as much as I thought. In the wake of his being killed we learned that he was involved with a think tank here in Paris that is jointly sponsored by the French government and the CIA. This could be another reason he was targeted along with the fact that he was weaponizing and implementing the use of super recognizers for French counter terrorism efforts.'

'Are you thinking he was working directly for the CIA?'

'All we know at this point is that he was on the payroll by way of the think tank and also spent a great deal of time in Paris. John owned an apartment in the eleventh arrondissement near the Bastille and over the years maintained a casual and at times extended presence in the city. What concerns me is how much risk his past brings to our doorstep, and by the way have you spoken to Dan since we arrived back in Boston?'

'No, and I don't have any intention of doing so. Dan will act in the manner stated and doesn't need to be coached by me.'

'Fair enough.'

'Sorry, Jack. I don't mean to be rude, but it would be best for all involved to give Dan some space.'

‘I’ll pass that along.’ Jack stood to leave. ‘I’m here if you need me.’

When Kris returned to her makeshift office in the interrogation room it was with the knowledge that Jack’s perception was correct, and that the vertigo was raging nearly to the point of nausea and the room swirled with the slightest movement of her head. The extended bout in front of the computer screen was only making matters worse, but they were too close to back off and risk losing the momentum the partial image from Luxembourg Gardens placed in motion.

It had occurred to Kris that the only reason the American couple remained alive was due to the close proximity of the yoga group, as the image indicated the runner noticed the camera pointed in her direction, and after two more hours of searching it became obvious the runner had altered her appearance in response. Apparently removing the hooded sweatshirt after passing the couple and stuffing it into her backpack, as no clothing items were reported during the search of trash bins in the immediate area. By the time the CCTV stream could pick her up again she may have created a totally different appearance.

Kris sent a text out for the crew to forget the backpack and focus on a woman wearing a large cloak, a poncho or any type of clothing that would allow a backpack to be concealed at the chest and a hat large enough to shield her face. And to also limit the search to both sides of the street along the shortest possible route leading from Luxembourg Gardens to the Saint Sulpice Metro Station.’

Another frustrating hour brought a flurry of images and Kris tagged a few for a second look while the

crew went back for another sweep of the connecting streets. O'Malley joined her in the interrogation room with more coffee.
'You babysitting, Jack.'

'I wouldn't characterize it that way.'

'I do appreciate your concern.' Kris smiled. 'You realize that don't you?'

'On occasion.'

Kris leaned back in the chair and looked up at ceiling. 'She's always one step ahead of us, Jack. You notice that?' She turned to him with an expression that lodged her disgust, and the scar running across the side of her face, a vivid reminder of the point being made. Kris returned to the silence of the computer screen and a few moments later, as if conjured from the depths of frustration, she put down her coffee. 'That's her Jack.'

The words came with barely a shred of emotion and O'Malley looked up at the monitor into the middle of a crowd of pedestrians to a woman in a grey poncho with the hood pulled tight around her face.

'The woman in grey?' O'Malley confirmed

'No.' Kris pointed at the monitor to a woman three steps to the right and a little behind the woman in the grey poncho. 'This is the runner.' The woman was wearing a light brown, military style cape with pleated shoulders and had both hands concealed under the cape, which offered ample space to clutch a backpack to her chest. The woman's head was tilted forward, but at enough angle to allow the bridge of her nose and upper cheekbones to be clearly visible.

‘I’ll take your word for it, Kris. Crop the image and pass it along to the crew.’ When Jack left the room, Kris leaned back in the chair and closed her eyes to relieve the strain, if only for a few minutes while awaiting the next round of images that would shortly be coming her way.

The crew scanned the street and picked the runner up a block earlier. Still, they couldn’t manage to get a clear shot of her face and the angles were too steep for Kris to get a better view than the first image provided. The woman possessed an uncanny knack of avoiding cameras and had obviously performed due diligence on the placements between Luxembourg Gardens and the metro station.

The last image of the runner was captured as she descended the steps at the Saint Sulpice metro station on Rue de Rennes at exactly eleven thirty-three, a few moments after the stations security cameras went down. The parting image was captured from a camera set high on a building fifty yards away and with that parting shot the runner disappeared once again.

The crew then began the arduous task of searching every metro station leading away from Saint Sulpice in both directions, but this time around they knew who they were looking for. Kris finally reached a point where she could no longer avoid some down time without repercussions, and Jack made arraignments to have her escorted back to the townhouse.

After more than twenty-four hours of scanning CCTV footage, the bedroom appeared like a mirage that threatened to disappear before she could kick off her shoes and crawl underneath the comforter. A full six hours later her eyes reopened, and it took a moment to grasp where she was before rolling over again in a futile attempt at more sleep. An hour later she was still awake with thoughts consumed by events of the last few days, and was finally forced out of bed by hunger and a dire need for a jolt of caffeine and a shower before returning to the office.

She checked her phone and there were no messages from Jack, which meant nothing changed since she left with exception of the vertigo, which had mercifully eased. The relief was immense even if it turned out to be short lived. She wolfed down an egg and cheese sandwich accompanied by half a pot of coffee. The shower afterwards felt like an indulgence with the hot water flowing endlessly over her head and down her back and she could feel her energy level beginning to rise. Afterwards she towel dried her hair making no attempt to avoid the scar placed there by the runner. Sometimes she just wanted to run her fingertips along the scar and to feel the rough texture and look into the mirror not to where the scar lay but rather to the stillness of her eyes.

The Suburban was waiting by the time she was showered and dressed, and Kris sat in the backseat looking out the window as they drove down Ridgeway Lane. The photogenic neighborhood a favored destination of tourists seeking pictures of the cobbled streets and historic townhouses, and as they approached the corner, a young man was standing on the sidewalk with a camera pointed down the street and an image immediately snapped back into her consciousness.

The image as vivid as though she was still looking at it on the computer screen, and when they arrived at the FBI garage she barely waited for the vehicle to come to full stop before bolting out of the door and heading straight for the elevator. O'Malley caught the intensity on her face when she entered the office and without a word continued towards the interrogation room and he fell in behind her.

'What is it. Kris?'

'A long shot.' She threw her jacket and bag on top of the table and opened the laptop. The paused image of the runner with her back to the camera was still on display, and Kris restarted the video at the point where the runner was approaching the Saint Sulpice stairwell and as she started down the steps into the metro, Kris stopped the video.

'What are we looking at?'

'The tourist in the upper frame leaning against the railing with her cell phone pointed down the street and over the top of the stairwell.'

Jack for the first time noticed a woman with short, white hair standing at street level above the stairwell who was holding an iPhone away from her body and appeared to be taking a picture.

'It didn't register earlier because I was focused on the runner.' Kris said as she cropped the image of the tourist's face and dragged it into the facial recognition software. Within a matter of minutes, they had hits on Facebook, Twitter and LinkedIn.

Kris then began sorting through her postings on the day Davis was killed and there in a group of three images on Facebook was the one from Saint Sulpice Metro Station. The picture was taken above the stairwell and at the bottom of the image was a woman with ash brown hair, sunglasses and wearing a light brown, military style cape with pleated shoulders. The runner looking up at the photographer knowing there wasn’t a goddamn thing she could do about it.

Thirteen

Black Hills

Dan Walker was a man who enjoyed routine. No matter how vehemently he denied the accusation, and there was no separating Dan from the daily schedule envisioned the moment his feet hit the floor each and every morning. The routine was followed meticulously throughout the day until all six foot seven inches of the man leaned back on the headboard of the bed at exactly ten o'clock in the evening. Dan would then read the book that awaited on the nightstand and that would remain open until five minutes before eleven at which time the lamp on the nightstand went dark, and he laid his head on the pillow and fell immediately into a deep sleep.

Anne Walker would continue to read beside him until her eyes became heavy and she too turned her light off and lay next to the big man. Often, as she lay awaiting sleep, wondered how she got so lucky and how happy she is with life and the man she has come to know and love.

The scare with Kris enabled what was truly important in her life to crystalize and become so vivid she could nearly feel the sting of the bullet that was meant to kill her daughter. The same bullet that claimed her daughters partner, and the only man she had known Kris to allow close to her heart. The joy she experienced for her daughter was now replaced by a profound sadness for all that was lost and never to be. Anne would move ever tighter to Dan and after a while drift off to sleep.

In the hush of the predawn on a chilly September morning, two days after the killing of John Davis in Paris, the runner made her way up through a thin forest of ponderosa pine dominated by the outsized granite formations that characterize the Black Hills of South Dakota.

She was moving parallel to Highway 244, which snakes through the tiny village of Keystone, an old west style collection of hotels and tourist shops clinging to the walls of a narrow ravine. At the edge of the village the highway climbs towards the pinnacle of Mount Rushmore, then continues past the entrance to the national memorial in the direction of Crazy Horse, the second Black Hills memorial, a Native American tribute in progress, ten miles further down thc road.

The runner was somewhat amused by the irony of a Russian climbing the flanks of Mount Rushmore, the much touted shrine of democracy with the clear intention of killing a Native American on the sacred lands that the American government had brutally stole from his ancestors. In days past, she may well have sold his scalp to that same government he now represents, which would have been apropos, if not for the weary symbolism.

Her research was thorough, and she gave wide berth to the Xantarra employee housing complex located halfway up the mountain to avoid security cameras monitored by the Park Service police headquartered a quarter mile further up the mountain. She worked slow and easy up the steep incline and beyond Xantarra to a point where a park service utility road branched away from Highway 244.

The weather was especially cool, and she needed to avoid building up a sweat and waited with her back pressed against a retaining wall of the service road, which loomed ten feet above. A few minutes before 7:00 AM, a pair of maintenance personnel made their way along the service road to the supply depot. The early arrivals were new seasonal employees assigned to the restroom detail, and would proceed to stock a golf cart with cleaning supplies for the day, then drive back along the service road and up to the Grand View Terrace to begin cleaning and sanitizing the public areas of the monument, and in so doing passed above the runner for a second and final time.

Activity on the service road would not resume again for another hour, followed by a lull while the entire maintenance staff huddled around a wood stove, debating who would be the first out the door and with whom in a process that often consumed an hour or more. The runner used the opportunity to embark on the last leg of her trek up the mountain.

The destination was a viewing platform tucked aesthetically into the landscape, a few steps down from the Grand View Terrace, the wide open and granite tiled expanse with unobstructed views to Mount Rushmore. The terrace would be thinly attended by a scattering of early morning visitors with steaming cups of coffee in hand, and eyes glued to the colossal faces carved into the mountain.

Dan Walker made his way across the Grand View Terrace from the administration building at 9:45 each morning with the margin of error being a minute or two. He walked the half mile loop of the Presidential Trail with vigor, and in reverse. The preferred route follows a rambling series of stone steps descending to the Borglum View Terrace, then continues down past the Sculptors' Studio where the trek bottoms out and winds its way back up along a faux wooden boardwalk interspersed with a series of steep staircases climbing steadily towards the monument and finally looping back around to the Grand View Terrace. On mornings when his schedule was light, he allowed himself another round.

Dan became the sudden recipient of a heart valve stint the previous spring, which prompted an abrupt change of diet and the self-mandated regimen involving the Presidential Trail. He even extended the regimen to include weekends and drove up to the memorial from their home on the edge of Keystone. The results were positive with his weight down, energy levels rising, and he never felt better in his life. The irony of a near-death experience as a pathway to achieving optimum health was not lost on Dan, and his overriding sense of being on borrowed time was powerful motivation.

The runner had spent the previous two days sequestered in a hotel conveniently perched on a bluff overlooking Keystone. Her room offered an uninterrupted view towards Mount Rushmore, and more importantly it allowed the opportunity to monitor the movement of people as they passed through the village. This was the third trip up the mountain and would be her last if everything went according to plan.

With the entire maintenance staff gathered in the basement of the Sculptors' Studio, the moment she was awaiting finally arrived and the trek up the mountain resumed by following the retaining wall to the point where it became low enough to scale and then she quickly crossed the service road, and continued up through the last stretch of forest while remaining safely beyond the reach of the security cameras mounted on the Borglum View Terrace.

At 9:40, the runner was sitting on a bench at the viewing terrace overlooking the Mount Rushmore amphitheater, and six minutes later she observed Dan Walker proceeding across the Grand View Terrace. His momentum was interrupted briefly by an inquisitive tourist, but less than five minutes later he started down the rambling stone staircase that marked the beginning of his daily trek. Twenty yards down the staircase the trail wound tight to a tall, granite outcropping at the entrance of the spur trail leading to the amphitheater viewing terrace.

Dan tipped his hat to a young woman coming away from the terrace and about to leave the spur trail. Although, he was unaware that the young woman had falling in behind him, as they both descended the trail towards the Borglum View Terrace. Nor did he realize she was rapidly closing the gap between them when a loud and unexpected, 'Dan Walker', rang out from above. He turned to face the shout and was immediately confronted by the young woman who was nearly upon him and was forced to sidestep in order for her to pass on the narrow pathway.

'Dan Walker,' the voice bellowed out again and he waved an acknowledgement to the figure of a man standing on the stone staircase, a few meters down from the Grand View Terrace. The man then reached into his jacket and held out a badge in the arrogant manner that Dan associated with the FBI, and immediately caused a searing jolt of fear to course through his entire being with thoughts racing to Kris and all that transpired recently. 'Hold on. I'm coming up.' His distinct, baritone voice echoed through the thin mountain air and Dan rapidly closed the distance between them in a rage of emotion and was in no mood to shake the outthrust hand of Will Jenkins.

'What happened?'

'Kris is fine.' Jenkins acknowledged the imperative. 'She's still in Ireland but Jack O'Malley will be transporting her to Boston, and we need to talk.'

'Follow me.' Dan turned and headed back to the administration building with Jenkins in tow, and while relieved to hear Kris was safe, there was no escaping the thought of something being radically wrong. Although, the realization that he had been only four short steps away from a fatal heart attack would remain in the wind, and the tiny, red pin prick destined to appear on his upper back would have to wait for another day.

With her target so rudely snatched away, the runner paused forty yards further down the stone staircase with feigned interest in a placard touting the flora and fauna of the Black Hills, and as soon as Walker and the FBI agent ascended out of view, she left the trail and cut across above the Borglum View Terrace, then retraced her steps to the service road and back down through the forest to Keystone.

There was ample time on the trek back to the hotel for her to consider exactly what transpired on the mountain. She was not only unable to complete the task, but also embarrassingly went face to face with the subject. A development she would allow to stand for the time being. Dan Walker was now a threat and a loose end that needed to be tied off, but with the FBI brought into the equation, the only consideration at the moment was to get off the mountain and out the Black Hills, as quickly as possible.

It was also painfully clear that the time had arrived for a face-to-face conversation with Alexei Orlov, otherwise known as Pablo Ortiz. A meeting to be arraigned the moment she arrived back at Brighton Beach, and the bastard better have the right answers to the serious questions he needs to address. Orlov's stated purpose in life involved keeping her one step ahead of all risks associated with the task at hand, and that goddamn well included the FBI, Scotland Yard or any other son of a bitch standing between her and the subject of her pursuit. She was sorely tempted to permanently annul the relationship with Orlov, but unfortunately this was another matter to be revisited.

Orlov came highly recommended by her father and performed flawlessly during the early stages of their collaboration in France and Germany. His ability to hack into John Davis's laptop and phones was indispensable to the successful outcome of her efforts until that morning. She was in the Black Hills for the express purpose of killing Walker. The act sure to flush Kris Shepard out of hiding and who according to Orlov, had completely disappeared.

The Shepard woman would undoubtedly be drawn to South Dakota for the funeral service and in a matter of days, the multifaceted contract would have been completed and 'The Runner,' as she was so rudely referred to by the FBI, could simply melt away. And although acutely aware of the imperfect nature of the world at large, this was not the one she occupied, and her version of reality extended to all with whom she associated and there could be no exceptions to this rule, a lesson her father went to great lengths to impress upon her.

A philosophy that wouldn't be lost on Dan Walker, as he took a seat at his desk across from the FBI Agent who introduced himself as Will Jenkins, a member of the team Kris was working with when Sam Bordeaux was killed, and she barely avoided the same fate. The moment he heard from Jenkins that Kris was once again working with the agency he demanded to speak directly from Kris before their meeting progressed any further. Prompting Jenkins to inform him that it wasn't going yo happen, although for reasons Dan was willing to accept.

'We're not sure of the extent of the hacking involved.' Jenkins continued with his explanation. 'But we do know they penetrated every source of Davis's digital world with an impressive degree of efficiency, and to be honest we can't be sure the same thing hasn't occurred with both you and Mrs. Walker.'

Jenkins paused to allow Dan a moment to absorb the risk factors involved. 'We need to monitor your computers, phones and any devices connected to the internet. Our first priority is to keep everyone involved safe and with any luck also capture a digital trail to follow back to the source.'

'Do we need to sign off on anything?' Dan had moved reluctantly onboard.

'No. It's already happening.' Jenkins leaned forward on the desk. 'Dan, we firmly believe that you and your wife, along with Kris are in imminent danger from the suspect we refer to as the runner. The last correspondence between John Davis and your daughter placed her squarely in the Black Hills with you and Mrs. Walker and wouldn't be a huge leap of faith to assume that the runner is going to show up here looking for Kris. And until we can apprehend this individual or it ends by other means, we'll need to keep our people with you twenty-four seven. Is that a problem, Dan?'

'You best believe it's a problem and I'm not happy about anything the FBI has shown me from the first day Kris has been with you. That said, I have no option, but to facilitate whatever you need to do. But listen very carefully to what I have to say next.' Dan rose to the full measure of his six foot, seven inches and then leaned forward with both hands on the desk. 'If anything happens to my wife or daughter on your watch, Mr. Jenkins, be advised that I will hold you personally responsible and there will be consequences.' Dan eyes were stone cold and riveted on Jenkins as he walked over and opened the door to his office. 'We're done here.'

The following day after arriving back in Brooklyn, the runner arranged to meet Alexei Orlov on the boardwalk near the Tatiana Grill. The pedestrian traffic on the normally busy boardwalk was light with only a scattering of walkers, joggers and the occasional retiree with a dog on a leash.

She allowed Orlov to stand for close to an hour with a group of Russian men watching a chess game unfold on a bench outside the Tatiana Grill. Orlov was entirely out of his element and hard pressed to blend in with the other petty thieves crowded two deep around the bench. The Rolex, layered haircut and Brooks Brothers suit made a dangerous impression and not the best choice of attire in light of his present company. She enjoyed watching his anxiety level rising by the minute and the fear she sensed on Orlov excited her predatory instincts and there would be no effort made to relieve the slow burning agony that his taunt nerve endings were experiencing, a process she would soon escalate.

The runner sat a corner table inside the Tatiana Grill, one row removed from the windows overlooking the boardwalk and when she became bored with his discomfort, a text went out and Orlov quickly broke away from the entourage surrounding the chess game and a few minutes later was ambling towards her across the empty dining room. She owned the entire space for the next two hours and afterwards they will have never been there. Nor will the waiter who brought lunch and the bottle of vodka or anyone else on the boardwalk ever testify to having seen either her or Orlov and this was a guarantee written in blood by men like her father, not so long ago.

Anna Volkov was born at Park Slope, a half-hour drive away from where they sat in the Tatiana Grill. She started life as an American citizen, unlike Orlov who arrived by boat, indentured and enslaved in return for a safe harbor and lucrative contract with the Russian mafia. Orlov, as promised would return by the same route one day with a pocketful of cash or so he believed. Of course, at this stage, Anna didn't envision that happening in quite the same way.

Her father, Petr Volkov, a military man of high standing within the Russian Federation also held a tight grip on the mafia enterprise operating out of Brighton Beach. A dedicated Pakhan within the Russian mafia, who commands an elite group of ex-military personnel with full access to the slowly disappearing Russian stockpile of military grade weapons.

Although, the main business enterprise under his control was the persistently lucrative, heroin trade by way of the Taliban, who currently held possession of the opium fields in Afghanistan. The heroin was shuttled unimpeded through Russia and funneled directly into the pipeline feeding the North America drug trade under the watchful eye of her father.

In his official capacity, Petr Volkov worked as a military attaché with the Russian Embassy while maintaining an unofficial residence in Brighton Beach. It was there Anna Volkov had lived with her mother, an unmarried second generation, Russian-American. When she reached the tender age of five years old, she and her mother were escorted back to Odessa. And there they would remain under the full protection of her father's associates.

Orlov took possession of the seat opposite Anna, who remained silent long enough for Orlov to start talking non-stop in a staccato rhythm. He was displaying an even higher level of fear, than Anna anticipated and the more he rambled, the less likely he was to survive in the long term. 'Alexei.' She broke into his breathless rendition of why she endured a close encounter with the FBI, and how such a thing couldn't possibly happen again. 'The only words I want to hear pass through your lips,' she continued, 'are those directing me to the Shepard woman.' Anna looked into his eyes and waited for an answer.

'I'm guessing,' he began.

'You don't want to use that word, Alexei.'

'Sorry, I now believe that Kris Shepard is with the FBI at the Boston headquarters.' Orlov assumed a more authoritative tone.

'And why do you believe this?'

'The only reason the FBI would bother to put Dan Walker and his wife under their protection, is if they realized I hacked into Davis's computer, which left little to the imagination concerning your next move, and by now the FBI is well represented in the Black Hills. You were lucky to get out when you did.'

'I don't traffic in luck, Alexei.'

'I'm not infallible.' Orlov was starting to sound testy, which Anna found rather amusing.

'Let's order I'm starved.' She signalled to the waiter who then approached and took her order of a Tatiana salad followed by the herring with onions and olives, accompanied by a bottle of vodka for Orlov to abuse. She then moved the conversation to where it needed to be. 'I want you to hack into Jack O'Malley's lines of communication, as we've discussed on more than one occasion, and I want every type of equipment that he uses to be included. '

'Anna, we're discussing the FBI, which is a far cry from the security John Davis was able to muster.' Orlov paused for effect. 'I need more time to nail it down.'

'You have one week.' She reached across the table and took both his hands in hers. 'Do not let me down again, Alexei.' She tightened the grip on his hands and pulled him closer to her. 'And if you ever bring a weapon into my presence again, it will be your last act on this earth.' She let go of his left hand and placed her own under the table. 'Use two fingers to remove the gun from inside your jacket and place it on table, then sit back where you belong.'

The color drained from Orlov's face and he didn't hesitate to do as instructed. 'I carry it for protection. Please, Anna, I didn't mean any disrespect. It won't happen again.'

'I am the only protection you need.' She removed the gun from the table. 'Have a drink Alexei. You don't look so well.'

Orlov drank deep from his glass of vodka and waited a few minutes for the effects to settle. 'One week is not possible?'

'There's the attitude again.' Anna straightened out the napkin on her lap and after a brief pause her steel grey eyes bore into Orlov, riveting him to his seat. 'One thing of absolute certainty. Is that I will see you next week, and at that time you will tell me what I want to hear. Now get up and return to the chess game on the boardwalk and stay there until the last man has left the bench.' Orlov hesitated for a heartbeat then rose from his seat. She watched him walk across the dining room with the awkward gait of an extremely nervous man, and he had a right to be.

Two hundred and twenty miles away, at One Center Plaza in Boston, the runner's face was on the big screen in the conference room, with the entire crew gathered around the table. O'Malley entered to start the proceedings followed a few minutes later by Kris who took a seat at the back, too exhausted to even acknowledge the approving looks directed her way. Jack stood next to the runner's image on the screen and went right into the business at hand.

'This individual, as your all aware by now is the woman who shot and killed Sam Bordeaux and John Davis and made an attempt on Kris. We believe she has every intention of returning to finish what she started. I'm aware of the effort it took to get this far and how desperately everyone in this room wants to put a name to this face.' He paused and looked around the room. 'Nor do I have any doubts concerning the talent gathered around this table. That said, I need everyone to refocus their attention under the leadership of Anthony Russo who is now coordinating this effort and will be keeping me updated concerning any new developments, and with that I'll leave you to it.' Jack headed for the door and motioned for Kris to follow him out of the room.

'I need a moment to discuss what's happening in the Black Hills.' They continued down the hallway toward his office and Jack took a seat behind the desk while Kris walked over and stood looking out the window.

'How you feeling?'

'Fine. And you don't need to ask me all the time. I'll let you know if there's a problem.' Kris turned and sat down across from him.

'Fair enough.' Jack retreated.

'I appreciate your concern.' Her tone softened. 'But you have to trust me on this.'

'I'll do the best I can. No promises.' He sat back in his chair. 'Have you spoken to Dan or your mother recently?'

'A few days ago. Why do you ask?'

'Dan's having more than a few problems adjusting to the security we put in place, and I want to make sure everyone stays safe.'

'What's the issue?'

'He takes daily jaunts into the Black Hills and at times, the team can lose him completely. They sent a drone up the other day and he pointed a weapon at it when they found him.'

'Give him space.' Kris continued. 'Dan can take care of himself, and if someone is going to get hurt out there, it won't be Dan Walker.'

'Do you think it would it help if I went out and had a talk with him?'

'Hardly. And besides, the issues he has are long standing and not something you could ever address. I'll give him a call, but the crew really needs to back off, as much as possible.'

'Alright, I'll touch base with the crew.'

'Anything else?' Kris stood up.

'No, we're good.'

Kris stood and left the office and Jack hadn't failed to notice the edge she had acquired since the day she first informed him of her intention to join the agency, or perhaps it had just become more apparent, but in any event made things simpler and safer for all involved, and whether or not this was in her best interest long term was a moot point, and he felt bad about that.

Fourteen

Black Hills

A covered, wooden walkway runs along the back of the administration building at Mount Rushmore. The walkway overlooks a grove of Ponderosa pine, which provides a hundred-yard buffer between the administration building and Highway 244 winding past the memorial. The pine grove is also Dan Walker's favorite route into the Black Elk Wilderness.

The rear exit of his office leads onto the walkway, which allows Dan to leave his inner sanctum without running the gauntlet of staff and tourists waiting beyond the front door. His secretary, Elizabeth, knows when the office door closes each afternoon that Dan is wholly unavailable until it returns to an invitingly open position, signalling his willingness to once again entertain the various factions vying for his attention.

The public relations aspect of his position devours much of his daily schedule, but Dan is fortunately well suited to the task and seizes every opportunity to spread his message of inclusion and further his agenda of Native American advancement through education. Being both charismatic and articulate allows his passive aggressive stance to gain a wide audience within both regional and national news outlets. A circumstance that leads to an equal number of admirers and detractors, whom Dan holds in equal esteem. His ability to listen and absorb various points of view is one of his greatest assets and allows for an engaging conversationalist and distinctly formidable opponent.

The mid-afternoon outings began shortly after he arrived at Mount Rushmore and are essentially a stroll punctuated by extended periods of sitting with as little outside interference into his thought process, as can be achieved. His ability to be at peace within the landscape and to derive a sense of renewal by simply walking through the forest is something Dan considers a gift, which demands the same degree of respect, as any other element in his life.

The walkabouts often culminate upon a granite outcropping with his back to the stone, eyes shut listening to the sound of the wind coming off the plains or a mule deer moving nervously downwind, and at such moments there is neither past nor future and the present lay stilled within the company of one.

Moments such as these became increasingly difficult to attain following the intrusion of the FBI into every aspect of his life, and if there was one constant Dan had observed in his ongoing passage through the world according to the white man was that change never happened in a void, and that a sudden lack of interest in his daily excursion by the agents assigned to him was cause for concern.

'Hey.' Kris picked up on the first ring.

'Can we speak freely?'

'I believe so.' She answered.

'Is there a reason the security detail has lost interest in my whereabouts?'

'Yeah. O'Malley mentioned the incident with the drone.'

'It didn't actually rise to the level of incident, although there is potential, if they insist on invading my privacy.' Dan interjected.

'O'Malley has instructed the security team to back off when you move about in the afternoons.'

'I see.'

'He says it's the best he can do, and I believe him.'

'I can live with that for however long he keeps his promise.'

'I'll pass that along.'

'Has there been any progress in the investigation?'

'We have a suspect from a related shooting in Paris. A woman around thirty years old.'

Dan hesitated before responding. 'Brown hair about 5'10 and a hundred thirty pounds?'

'Where did you see her?' Kris' blood ran cold.

'On the Presidential Trail, halfway down to the Borglum view terrace.'

'How long ago?'

'The same day and at the exact moment O'Malley's guy showed up.'

‘Check your phone, Dan. I just sent you an image.’ She continued after a few silent moments.

‘Yeah. That’s her.’ He concurred without hesitation.

‘How close to her were you?’

‘Close enough to see her cold, grey eyes when she walked past me.’

‘Anything else you can recall?’

‘A thin scar on the edge of her upper lip.’

‘Is that it. Grey eyes and the scar?’

‘For now. I’ll let you know if I recall anything else.’

After they ended the conversation, Dan walked up one flight of stairs to Anne’s office, while Kris made a similar trek to O’Malley, and neither one of them was prepared to hear exactly how close the runner managed to get to Dan.

‘Jenkins is the only reason he’s still around. I hope Dan realizes that?’ Was O’Malley’s terse response.

‘I’m sure. And he’ll act appropriately.’

‘Well, that’s almost reassuring.’ O’Malley needn’t say more in that direction. ‘I’ll have Sarah update the runners profile to confirm the grey eyes and to include the scar and then pass it along to our counterparts in France and Germany.’ He paused. ‘You OK?’

‘Yeah. Just shook me up thinking about what nearly occurred and whether the runner is still in the Black Hills, waiting for another opportunity.’

'I don't see it. There are few places she could blend in and doubtful that she would risk remaining in place after Dan had a good look at her face, which isn't the same as saying she won't be back at some point. Unless we get to her first.'

O'Malley's words stung, but Kris knew he was right, and no amount of fear or anger would change the outcome. She needed to maintain a clear state of mind, if there was to be any chance of preventing Dan from having another encounter with the runner and knowing that he wouldn't see her coming the second time around.

The crew settled into what became a four-day siege focused on putting a name to the woman in the stairwell, the same one Dan encountered on the footpath at Mount Rushmore and despite intensive efforts that included a degree of cooperation from their European counterparts, the runners true identity remained as elusive as it was the day she killed Sam Bordeaux.

'Are you comfortable with the European response? Kris felt the need to pose the question.

'To a point.' O'Malley was quick to answer.

'What are the chances they're withholding information?' Kris was standing at the window in O'Malley's office watching a plane lift away from Logan International Airport.

'Normally, I would say fair to good, but I don't see that happening in this case for a variety of reasons. Foremost being the manner in which the runner sliced through the European counter terrorism defences, as though they didn't exist. The display of technical sophistication which allowed her to move around undetected is a wakeup call and demands a sustained level of cooperation to close the gaps that exists in the individual surveillance apparatus.'

'Has anyone considered a Russian connection?'

'It hasn't specifically been mentioned, but the question is never far from anyone's mind. Why do you ask?

'The runners appearance suggests a Slavic origin and her skill sets are consistent with a military background, wouldn't you say?'

'I wouldn't argue concerning her abilities, but I can't see the Russian military immersing themselves in an attempt to thwart terrorist attacks anywhere but on their own soil. It's not in their DNA for one thing.'

'That part I understand.' Kris continued. 'And the theory of Isis or Al Qaeda eliminating sleeper cells as a way of protecting a specific objective is likely to be correct. But what if there is a third party involved?'

'I'm listening.'

'Could we be looking at murder for hire with the runner aligned with the Russian Mafia?' Kris posed the question in a rhetorical fashion, as much to herself as to Jack. 'Which means that she wouldn't appear in the archives or on the watch list at any of counter terrorism bureaus.'

'And what would be the Mafia's motivation to get involved?' Jack sat back in his chair.

'To send a message like most other Mafia hits. The fact they're moving heroin out of Afghanistan in collaboration with the Taliban is common knowledge.'

'Alright.' Jack answered after a moments silence. 'I'm going to have Russo point the crew in that direction and we'll see where it leads.'

Kris turned to leave the office and stopped short of the door. 'Thanks, for hearing me out.'

O'Malley looked at her for a moment and nodded. 'You have good instincts. But then we knew this, didn't we?' And he was still looking at door after it closed.

Fifteen

Boston

The crew embraced the new direction with their usual intensity and for the first time since the operation went so radically wrong in Springfield, the underlying basis of the investigation felt right, and a sense of forward momentum took hold in spite of the tremendous work load they were facing.

The main task involved sorting through countless images gathered from sources including the FBI and NYPD Organized Crime Task Forces. The crew worked within the limitations of the computerized facial recognition system by breaking down the various mafia factions into groupings, which provided a semblance of order that Kris found easier to absorb.

The clear, frontal images gathered from mug shots and past surveillance operations, provided a basis for identifying individuals from subsequent images captured at difficult angles or containing partial profiles. The quality of the images were often poor due to bad lighting, subjects in motion, or the level of risk the agent behind the camera was in the midst of experiencing at a given moment.

O'Malley called in a favor and arranged a meeting with a source working undercover for the Organized Crime Division of the FBI in New York City. The man was born and raised in Brighton Beach by Russian parents and had placed himself in a difficult position between the FBI and the Odessa Mafia.

The source had previously been targeted in an undercover drug operation, which revealed that he was skimming money and drugs from the Odessa Mafia through his position as a regional distributor. The damning information that the FBI now possessed, held the greatest threat to the man' survival in light of the unforgiving nature of the mafia and formed the basis of his indentured relationship with the agency. The meeting took place mid-week in a parking garage on 42nd. Street at 4:00 A.M., with Kris in attendance.

Erik Petrov sat across from O'Malley in the back of an unmarked van with Kris in the driver's seat and turned to face the conversation. Petrov was not what O'Malley was expecting. He placed him somewhere in his early forties. Tall, thin and articulate with no apparent addictions that may have caused him to be sequestered in the back of a van with the FBI. This to O'Malley's way of thinking made him all the more dangerous. 'Have you ever seen this woman?'

'No.' Petrov answered after much deliberation and handed the photograph back to O'Malley. 'She must be popular to draw this much attention and from the background I'd say all the way from Paris, no less.'

O'Malley didn't respond to the open ended question. 'Have you any knowledge of a woman working as a hired gun for the mafia.'

'Not personally, but I've heard rumors on occasion about the daughter of one the warlords who works out of the Kremlin, but then how much of that type of thing does one take onboard. You know what I'm saying.'

'You have a name for this warlord?' Jack continued.

'No. That's not something one speaks out loud, even if you do know. It's the kind of thing that gets your name on the wrong kind of list.'

'You're not talking to the mafia now.' Kris joined the conversation.

'And how would I know that?' Petrov turned his attention to her. 'But don't take that personally, miss?'

'How closely do rumors resemble the truth in your world?' She ignored the question.

'Much closer than the one you inhabit.'

'And the Kremlin connection?' Kris continued.

'I would say that aspect of the tale has a certain ring to it. As you know, the biggest worry before the collapse of the Soviet Union was that the mafia would infiltrate the military. But as it stands now, you best learn how to salute if you intend to do business with the mafia.'

Petrov put his hat on and looked across at Jack. 'We won't be having further conversations of this nature. The has been a one-off event, and far too dangerous for all concerned, and quite frankly, Mr. O'Malley, I often wonder if your comrades possess a true understanding of the nature of the threat your dealing with.' Petrov started to leave then stopped and turned back. 'Tell me something. This woman in Paris. Did she get one of your own?'

O'Malley gave an affirmative nod. Petrov looked back and forth between him and Kris. 'I'll see what

I can do. No promises and don't attempt to contact me.' Then he was out the door and gone.

'Any chance he'll follow through?' Kris asked as Jack settled into the passenger seat of the van.

'I don't have a track record with this guy or reason to believe that he'll actually try. But I do, and in the meantime, the crew can make a run at finding high ranking Russian Military personnel working stateside that have daughters around the same age as the runner.' Jack looked over at Kris. 'But first I want everyone to back off for a few days. We've been pushing hard, and some down time is in order.'

Kris kept looking at the road ahead and after a while turned to Jack. 'You doing this for me?' It was as though the thought suddenly occurred to her. 'I'm perfectly capable of maintaining a normal routine?'

'Not the case. I would tell you if it was otherwise and actually I'd like you to accompany me to New Hampshire in the event something material comes out of the New York office that requires both of us to get involved.'

'What's in New Hampshire?'

'I have a cottage in the White Mountains that I prepare for winter around this time each year. There's plenty of room to stretch out and enjoy the scenery. Have your ever been to New Hampshire in autumn?'

'Just once when I was in college.'

'And?'

'Loved it, but the thing is Jack, I don't do well in those circumstances.'

I realize that Kris, but for the moment it's best that we stay in close proximity and if you prefer we can remain in Boston.'

'No. I don't want to do that. New Hampshire is fine and the cottage sounds lovely.'

'I believe rustic is the general consensus, but the foliage and mountain air will more than make up for the lack of creature comforts, and besides, I have every intention of putting you to work.'

The following afternoon the ride from Beacon Hill to Bristol, New Hampshire took a little more than two hours, the traffic being light once they moved beyond the greater Boston area. Kris was concerned the journey would be long and silent with not much to talk about beyond the operation. Surprisingly, the time passed quickly, and they spoke of unexpected things from their backgrounds, college and even the art of winemaking, a subject Jack was passionate about.

Kris thought about how seldom people surpass her expectations and wouldn't have considered Jack to be among them. She hadn't laughed in so long that it felt strange to hear the sound of her own voice, and he was right about the foliage, the effects were mesmerizing, and she felt a strange blend of exhilaration and comfort from the mile upon mile of intense colors that encroached upon the highway.

She was glad to be there despite initial reservations. Her natural inclination is to avoid situations that involve extended contact with other people and this aversion wasn't directed at Jack or anyone else. But it was a real concern and mattered in ways she found difficult to get past.

O'Malley's lakeside cottage was a few miles outside of the quaint and tiny village of Bristol, New Hampshire. As they passed through on the way to the lake, Jack pointed out landmarks from a childhood vividly recalled, and seemed especially pleased with the age defying wooden boardwalk running the length of an equally dated grocery store with floorboards that squeaked underfoot. A lumber mill on the edge of the village was a favorite stop when he was young and a place he said he still visits at times, just for the hell of it.

After gathering a few staples that consisted mainly of coffee, eggs and bread they continued on their way and about a mile outside the village drove past 'The Old Mill Stream', a former lumber mill built tight to a swift moving stream flowing away from Newfound Lake. The derelict building having been refitted in the late nineteen fifties took on a new persona as an ice cream parlor. The iconic foot-long hot dogs served out of a walk up window became an overnight sensation that continued unabated until recent times. New owners had stepped in with a vow to carry on with tradition, although the building to Jack's dismay was boarded up once again, another casualty of the recession.

Two miles further up the road they turned towards the lake, passing a stone chapel then down a slight incline and across a narrow bridge that offered Kris her first view of Newfound Lake. A thin scattering of cottages dotted the far shoreline while others clung precariously to the steep, heavily wooded hillside rising above the lake. The road continued to hug the shoreline and the initial impression of a small lake in the mountains gave way with each twist of the road. Waterfront cottages and wooden boathouses were randomly placed and separated by towering pine groves that stretched to the water's edge, and finally they pulled off the road and parked next to a small metal sign that proclaimed the rough, lakeside patch of land as a public beach for residents of the Village of Bristol and for Kris, the lack of amenities held a certain charm, not unlike the Black Hills.

How much the lake and tiny village were a part of Jack's sense of identity was becoming increasingly obvious to Kris, and she was no longer sure of what to make of him. The man wasn't adhering to the script running through her head since the first moment they laid eyes on each other, in what was now another life, as they both knew it to be.

They got out of the car and walked down to the shoreline, the water was pristine and cold to the touch. A small island lay about a quarter of a mile offshore and beyond there appeared to be no end to the lake. 'Mayhew Island.' Jack answered her unstated question, and although he really wasn't much of a tour guide, certain places seemed to draw him out.

'Is it inhabited?'

'Only in July and August. The island serves as a boy's camp with a timber framed lodge and a cluster of small cabins along the edge of the water. A place for wealthy parents to sequester their kids for the summer.'

'Did you ever go out there?'

'Once in a while I would swim out or borrow a canoe from the marina. The counsellors always chased me off and that was probably the best thing for everyone involved.'

The scent of firewood filled the air in a way Kris found pleasant and reminiscent of the Black Hills, although never with a backdrop as colorful as the one in which she was now immersed. 'This building across the street.' Jack pointed to a long, rectangular shaped building with the same rustic demeanor as the white, shingle clad bungalows scattered across the adjoining hillside. 'My parents operated a restaurant and gift shop there during the summer months when I was a kid. Actually, it was my mother's project with my father making weekend appearances to restock merchandise from a South Boston distributor.'

'Sounds like a charming childhood.'

'I never thought of it that way but appreciated being here and spent most of my time on the lake in some fashion.' He picked up a small flat stone and skimmed it across the water then turned back to Kris. 'I imagine the Black Hills offered you much of the same.'

'It still does. I don't believe that will ever go away.'

'And you feel the same way about Ireland?'

'I do, although Ireland and especially Inis Meain appeal to me in ways not possible anywhere else. I find the barren landscape and degree of isolation on offer holds a certain appeal, and it would be difficult if I was forced to choose between the Island and the Black Hills.

'You seem to value solitude more than anyone I've ever known.'

'Is that a question?'

'No. Just wondered if it has always been that way for you?'

'It has.' Kris seemed amused. 'Although, I don't know if value is the right choice of words. It's not that simple, nor as unusual as you may think and actually, I haven't sensed an overwhelming amount of people traveling in your orbit either. But perhaps you don't see it that way.'

'I'm sorry. That came across like a criticism and not what I intended.' Jack held her gaze. 'And your right about my lack of fellowship for lack of a better word, and to your point, I would say my comfort level for being alone is especially high, but not always my first choice. That said, I do prefer to drink alone, if that qualifies.'

'Only if it works for you.'

'Maybe we should call it on the grand tour and get some dinner. There's a little place down the road with a decent menu and better the wine list than most. Sound good?'

'Food always sounds good?'

'I like that about you, Shepard.'

The little place down the road turned out to be a lovely, two story cottage set high on a wooded hillside above the lake. The owners had never changed the original layout, and the seating areas rambled through a series of small interconnecting rooms with antique furnishings and colorful wallpaper that appeared straight out of the nineteen twenties.

They sat in a small nook with a view over the lake as dusk began to settle. The lighting was soft and the fire in the wood stove created a warm, cozy atmosphere. Jack made a few suggestions for dinner and Kris was happy enough to follow his lead, and they ordered a half carafe of white wine and the waiter lit the candles on the table.

The intimate atmosphere with magnificent views of the lake and beyond to the White Mountains ablaze in the final throes of the setting sun only added to Kris's growing sense of unease. This having nothing to do with Jack, and if anything, he was a buffer between her and the feelings she had struggled to keep at bay from the moment they sat down. The quaint atmosphere had provoked an intense feeling of loss, a wave of emotion she was not prepared to confront or share and knew would pass, if she could wait it out, and it helped knowing that Sam would have understood her need to simply let it be.

'You seem quiet this evening.'

'Sorry, I get that way once in a while.' She didn't realize her feelings had been so transparent.

'No reason to apologize. I know the feeling.'

'Of course.' She took a sip of wine.

'We don't have to talk.'

'Really Jack, I enjoy our conversations. It's just that sometimes I drift into myself and find it hard to come back. If that makes any sense at all.'

'Sam?' He waited for a response that wasn't going to come. 'You don't have to answer that Kris, I shouldn't have asked.'

'Your fine, Jack. But I really don't want to talk about Sam, if you don't mind.'

'Not at all. What do you think of the wine?'

'It's lovely. Perhaps we could get a bottle to take back to the cottage, which I assume is being cleared at the moment.'

'It is indeed, and the wine is good thought. Russo will text me when the cottage has been inspected and the security detail is in place.'

'You seem to hold a high opinion of Russo.'

'I do and one he deserves. Russo came out of Chicago with an impressive arrest and conviction record, along with the scars from being knifed and shot on two separate occasions. His last partner didn't come off as well and I believe that's what brought him here, and by the way, Russo refused to take the weekend off when he found out we were leaving town.'

'Sorry to hear about the partner.'

'Yeah.' The waiter arrived with dinner and then refilled their wine glasses. Two hours later they finally arrived at the cottage and settled into a pair of Adirondack chairs on the front porch, where they remained bundled up in hooded sweatshirts with a bottle of Château Sainte-Marie Bordeaux Supérieur 2007 on a small table between them, uncorked and untouched, waiting for the moment Jack declared it fit to drink. Inside the cottage a wood stove groaned and shuddered to life with a belly full of dried oak cut and split the previous year.

Murphy O'Shea had made a proper entrance and introduced himself to Kris before stretching out in front of the fire, as though a permanent resident of the cottage, which in all the important ways he was. At the edge of the short cart road leading up to the cottage, Russo was engaged in a discussion with the occupants of a second Suburban and shortly afterwards, Jack received a text and replied, which caused the other Suburban to pull away and Russo's to go dark.

When satisfied the wine had achieved the desired threshold, Jack poured two glasses and they remained on the porch in the dark with a full moon floating on the surface of lake, the night sky as bold and startling as the air was crisp and barely a word passed between them. The wine was as perfect as Jack predicted and Kris draped a small blanket over her legs, content to remain in his company.

The lonely call of a whip-o-will drifted out of the darkness, as the wine began to take the edge off the lingering effects of the gruelling schedule in the days leading up to that moment. The soft, rustic ambience of the timber framed cottage appealed to Kris and it was easy to share O'Malley's love for the place, and when the cool night air finally drove them inside, she sat on the floor and leaned back against the sofa with Murphy curled at her feet in front of the wood stove, and every once in a while he made a high pitched yelp in his sleep without waking up. And between her and Jack there was little need to speak, but conversation flowed for hours and felt as though much remained unspoken when they called it a night.

Kris heard the handle of the back door rattle shortly after the lights went out and then footsteps moving down the gravel path towards the warmth of the Suburban and a long vigil for the security team at the end of the driveway. She fell asleep with no memory of doing so and hardly budged until she heard Jack stoking the fire and then rolled over and fell back to sleep as daylight began to glow along the edges of the heavy, green window shade that nearly defied the sunrise.

She emerged from the bedroom late morning to be greeted by the scent of coffee. Jack was sitting on the porch with Murphy at his side and who noticed her the moment she stepped away from the bedroom and nosed up to the French doors with tail wagging and something between a whimper and a bark until Jack stood and they came inside.

'Morning. How'd you sleep?'

'Like a child.'

'Hungry?'

'Not really.' Said while Murphy lay on his back with eyes closed as she rubbed his belly.

'Coffee?'

'That sounds better.'

'I was planning on taking Murphy for a walk up the mountain after breakfast and your welcome to come along.'

'Sounds lovely.' Kris took a slice of cheese from Jack and Murphy followed her out to the porch. The lake was bristling with whitecaps and the wind brisk and chilly and Jack came behind with her sweatshirt in one hand and a coffee in the other.

'You're going to spoil the lad.'

'I think it's far too late for that to happen.' She smiled and it felt good to feel normal again. The mountain air was invigorating, and the vertigo didn't stand a chance on such a day. They sat in silence with the lake glistening below and the mountains rising smooth and layered towards a jagged, pale white horizon and after a breakfast of yogurt, blueberries and a toasted egg sandwich, Kris returned to the front porch with a second cup of coffee, the morning sun warm on her legs and watched Jack walk down the gravel driveway towards the Suburban. Murphy waited patiently beside the vehicle for Jack to emerge then ran ahead and pawed his way through the back door to greet Kris as though for the first time that morning and his excitement was contagious.

'Everything alright, Jack?'

'Yeah, everything's fine. I'll fill a couple of water bottles for the hike.'

'It's going to feel really good to hike again.'

'Good, then let's get out of here.' Jack shoved the water bottles into his backpack and snugged up his hiking boots. Murphy ran ahead as they started through the stand of sugar maples behind the cottage. Murphy stopped often and looked back to assure himself that Jack and Kris were following, although the further they progressed up the mountain the less they saw of Murphy. His excitement was such that he would arrive suddenly from behind and dash past only to disappear again into the rise and twist of the trail.

Kris was captivated by the vivid colors and musky scent of the leaves clinging to the trees and littering the floor of the forest, but still it felt strange to be there and walking behind Jack, and both of them so removed from the other world they occupied, the one they could never escape for long.

Murphy was waiting when they arrived at the bare granite peak and there they sat with an unfettered view of Newfound Lake and the northbound mountains rising from the water's edge. The sun was warm and the spring water from the cottage was cool and delicious and Kris could feel it travel to the pit of her stomach.

'It's very peaceful here, Jack.'

'Yeah.'

'I can see why you love it so much.'

'I do. But not unlike my father before me, I arrive back in Boston sooner rather than later. I don't believe I could handle all this peacefulness on a full time basis, as much as I might like too.'

'Good to know.'

'Yeah. Obviously, you don't have a problem with quiet places.'

'No, not at all.'

'Do you miss Provincetown?'

‘I miss Tyler. Do you know he leaving my studio as it was the day I left Provincetown? I could walk back into it tomorrow and pick up as though I had never been away.’

‘I never heard you speak of anyone that way before?’

‘And what way would that be, Jack?’

‘As someone your close to.’

‘Nor you.’

‘Point made.’ Jack smiled.

‘Even though you live in the big city.’

‘Right again.’

‘To be fair, I thought I would miss Provincetown more than I do, but now I don’t believe I’ll ever return and I’m good with that.’

‘What’s it like to never forget a face?’ Jack changed the subject.

‘I never really thought about it before John Davis made it an issue. I always believed everyone was the same, although I was aware that people I encountered casually often wouldn’t recognize me again. So, if I happen to bump into somebody from a grocery store two years earlier and they don’t offer a hint of recognition, I avoid any chance of embarrassment by not saying a word.’

‘And that works?’

‘Usually.’

Murphy had been among the missing as he explored the back side of the mountain and finally made his way back to the peak and Kris cupped her hands while Jack poured in water from his bottle and Murphy lapped it up as quick as it arrived, and then settled down next to them for a breather.

'The carving you were working on when we left the island. Was that someone in particular.'

'Samuel Beckett.'

'Why Beckett.'

'Beckett had a way of moving through the world in spite of himself or the world, and it helps me to understand or at least gain appreciation for what that was about. A persons face can tell you more than you want to know sometimes. He's not one of them.'

'Why is it you only sculpt faces?'

'It's all that interests me, and I don't know what that means either.' Kris stood up.

'Fair enough.' Jack was looking up at Kris silhouetted by the sky behind her. 'I won't ask you to explain your existence any further.'

'Sorry. I didn't mean it to sound that way.'

'Does that happen often.'

'Afraid so.' Kris offered her hand, which Jack took, and she yanked him up in a move that also brought a startled Murphy to his feet and together they began the trek back down the mountain.

The footing on the descent was more challenging with loose stones and the tips of granite boulders protruding randomly from the trail and made for a slow pace. Murphy had temporarily burned out and remained at their side until they arrived back at the stand of sugar maples behind the cottage and then caught a second wind and made a dash for the back door.

His two hiking companions lagged behind and were barely clear of the sugar maples when Murphy reached the cottage. He attacked the lever handle of the back door with the usual flurry of paws until the door swung open, and his madly wagging tail barely made it across the threshold when the explosion ripped through the cottage, the force of the blast knocking Kris and Jack to the ground. Debris and shrapnel ripped through the grove of sugar maples and they lay stunned and writhing on the ground with every move they made exaggerated and incomprehensible, as they struggled to catch their breath.

The deadly silence that followed lasted only a matter of minutes with black smoke and flames rising from the shattered, burning remains of the cottage that had collapsed upon itself. A Suburban careened up the driveway stopping short of the blaze, the call for emergency services went out and the crew with no idea whether Jack and Kris had become part of the inferno. The second Suburban arrived in a matter of seconds and the four men made a wide circle around the burning cottage and only then realized the extent of the blast.

The entire back section of the cottage was missing. One of the crew stepped over a foreleg and paw from the dog that hung around with O'Malley, and they feared more gruesome news awaited. The heat and smoke from the burning cottage was intense and forced a wide birth to the frantic search that seemed to drag on forever. They continued along incline running parallel to the cottage then back towards the tree line and past the cottage with the smoke blowing and circling in the wind, moving past the point where hope had brought them and then with eery calm from the edge of the forest, Russo voice came over the headpiece. ‘I found them. Call for a chopper.’

Sixteen

Boston

The direct impact of the blast that took down Jack and Kris was diminished by the configuration of the landscape with the most damaging aspects absorbed by the steep rise directly behind the cottage. The main thrust of the blast reverberated back upon itself shattering the cottage, and although far enough away to avoid the fate visited upon Murphy, the force that hurled them off their feet had also saved them from becoming victims of the fragments of timber and shards of glass embedded at various heights into the stand of sugar maples they walked out of only moments earlier.

Jack was the first to be reached, and struggled to sit up and could see Russo's lips moving as he knelt down next to him but heard nothing but the sound of rushing air and every word spoken triggered a stab of intense pain, and Kris was on the ground a few feet away with her knees curled up and both hands covering her ears. He crawled towards her on his hands and knees as another agent was trying to roll her on her back. She was bleeding from one ear and Jack waved the agent away and sat holding her head in his lap as they waited for the helicopter to arrive.

Thirty five minutes later, the helicopter carrying Kris to the hospital in Plymouth lifted away from the public beach. Afterwards, Jack stood in the gravel driveway looking at the smouldering remains of the cottage, and with the image of Murphy going through the back door seared into his consciousness. The fire crew had dropped pumps into the lake to extinguish the flames and were continuing to wet down the area surrounding the cottage. An ambulance was waiting at the end of the drive, which he refused to take until the volunteer fire brigade backed off and his crew assumed total control of the crime scene. He arrived at the hospital in Plymouth barely in time to board the helicopter airlifting Kris back to Massachusetts General Hospital in Boston.

When they touched down at Mass General, the two agents were whisked away by separate medical teams waiting on the helipad. Jack bristled at the amount of attention going his way, and once inside the treatment center refused to be examined until the extent of Kris's injuries were known. He planted himself outside of the treatment room and waited while the medical team conducted their initial examinations.

'How is she?' Max Cooper knew exactly where to find him, and this wasn't the first time they met in a hospital corridor. As the Special Agent-in-Charge, Max Cooper held responsibility for the counter terrorism task forces positioned on the east coast, and the only man Jack answered directly to within the agency. At six feet four inches and one hundred and ninety pounds, the sixty two year old former tight end for the University of Oregon remained an imposing figure. The scar above his right eye testament to years of working undercover, and there wasn't another man whom Jack respected or trusted more than Cooper. The feeling was mutual.

'Don't know yet.' Jack was glad to see him.

'And yourself?'

'I'm fine Max.'

'You don't look so fine.'

'What's going on at the lake?' O'Malley stood up.

'Russo still has the site locked down and forensics is combing the debris and I wish to hell you'd take care of yourself. Do you hear what I'm saying?'

'I hear you Max.'

'I hear you Max.' Cooper repeated. 'What the hell does that mean?' He attempted to press on but the door to the treatment room opened and two doctors emerged.

'One of you Jack O'Malley?' When Jack nodded the woman introduced herself as Doctor Rachel Moore, the ear specialist called in by the staff physician who introduced himself as Doctor Robert Montreau.

'Your colleague, Kris Shepard suffered a perforated eardrum. We started her on a course of antibiotics, and she is being monitored for the effects of a minor concussion. In a few days after her condition has been fully assessed, I'll operate to repair the eardrum. Do you have any questions?'

'Can we see her?' He gestured towards Cooper. 'This is Max Cooper, the head of our department.'

'No, she needs to stay quiet for the time being. I'm going to limit the visitations to five minutes every hour and we'll let you know when the visits can begin.'

‘We will be posting security around the clock for her Doctor Moore.’ Max interjected. ‘And I request Kris be moved to a more secure location away from the emergency department.’

‘We’ll arrange for the move as soon as I feel her condition is stable, Mr. Cooper.’ The specialist turned back to O’Malley. ‘I understand you were also injured in the explosion.’

‘I’m fine Doctor.’

‘I’m a better judge of that Mr. O’Malley.’ She turned to the other doctor. ‘Doctor Montreau, please have another examination room prepared and I don’t want any visitors allowed into Ms. Shepard’s room until after I have a chance to examine Mr. O’Malley’ She turned back to Jack with a look that clearly stated her position.

‘I like your approach, Doctor Moore.’ Max couldn’t resist. ‘I’ll be right here Jack until our people are in place. So, go take care of yourself.’ Max returned to his seat outside of Kris’s room.

The examination revealed that Jack was also exhibiting symptoms of a low-grade concussion, but his ears drums were intact, and after agreeing to a follow up appointment, Doctor Moore granted permission for him to visit Kris in the next room. The shades were drawn, and she was laying on her side. He went in and sat down beside the bed and when her eyes opened whispered, ‘I didn’t mean to wake you.’

‘I wasn’t asleep.’ She adjusted her pillow to see him better. ‘Murphy?’

Jack shook his head.

She reached out and squeezed his hand. ‘I’m so sorry.’

‘It shouldn’t have happened, and I have no one to blame but myself. I let my guard down thinking the runner would never find us at the lake.’

‘We were all there, Jack. So, there’s plenty of blame to go around.’ Kris moved on before he could answer. ‘Do you have any idea how she got in and out of the cottage without being noticed.’

‘The crew tracked her over the mountain. She had a car parked on a forest service road and hiked to the cottage and entered from woods when we were on the mountain. She managed to allow herself enough time to make a clean break before Murphy went through the back door. If she had attempted her usual method the outcome would have been different with no place to hide after the first shot was fired.’

‘She was so close to us, Jack.’

‘Yeah.’ His response nearly a whisper, a moment later the nurses arrived to move Kris to a secure location. Jack followed along with Max and they waited together until she was settled and the FBI security detail in place. An hour later they were in Cooper’ office one floor above his own at One Center Plaza in Boston.

Jack stood at the window looking down over the city, and the lights of Faneuil Hall and only then acknowledged the darkness. His thoughts kept racing back to the moment Murphy went through the door of the cottage and the image of Kris curled up in pain, and each time he revisited the moment only deepened his sense of vulnerability to a force he didn't understand and probably never would.

The world he knew as a young man and occupied for most of his adult life had vanished, replaced by something that seemed to move below his feet, carrying him along, always faster, never the same for long, and becoming more dangerous all the time. He would be happy enough to let the world move along without him, if only that simple and affected no one but himself.

'You want to talk about it?' Max broke the silence.

'No.' Max waited and a few moments later Jack turned away from the window, as he knew he would.

'I'm going to need more tech support Max?'

'I don't have a problem with that.'

'Well you should.'

'What's on your mind, Jack?'

'What's on my mind is that I can stand here and request more tech support and you say no problem. But there is a problem. You and I are fundamentally unqualified to even ask for exactly what it is we want or need so badly, and any doubt that we need it disappeared today.'

'I see.' Max took off his glasses and sat back in the chair.

'I don't know that you do, Max. Your too far removed from what's happening on the street.'

'Which is why you're out there.'

'The fact that it works for you doesn't make it right and won't keep people from getting hurt.'

'It's been a long day, Jack.'

'We don't get out of it that easily. A tipping point is going to be reached when all those years of experience we bring to this job become a problem and get in the way. We're operating from another time and place, a slower and less fluid place that no longer exists and we have to know enough to call it before we cross a line that we'll both regret.'

'I hear what you're saying, Jack, and at times I feel the same way. Thing is, we have more going for us in the way of instinct from that other and much slower world you speak of. And those instincts were hard earned and remain intangible, not unlike the ability Kris Shepard brings to the table, and try as it might, technology simply can't compete. I doubt it ever will.'

'We can buy into that theory for the moment, but let's not bullshit ourselves into believing instinct exists without limitation or can survive without relevance.' Jack turned to leave. 'I'll have Sarah O'Sullivan give you a list of what she requires on the technical end, and I also need more people assigned to security for Kris.'

'You got it. Now get some rest.'

The thought of going up to the apartment held little appeal and he decided to spend the night at the townhouse instead. He took the elevator down to the lobby and walked out into the night air that had turned cold but felt especially good and he started walking up the plaza in the direction of the townhouse and abruptly changed his mind. Instead he took the staircase down towards Cambridge Street and over to Faneuil Hall. The last remnants of the nine to five crowd had petered out and the shops adjacent to Faneuil Hall were shut with a scattering of tourist's window shopping. He cut straight across Merchants Row and turned the corner onto Chatham Street towards The Black Rose pub, and the moment he took the corner noticed a group of young guys standing in a darkened section of the street close to the dumpsters from the Chinese and Greek restaurants fronting South Market. The likely occasion for the gathering was to intimidate a bit of cash out of hapless tourists, who strayed off course.

As a group, they decided in a heartbeat that he wasn't for them, and this he knew from their body language. The kneejerk reaction to the image he presented gave testament to the predatory nature of instinct and this bothered him more than their presence. They kept their backs to him when he walked past.

The Black Rose was unusually quiet with the exception of the barkeeps who were still arguing the results of the All Ireland football championship match between Co. Kerry and Co. Donegal that took place a month earlier. Jack had lost interest in the chase for the Sam Maguire Cup, after Kerry eliminated Mayo in a hard fought replay at the end of August. For much as his father before him, it was Mayo or nothing, but he still enjoyed listening to the banter going back and forth between the lads defending their home turf.

County loyalties are not taken lightly in Ireland, and perhaps less so with the Irish diaspora, as they already feel as though they lost too much. His father, Sean never gave up hope of seeing a Co. Mayo, All Ireland victory in his lifetime, a dream that followed him to the grave. Mayo hasn't lifted the Sam Maguire since 1951, when as the story goes a curse was placed on the Mayo team celebrating their victory by a widow who felt they failed to offer a proper degree of respect as they passed by her husband's funeral procession.

The widow vowed Mayo wouldn't win another All Ireland until every member of that winning team was dead and buried. Mayo has yet to place a glove on the Sam Maguire since the curse passed her lips, and two members of the team are still alive. One in Kerry and the other in America, and they best stay there.

Jack ordered a pint of Guinness, took a copy of the Irish Examiner off the bar and sat down at a corner table facing out towards the door. Both the Guinness and the Examiner were rare occurrences, and the combination reserved for moments requiring a change of venue, and nothing brought him out of himself more completely.

He scanned the front page then headed for the sports section out of force of habit. The pundits were still dissecting the outcome of the All Ireland, while the Kerry senior football squad slow danced the Sam Maguire around the county in a long standing rite of passage within the Kingdom, and there was something noble and timeless about the concept of sport purely for the sake of competition. The lads not making a dime for the effort, yet waging battles on the pitch like Celtic warriors, drawing blood and sustenance from the purity of the moment, as the dream of bringing home the Sam Maguire passes unabated from generation to generation across every county in Ireland.

These ingrained and well-honed concepts of honor and sacrifice extend beyond the pitch in ways that don't require the spoken word to convey pride of place, or a sense of being part of something bigger than oneself. And one needn't be Irish to appreciate the concept, nor its effects on a society.

It occurred to him that he rarely had a conversation in relation to Ireland with Kris. But that would be the way of it, and even within his own family the discussions rarely strayed beyond football or the weather in Mayo. Although his early memories include discussions between his father and grandfather, which were off limits to him and had everything to do with the troubles back in Ireland.

His grandfather, James J. O'Malley came out of Belmullet in Co. Mayo, and the first of his family to make their way to Boston in the early nineteen forties. A sister and a younger brother followed and together they forged a new life and there wasn't much talk about the one left behind. His grandfather died when Jack was only ten years old, and although he didn't know the man that so many have since described, their unusual bond was forged before he could walk, and he can vividly recall the first time he looked into his grandfather' eyes and encountered his own looking back.

The tri-colored funeral in South Boston had a massive turnout and respect for the man was obvious even to a ten year old. His grandmother, Kathleen, also from Belmullet moved in with his parents shortly afterwards and became a big part of Jack's life. He loved her sense of humor, and she was a constant source of advice in ways that only seem unusual in retrospect, and she left a big hole in his life when her time came.

Jack nursed the pint of Guinness for the better part of an hour and before leaving the Black Rose, he checked in with Will Jenkins who was leading the security detail at the hospital. Kris was asleep and having Jenkins in charge put his mind at ease. The Kerry and Donegal debate was still raging when he walked out to State Street and waited at the curb for the security crew, which he knew Max assigned in spite of his request otherwise.

Eight minutes later he was dropped off at the door of the townhouse on Ridgeway Lane. Cooper's guys would have already cleared the building, but he went through the routine anyway, assuming responsibility for his own space, which was something he let slide back in New Hampshire and the toll was heavy.

Sleep came quick but didn't last long, and at 5:00 a.m. he relieved Jenkins at Mass General. The entire wing was sealed off and Kris was up and pacing the corridor. At noon she was cleared for surgery and the following week stood with Jack on the gravel drive leading up to the charred remains of the cottage. The scope of what was thrown at them and how fortunate they were to have survived was stark and brutally manifest within the tranquil lakeside setting.

'Thanks for bringing me here. I needed to see it for myself.' Kris had slipped back into the throes of vertigo and her arm was wrapped in Jack's to maintain balance. She tugged him a little closer to the rubble. 'Did the forensic team come up with anything useful?'

'Nothing beyond the obvious fact of the bomb being constructed by someone who knew what they were doing.'

'And that leaves us where?' She turned to face him.

'Max has agreed to give us more support on the technical side and the crew will be able to expand their reach. Sarah has been working closely with our people in Russia to nail down the identity of the military official in control of the Brighton Beach mafia. When we get back to Boston, you and I will sit down with the crew and talk about where we are and where we need to be with the operation, if you're up to it.'

'I'm ready.' Kris offered in spite of the intense bouts of nausea, which were showing no signs of abating. At this point, she had acquired enough coping strategies to get past the worst of it and was glad Jack had understood her desire to revisit the cottage. Now all she really wanted and needed was to get back into the search for the runner.

By evening they were back in Boston at the townhouse. Kris sat with her feet propped on the footrest next to the gas fireplace while Jack poured wine in the kitchen. She stared at the flames and thought about their last evening in the cottage with Murphy sound asleep in front of the wood stove, and how fast everything changed and how easy it would be to resent change in any form.

Jack came back with the wine and sat across from her and waited for reaction to the wine.'

'It's not for me. Sorry, Jack.'

'You're tough.'

'Don't give up.'

'Alright.'

'Tell me something.' She hesitated. 'Your aversion to technology. Where's that come from?'

'Actually, it's more avoidance than aversion, and if I had to choose a reason, I suppose it would be the speed of change. At some point, I realized it was possible to coexist with the latest advancement by skimming the surface, and simply waiting for the next new thing to come along. Now, it's so far ahead of me that I'm entirely dependent on people like Sarah O'Sullivan and Will Jenkins who are truly brilliant. How about you?'

'I enjoy the freedom technology brings to my life, but my passions reside elsewhere. I don't feel the need to either embrace or avoid the changes, as you say and until now it hasn't really mattered.'

'Why did you bring it up, Kris?'

'I was thinking about the runner and the way she has absolutely no electronic, digital or cellular profile, as though she lives in a parallel world even more extreme than yours. But doesn't it feel like we're dealing with someone as knowledgeable as Sarah or Will Jenkins?'

'You're not the first one to raise that question, and it's becoming more and more obvious with each new encounter that we're being dangerously outmanoeuvred.'

'Where do we stand with the Russian Mafia investigation?' Kris changed the subject.

‘The crew has established a few interesting connections between the Russian military leadership and the mafia that warrant a closer look. There appears to be a serious amount of Russian military involvement throughout the entire procurement and distribution chain of the Taliban heroin coming into North America.’

‘Do we have much background information on the leadership?’

‘We have profiles from the military side of the ledger but only within their official capacity. Their diplomatic immunity allows for easy access to all things American and they know how to work the grey areas. We do know that a number of them came out of a place called Reni, which is a small port town on the Black Sea in the Odessa Oblast. Some of these guys have been comrades from birth.’

‘I find it hard to believe more information isn’t available about an operation of this scale operating in Brooklyn.’

‘The scale is precisely the reason everyone is being cautious and protecting their own turf, and when you blend diplomacy and politics, the concept of making sense isn’t the first priority.’

‘And that leaves us where in terms of the investigation.’

‘I believe we’ll get more cooperation from our own government agencies, such as the CIA when they feel we know as much or more than they do, but until then we’re on our own.’

‘So, we have nothing on the mysterious daughter that Erik Petrov mentioned.’

‘No, and at this point all we can do is make a run at unraveling the digital trail and Max is in the process of assembling a task force from the cybercrime divisions of both Quantico and Silicon Valley to help track down the hacker and they should be in place within a few days.’

‘And in the meantime?’

‘We step back until the task force has a chance to do its thing, and for the moment I’m going to bake the cod I had sent over earlier. You must be starving?’

‘Not until you mentioned it. Can I help?’

‘No. I got it.’

Jack baked the cod in milk and steamed a side of broccoli then opened another bottle of wine, poured two glasses and sat down at the breakfast bar across from Kris. He was halfway through answering the question of how he acquired the cooking skills that he was trying his best to diminish when Kris received a text message.

‘It’s from Tyler Frank.’ She looked across to Jack. ‘He wants me to call as soon as possible.’ She took the phone into the living room and came back ten minutes later. ‘I think we have a problem, Jack.’

‘What happened.’

‘One of the artists from Provincetown was walking past our studio last evening and noticed what appeared to be someone moving about with a flashlight and she knocked on the door thinking it was Tyler. But nobody came to the door and the light went out, so she left and notified the police.'

'Did the police go into the building?' Jack stood up.

'No. They checked the doors and windows for forced entry and everything appeared in order, so they contacted Tyler to make sure he was alright.'

'Where's Tyler now?'

'He's still in Texas. But he's shook up about the prospect of having his work stolen or vandalized.'

'Tyler may have more immediate things to worry about. I'm going to have a crew from Austin keep an eye on him. In the meantime, we need to lock down the studio and get the bomb squad in there.'

'I need to go to the studio, Jack.'

'Not a good idea.'

'That wasn't a request and you can either come with me or not.'

They stood six feet apart with eyes locked and finally, 'If it means that much to you, Kris, we can go out there in the morning. I'm sending in the bomb squad followed by a forensics response team before we can have access. That work for you?'

'Yeah, it does. Thank you.'

The helicopter landed at the Provincetown Airport late the next afternoon and they were met by the local police chief and escorted to town where the yellow tape was still in place across Commercial

Street and a large segment of the population remained traumatized by the forced evacuation that stretched from the wharf to three blocks above and either side of the studio. The bomb squad and forensics team had cleared and released the site a half hour earlier and the police chief wanted his town back. Although, Jack didn't offer any relief by informing him that both his crew and the yellow tape would remain in place until after Kris viewed the studio.

Russo met them at the tape, and they walked down the deserted Commercial Street to the studio where the response team had been in position overnight, and the moment Kris walked through the door she knew that the runner had been there. 'Did forensics come away with anything?'

'The initial assessment doesn't look good.' Russo answered her question. 'The team in Austin is processing the Tyler Franks DNA sample and forwarding his fingerprints while the Boston lab sorts out what little they were able to gather from the studio and apartment.'

Kris made her way through the common area separating their studios and upon entering Tyler's went directly to his print locker, a deep, chest high wooden filing cabinet as wide as it was high that held prints, charcoal sketches, pen and ink drawings and in the right hand side of the bottom drawer, a sketch book that Kris removed and closed the drawer again.

'What is it?' Jack had followed her movements.

'An important sketch book.'

'Important to who?'

'This sketch book contains the only images of someone Tyler was close to and I promised him that I would keep it safe.' Said as she slipped the sketch book into the canvas bag that had been slung over her shoulder.

'Is this person someone of interest?'

'Not to us. His name was Bill Mansur. An artist that Tyler was involved with for over ten years. Bill was an extremely private man and would never allow his picture to be taken. Four years ago, he left for an exhibit on the west coast and never came back. This is all that remains from that relationship for Tyler.'

'Where is this guy now?'

'He traded California for the Costa Blanca in Spain and died there last year.' Kris put the canvas bag back over her shoulder. 'I would like to see my apartment now, if you don't mind.'

The apartment was cold despite the sun blaring through the bank of windows facing the harbor and Kris moved slowly through the apartment, opening drawers and closets and when she entered the study, stopped suddenly and turned to Russo. 'Has anyone touched any items in this room?'

'No. Everything was left as found.'

'You're sure of this?'

'Absolutely.'

'What's wrong?' Jack moved next to her.

'This.' Kris stood up two picture frames that were facing downwards on top of a wooden bookcase.

The first held a photograph of Dan Walker and her mother on the viewing terrace at Mount Rushmore, and the second was of Kris and Dan at Medicine Wheel in the Bighorn Mountains of Wyoming.

'Now, I would say this is getting personal.' Russo stated what appeared to be the obvious conclusion. 'And she's toying with us by simply being here.'

Kris placed both frames in the canvas bag with Tyler's sketch pad and turned to Jack. 'I need to leave now.' And they didn't speak on the way back to the airport, nor in the chopper, and it wasn't until they reached the townhouse again that Kris broke the silence. 'I don't believe this is personal for her Jack. The woman is utterly focused on her agenda and she won't allow interference of any nature to exist. I know that level of obsession painfully well, and at this point there's nothing for it.' Kris turned and walked down the corridor to the bedroom and a few minutes later, Jack heard the shower running and he left the townhouse.

The Provincetown event created an even greater sense of urgency to increase the security around Kris and the crew began working out of the townhouse to allow Kris more down time whenever the need arose. With new faces on the crew they rebooted by reviewing everything that transpired since the day Sam was killed, including the forensics associated with the case, which ranged from slim to non-existent depending on the particular location.

The investigation had repeatedly imploded due partly to way the runner conducted her life in a manner consistent with the nineteen fifties and in doing so rendered the latest tools of surveillance and detection mute. That said, she could no longer walk down any street in Boston, as simply another face in the crowd. And this she knew as clearly as the image Kris held onto each night when she closed her eyes.

Four days after returning from Provincetown, in what was either failed karma or a solemn dose of irony, the long awaited break in the search came from an unexpected source, the hacker. In an apparent bout of hubris, the man bragged in a chat room on the dark web about bringing the FBI to their knees without leaving a trace, and although the statement was essentially correct it had also managed to capture the attention of Patricia Ward who was prowling the site and remained in attendance for the entire duration of the his rant. Patricia was a founding member of the Cyber Warfare Task Force and not someone the hacker would be especially pleased to have shared his exploits, and by extension placed his days on the loose in serious jeopardy.

Kris was the first to question whether the mistake wasn't actually the act of a desperate man. She felt the guy was too smart for such a blunder, and instead may suggest a need for the financial means to sever the connection with the runner. Certainly, this individual had ample opportunity to realize the nature of who he was dealing with and every reason to be concerned about drawing his next breath.

The task force led by Patricia Ward began an intensive effort to uncover the identity of the hacker, and forty eight hours later a name was placed on O'Malley's desk. He immediately went to Ridgeway Lane and woke Kris at 7:30 A.M., on a Sunday morning. An hour later they were back at One Center Plaza in the conference room surrounded by both the new and original members of the Springfield crew. The hacker's image was on the big screen above the name, Alexei Orlov.

The man was an undocumented Russian immigrant living in Brighton Beach under the alias, Pablo Ortiz. He had studied the art of hacking at a makeshift school operating out of a rundown apartment building in the heart of Moscow. The longhaired and bearded headmaster of the school is considered a computer genius by an entire generation of young Russian hackers. The unofficial university led by the young guru has a reputation of attracting the elite within the overeducated and underemployed legions of Russian hackers in waiting. The entry exam to the pop up university was notoriously difficult and designed to identify the truly gifted from within the hordes of applicants.

According to his disciples, the self-appointed headmaster preached the virtues of staying within the letter of the law, and insisted he only instructed individuals in the fine art of defending themselves from cybercrime. The oddest part of the statement was that he spoke the truth, as he perceived it.

Patricia Ward' task force was assembled from an international pool of the best talents available including a young Israeli out of the Team 8 think tank, as well as two Russian asylum seekers who came on board through an act of self-preservation. They had previously refused to put their talents to work for the military, and rightly concluded fleeing Moscow to be a matter of upmost urgency and the FBI awaited with open arms.

Both defectors attended the Moscow hacking school and recognized the unique methodology Orlov used to cover his footprints following the chat room encounter. Although disappointed with their former comrade, they were aware of the rumors floating around Moscow suggesting Orlov was recruited by the Russian Military, or an affiliate with the implication being organized crime or more specifically the Odessa Mafia. Orlov had disappeared from Moscow shortly before the defectors crossed over to the FBI.

One point the defectors made perfectly clear was the extent of Orlov's talents. A man they considered a truly gifted mathematician with computer skills to match. They suggested the task force use artificial intelligence to create a fake chat room with the intent of luring Orlov. Although, to the defectors way of thinking, the fact that Orlov was able to be sourced at all, coincided with the now prevailing theory of his seeking a way out of the association with the runner and if correct, Orlov was indeed a desperate man.

O'Malley opened the impromptu meeting with an acknowledgement. 'The first thing I want to mention is the debt of gratitude we owe to Patricia Ward and the task force who uncovered Alexei Orlov.' He took a drink of water and looked around the conference table and there wasn't an empty seat. 'It's become apparent that without the assistance of Orlov, that the runner would be essentially blind and her ability to function severely hampered. That said, her penchant for leaving no witnesses, doesn't bode well for Mr. Orlov' long term survival, and the theory of fear being the primary motivation behind his actions in the chat room appears to be a valid assumption that needs to acted upon.'

'The runner.' Jack continued. 'By virtue of being completely off the grid, has limited means of communication at her disposal, and when she feels the need to converse with Orlov it must be done face to face. Our goal is to have everyone in this room present when that next meeting occurs.'

'Are you comfortable with leaving him out there?' Sarah O'Sullivan posed the question.

'Not at all. But Orlov is the shortest route to the runner, who at this point has no idea that we found her man. But there is going to be a time limit on the live surveillance. If the runner doesn't attempt to contact him over the next ten days, then we have no option except to bring him in. The risk of waiting any longer is significant, and another train of thought questions the extent of the runner's technical abilities and suggests that we can't simply assume her off grid lifestyle translates into the absence of technical ability. A real possibility exists that she could be well versed in this area, which raises the risk of our surveillance being exposed in the first instance by the runner herself, and we know from experience what follows.'

Jack paused and scanned the conference room. 'If there are no further questions, I'll turn this over to Anthony Russo to work out the logistics of the surveillance operation and form the crew into two person teams. I'll be working closely with Kris for the duration and everything passes through me.' Jack turned to Anthony Russo, 'send me the notes of meeting when you finish here and make sure every image collected is in front of Kris as soon as possible.' Russo stood up and took over as Jack and Kris walked out of the conference room.

Back in Brighton Beach, Alexei Orlov was impressed at how easy it was to attract potential clients for his services. His initial response was suspicion, although this was his default reaction and obviously he had been out of the stolen data market for way too long. There now appeared to be a profusion of willing buyers, and he thought of posting a cryptic response, but decided to hold back until he had an opportunity to chase down the sources. The most pressing issue at hand was how to cut loose from Anna Volkov. A few short jobs would put him financially over the top, and he could afford to disappear for whatever period of time it took her to form new alliances.

He initially agreed to work with Anna in honor of the long standing and lucrative association that he maintained with her father, Petr Volkov. The work for Petr began as simply a matter of tracking down and monitoring individuals who found themselves out of favor with the old man for one reason or another.

Although, his personal knowledge and exposure to the fate of those targeted was always minimal, but Anna was another matter altogether and he was now in the position of having to extract himself from a collaboration with a psychopath. He knew Anna's obsession for keeping her identity secret, offered the potential to be lethal and there could be no illusions about her willingness to silence anyone arbitrarily viewed as a risk. Not to mention the fact that her cold, grey eyes never failed to send shivers up his spine.

Unfortunately, another meeting with Anna was already scheduled for the il Fornetto restaurant, by way of a business card tacked to the upper left hand corner of the notice board at the Taste of Russia Deli. At exactly three-thirty in the afternoon of each and every Wednesday he was required to check the Deli's notice board for a possible face to face with the woman who has slowly become his tormentor.

The appointed time for the meeting never varied from one o'clock sharp the following day, and it was his job to make certain the surveillance equipment at whatever restaurant or bar she chose for the meeting was rendered inoperative at the appointed hour.

The last outing, he arranged in New Hampshire had less than the desired results, but the outcome had nothing to do with his work. One could only hope she would fold up the operation after the near miss or simply ease off until things calmed down. In any event the timing never felt better for a quick and unexpected exit.

The only departure for their meeting, which varied from the normal routine was the choice of location at Sheepshead's Bay. The il Fornetto Restaurant was beyond Anna's established comfort zone of Brighton Beach, a safe haven where no one saw, heard or spoke a syllable related to the Russian Mafia. This due to the fact that the majority of residents in the enclave have a relative or friend back in Russia with nowhere to hide, and even a perceived lack of respect for the code of silence held the real possibility of harsh repercussions in the motherland.

Disabling the industrial grade surveillance gear at the restaurant wasn't much of a workout, and Orlov decided to focus on getting his affairs in order for a swift departure after the meeting with Anna. He devoted a few hours to wiping down the apartment for fingerprints and was looking forward to moving on from the cramped and Spartan existence he had endured by edict of his beautiful and deadly Russian taskmaster.

That evening, an attempt to read a book had failed miserably and during the night he tossed and turned, as was the case before every face to face meeting with Anna Volkov. The imposing sense of danger kept his thoughts locked into a continuous loop of worry that went on relentlessly, and at daybreak he awoke startled and wondering if had really slept.

His thoughts turned to what lay ahead, and the fact that he would be expected to sit in the last car of the Q train, at a window seat facing the Brighton Beach platform to insure he wasn't being followed. Only once did he choose to disregard her instructions and wasn't about to repeat that mistake.

He was anxious to get online and discover whether more messages awaited from his marketing efforts, but resisted the temptation and would wait until he was aboard the train before connecting to the internet. Not once in the five years spent at Brighton Beach did he venture online or even power up the computer while in his personal space, and the IP address was never compromised, and the apartment remained a sanctuary where he could sleep with both eyes shut.

Time was heavy and seemed to come to a standstill, and after the longest hour and a half of his young life, a final wipe down of the apartment was followed with an obfuscation spray to add a mix of genetic material to cloak whatever DNA remained. And when he went out the door for the last time he carried only what was necessary for the transition in a small backpack, and the knowledge that life was about to become exciting again.

The Brighton Beach platform was sparsely populated between rush hours, and as instructed Orlov arrived exactly four minutes before the Q train was due to arrive at the station. He walked down the platform to the vicinity where the last car of the train would be expected to stop. Three minutes later he boarded and joined a handful of passengers in the last car, and sitting beside a window, performed the obligatory scan of the platform, as the train was slowly pulling away from the station.

The entire routine he considered melodramatic, and not once had he ever encountered anyone even remotely suspicious. Although, on this occasion he did notice a guy in a hooded sweatshirt standing beside the elevator at the end of the platform and decided to wait until the train cleared the station before pursuing his online agenda. The guy in the hood began to move as the last car approached the end of the platform and if by chance, Orlov realized the figure wasn't a man, it would have been the last thought to pass through his mind.

The undercover agent who boarded the last car ahead of Orlov pulled the emergency lever and brought the train to a screeching halt, then scrambled onto the platform with clumps of Orlov's brains still clinging to her coat, and there wasn't a soul to be found in either direction.

Two other members of the surveillance crew were already in motion towards the next station when Orlov was killed, and by the time they made it back to the Brighton Beach platform any potential witnesses had scattered, including the MTA staff who worked the platforms on either side of tracks.

O'Malley and Kris were at the FBI office in New York City when they received the message about Orlov's demise, and hardly a word passed between them on the way to the train station. Rail traffic on the Brighton Line was halted in both direction, and the last car of the Q train stood isolated at the end of the platform. The balance of Q train had been sent ahead and remained under lockdown at the next stop.

They proceeded directly to where Orlov lay slumped across the empty seat beside him. His iPad was on the floor in a pool of blood, and the revulsion O'Malley felt had less to do with the gruesome condition of Alexei Orlov, than the reality of the runner having successfully shut down their operation with a single bullet. He walked to the end of the car and sat looking out the window. Kris joined him and after fielding incoming phone calls from Max and Patricia Ward, they were on the way back to Boston.

At precisely one o'clock and within the shadow of the Brighton Beach Q stop, the runner sat down at a table in the Skovorodka Restaurant across from a sandy haired and well-dressed young man.

'Good to see you.'

'And you.' She smiled and reached over to touch his hands folded on the table.

'Our father has taught us well, No?' The man responded.

'Some more than others.' She offered without expression.

The waiter arrived at the table and her brother ordered two double shots of vodka then continued the conversation. 'We now have but one outstanding matter to attend.'

'Nyet, my brother. We have two'

'Two?'

'We must also attend to Jack O'Malley, otherwise he will persist, and we don't need a crusader at our backs.' Anna paused while the waiter placed two shot glasses on the table and poured the vodka. 'The bottle stays.' She demanded and waited for him to leave the table.

'I see.' He picked up the shot glass. 'Perhaps we should have allowed Alexei a little more time on this earth to repent and make amends for his sudden lack of discretion.' He held the glass of vodka out in front of him.

The runner touched her glass to his. 'We are allowed but one mistake in this business, Anton.'

'Spoken like a true Volkov. You make our father proud.'

'And you have a long ways to go, I'm afraid.'

'With your guidance, Anna.'

'Have the funds cleared from our associates in Afghanistan?' She moved on.

'Yes, the last series of transfers are accounted for and the balance awaits proof that the Shepard woman is dead. They are demanding images and a body part.'

'This can be arranged.'

'And so, I will confirm?'

‘Of course.’ She set the menu aside. ‘In a few weeks you will be returning to Odessa. Does he know you’re coming?’

‘Not yet.’

‘He will be pleased, I’m sure.’

‘And you, Anna. You remain pleased to be doing the bidding of Petr Volkov?’

‘Of course, and you should be as well.’

‘Easy to say when you remain always within his good graces, as the loyal and obedient daughter.’

‘I make no apologies, brother.’

‘Nor is one sought. But this doesn’t change the way things are.’

‘And how are things, as you say?’

‘One sided as always with our father.’

‘And with yourself, brother. And with yourself.’

The waiter reappeared before Anton could respond, as was the good fortune, and they ordered lunch and ate well and after a while laughed and talked softly until they parted two hours later.

Seventeen

Boston

The mood of the entire crew was somber after returning to Boston and required a fresh attempt to regroup while awaiting results from the forensics lab. They began by chasing down the scant bits of evidence at their disposal, consisting mainly of bullet fragments, which not surprisingly were confirmed to have been fired from the same gun used in the series of shootings associated with the runner.

Her latest outing in Brighton Beach hadn't produce a single witness, and the surveillance cameras on both the platform of the train station and at street level below the elevated tracks were disabled thirty minutes before Alexi Orlov was killed.

One bullet placed above his right eye removed the hacker from the equation and the fact that this was accomplished with a moving target was a point that didn't escape O'Malley's attention, and supported the theory of a military background, a possibility explored to no avail, and the only certainty going forward was that the operation was in serious disarray, and it was time to gather the crew around the conference table and forge a new approach.

Kris continued to struggle from the effects of the near miss at O'Malley's cottage, and the chronic bouts of vertigo had resumed in exaggerated form and relegated her to spend most days in the safe house on Ridgeway Lane. She was now being protected around the clock by a special crew brought in Max Cooper after cottage was sabotaged. Jack resumed residence in a one room apartment on the floor above his office at FBI Headquarters, a familiar and official point of refuge over the years. On most days Kris slept late, and this seemed to keep the vertigo at a manageable level, and according to the doctors she could expect longer durations of normal activity and improvements to her sense of balance, if she followed the suggested regimen of light exercise followed by periods of rest.

The sense of frustration and uneasiness leading up to the strategy meeting was palpable. The entire crew had gathered early at headquarters, and Jack opened the meeting by thanking all those present for the concern shown to Kris and himself following the event at the cottage, and the manner in which they continued to press on with the investigation to the extent possible.

The question of drawing out the runner was raised and immediately shot down by Jack. The thought being that her obvious fixation on Kris, would leave the runner exposed. 'I won't take that risk again, and we can do better than allowing ourselves to operate on her terms.'

'What became of Erik Petrov, the undercover agent out of the New York office?' Kris addressed the question to Jack.

'We haven't heard a word out of Petrov and he's apparently off the grid. I conducted a line of inquiry concerning his background with no results, and the consensus out of Quantico is that Petrov has formed or been drawn into an alliance with the CIA. What exactly that entails, I have no idea.'

'So, we can assume the guy is a dead end for now?' Anthony Russo weighed in.

'For the moment, but he's hardly the only way forward.' Jack responded. 'We need to shake things up in Brighton Beach, and I'm talking about our associates in New York. Max is pressing for more cooperation, but it'll be a hard sell, as they don't have a sterling reputation for being forthcoming in joint investigations, and I get that part. So, with that being a foregone conclusion, I want each of you to go over your list of sources and contacts to establish and connections that we could leverage.'

'There is something I would like to chase down.' Will Jenkins added. 'But I'll need direct assistance from the technical sector working out of Quantico.'

'What do you have in mind?'

'Just a hunch that involves more technical issues than I could explain in this setting.'

'Alright then. I'll make sure you get whatever it is you need.' Jack looked around the room again. 'How about you, Kris, something to add?'

'Nothing beyond the fact that I believe going after the Brighton Beach Mafia is the right way to proceed, and when this ends, it will have been about the drug trade from day one.'

'I agree.' Jack took over again. 'which is another reason to dig deeper into our sources and any past alliances formed within the narcotics unit working Brighton Beach. Also, make sure every image that offers even a glimpse of a wife, mistress or daughter associated with both the Russian military leadership and Odessa mafia is cleared by Kris.'

Jack ended the meeting on that note and turned to Kris, 'I have a few calls to make, so grab a coffee and let's say twenty minutes in my office.' And she could tell it wasn't the operation he wanted to discuss by the tone of his voice and the first words out of his mouth were, 'How you feeling?'

'I'm feeling tired of hearing that question.'

'Fine. Let's talk it then.' Jack didn't hesitate. 'I want you to return to Ireland for the time being.'

'I'm not running from this woman again, Jack'

'I'm not asking you to run.'

'Really. It doesn't sound that way to me.'

'I need to know your safe and doing the job you were hired to do. But we also need to free up some of the manpower currently employed to keep you safe around the clock on Ridgeway Lane. As it stands, our resources are overextended from Quantico's point of view, and the limited access to Inis Meain would allow the security crew to be reduced from six agents down to three and we need to use the extra manpower in the field before it gets snatched away.'

Kris remained silent for a few moments then stood and walked to the window and looked out over the city.

'You're right, Jack.'

'Not the answer I was expecting to hear.'

'Keep the images coming and I want to be here when anything of consequence takes place. Is that agreed?'

'Agreed.'

'When do I leave?'

'As soon as your bags are packed.' Jack sat back in his chair. 'I appreciate the cooperation.'

She walked away from the window and at the door turned to face him again. 'Cooperation has limits, Jack. Don't let me down.' She meant every word and it was his turn to remain silent.

The next morning Kris was sitting in a chopper on the tarmac of the Inis Meain Airport while two of crew members assigned to keep her safe cleared the cottage and outbuildings. The pilot sat patiently beside her while the third agent paced the tarmac, and it was good being so close to the stretch of beach that was part of her daily routine before Jack whisked her away, and she missed that time alone in the wind and the rain with cold hands and muffled ears and never a soul in sight.

Nearly an hour later, the van driven by Breda, the woman taxi driver from her first night on the island pulled alongside the chopper accompanied by one of the bodyguards, and shortly afterwards, Kris walked through the door of the cottage. The woodstove was ablaze with turf and the computer geek of the crew had commandeered the ground floor bedroom as a tech station, and all she really wanted and needed was to get upstairs and crawl under the duvet and sleep off the onslaught of vertigo brought on by the flight, and a particularly rough landing in Galway. Sleep came immediately and when her eyes opened again it was four o'clock in the morning, and she lay in the dark listening to the familiar howl of the wind, and the rain lashing at the windows and drifted back to sleep.

In the days that followed, Kris went into a cycle of long hours of sleep punctuated by bouts of utter starvation followed by more sleep. Slowly, the pattern began to adjust to the rhythms of the island and on day four, she awoke at sunrise and looked out the bedroom window to see the chicken she had previously named, Lady, moving like a roadrunner towards the back door of the kitchen. When she went downstairs one of the crew was throwing chunks of brown bread out the door to the scrawny chicken, who looked worse than Kris remembered, and it was obvious the pecking order had resumed after she left the island with O'Malley.

Kris was pleased to see the agent feeding the hungry creature and took it as a sign that perhaps she could coexist with this crew after all. The agent introduced himself as Brendan O'Leary and she pointed out that another O'Leary was just what Ireland needed, a statement he found humorous, and Kris had to remind herself that the sanctioned home invasion was a temporary condition to be borne for all the right reasons.

Her skill at remembering faces was countered by a sincere lack of desire to remember names, although she made the effort at times, but knew from experience that Jack would be rotating her guardians on a regular basis, and understood his reasoning and he was correct, it was easier on everyone. The statement sounded harsh to the uninitiated, but there was no animosity involved, simply the way it was, and really couldn't be any other way. He got that part and she was grateful.

The computer technician had mounted surveillance cameras at both the ferry and cargo piers, as well as various locations across the island, and the ground floor bedroom now held an entire wall of monitors constantly scanning the island, and he seemed quite proud of himself. 'Make sure you take all this gear when you leave,' was the only response she could offer to the liberties taken with the cottage. 'And talk to me, if you intend to bring in anymore equipment. Are we clear on that?'

'Perfectly.'

The man didn't appear fazed by her direct manner, and the crew had obviously been coached by Jack, which she may have resented in earlier times, and Kris knew that she needed to chill and would at some point, but the digital wallpaper was hanging in the bedroom where her grandmother spent her last painful days and died alone, and the only reason Kris allowed him to remain was knowing that her grandmother would have welcomed the young man to use the space, a natural sensibility that wasn't hers to offend, and least of all in that room.

By the beginning of the second week she was walking twice a day. A short outing before breakfast with increasing longer jaunts following an afternoon nap. The vertigo was beginning to flare sporadically during the course of the day, instead of one continuous bout. This was an encouraging development and a similar pattern emerged during her first encounter with vertigo, and she could only hope it continued to loosen its grip on her life.

For Kris, the impact of the FBI occupation was slightly offset by the constant supply of food and the endless warmth within the cottage. The crew was handling all the labor intensive tasks associated with the wet, windblown realities of island life, although it was also what she missed the most. There was solace to be found in waking to a cold, dark and silent cottage that perhaps few would appreciate, and she found difficult to live without.

The weather was especially challenging at the end of November, and the back-to-back gales shutdown the ferry service and grounded the air transport between the mainland and the Aran Islands. The weather hardly fazed the islanders whose lives are immune to extended periods of rough seas and the fierce winds that scour the landscape. For the security team the learning curve was accelerated by the persistent gales and required only one hungry night to guarantee it wouldn't happen again.

For Kris, the storms were a relief and allowed more freedom of movement around the island without the constant presence of her roommates, and she would be sorry to see them end. Jack checked in on a daily basis, but the best efforts in Boston were producing only a trickle of images for her to evaluate. Although, they were having slightly more success with the Russian mobsters from Brighton Beach than with the military leadership in Moscow. The FBI personnel stationed at the Russian Embassy, were making fresh attempts at capturing informal images of the leadership and their families, although the opportunities were infrequent at best.

There was an unmistakable sense of relief being on Inis Meain and away from the frustrating task that jack was facing. The forced cohabitation at the cottage was becoming more tolerable and less intrusive than anticipated and she credited the crew with that unexpected development. Still, it was a welcome change for all involved when she was able to spend time alone at her studio. The vertigo placed hard boundaries on her energy, and she made an attempt to ration the studio time to a few hours each day. Although, she often lost track of time and even when she didn't, it was difficult to stop working, but the risk of a setback was real.

The walks back and forth to the studio could stretch to an hour or more with frequent stops to spend time with whatever four legged creature she passed along the way. The evenings consisted of a daily briefing by Brendan O'Leary followed by extended periods of reading in her room and helped to relieve the stress of being exposed to the continuous presence of other people.

At the beginning of the fifth week, Jack called with news that the missing informer, Erik Petrov, had washed up on the shore of Sheepshead Bay in Brooklyn with two bullet holes in his head. The information was sure to travel quick and silence the other sources in Brighton Beach, and he feared that what little momentum they had was about to dry up completely.

Max Cooper was all that stood between Jack and the pressure coming out of Quantico to apprehend Sam Bordeaux's killer, and it was becoming harder to shield the crew from the criticism and second guessing he was being subjected to daily. Jack was not someone who required, nor would he respond to outside influences, and no one knew this better than Cooper. That said, the internal pressure he was placing on himself weighed heavily, and Kris could hear it in his voice.

‘Do you want me to return to Boston?’ She volunteered.

‘No. Nothing has changed in that regard, and I need to know your safe while I work out the way forward.’ Then he added the disclaimer. ‘Unless you feel the need to get away from the crew.’

‘No. I’m good for now.’

‘If you say so, but I need to be kept in the loop with how you’re getting along out there.’

‘You know I will, of course.’

Professor Davis had been thorough in the evaluation of his research subjects and had shared his findings concerning Kris with O’Malley prior to their first meeting in Cambridge. Although, he later came to believe that Davis held back more details than he provided about the nature of his recruits. But it was obvious even to Jack that the emphasis Kris places on solitude is intertwined with an intense need to create and influences the way she moves through the world, and on more than one occasion has questioned the decision to bring her on board regardless of her ability. The woman was perfectly suited to the life she was leading when Davis picked her out of the crowd and together they drew her into their own harsh reality, and he likes to tell himself it was her choice, but knows only too well that for Kris, the option ceased to exist at the finish line of the Boston marathon.

Three days later the knock on O’Malley’s office door came short and hard. Cheryl Wheeler, the computer forensics expert from Quantico was also well known for her deliberate approach.

'Doors open, Cheryl.' He offered even though the door was already in motion.

'Have a minute, Jack?'

'Sure, take a seat.'

Cheryl sat down across from him. 'I've been following up on the online activity of Alexei Orlov and found a person of interest who was also present in the chat room along with Patricia Ward, the day she discovered Orlov. This individual exited the chat room immediately after Orlov, but I didn't initially register this as noteworthy.' Cheryl adjusted herself in the seat. 'But I revaluated based on more research and I can give you the abbreviated version of what has transpired behind the scenes.'

'I'm listening.' Jack took off his reading glasses and sat back in the chair.

'Orlov changed locations repeatedly over the course of any given day, and by doing so created a new IP address from each location. He restricted the locations to those with public access to the internet, so conceivably we couldn't follow the digital trail back to his doorstep.' Cheryl stopped talking to determine if Jack was still with her.

'Don't stop now.' O'Malley sat back up again.

'We all create certain patterns in the basic things we do every day, and with time, these become habitual and subconscious actions. For instance, the way you shave your face or run a comb through your hair using the same motions each time. This process also occurs with people who spend a lot of time online. A subconscious methodology is established and guides the way the internet is navigated. Habitual and repetitive patterns emerge based on the way someone moves about from the moment they sign on. This is how we found Orlov in the first place. He visited enough locations with active surveillance cameras to allow us to pick him out of the crowd through a process of elimination.

'And why is this important?'

'Well, I went back over the research and this time focused on the IP address of the individual who checked out of the chat room behind Orlov, and what I found was a pattern that mirrored Orlov's exactly.'

'Are you saying this individual was in the same location as the hacker?'

'No. The person mimicking the hacker's movements online could physically have been anywhere. He or she obviously studied Orlov's online patterns as we did. Orlov was so predictable, it became possible to anticipate the order of his online movements, and to actually be waiting in a chat room for him to arrive. I believe it's what got him killed.'

'How so.'

'Orlov went from being an asset to a dangerous liability the moment he posted his comments online concerning the FBI. I believe he was being shadowed for just such an eventuality, but of course he was too sharp not to have realized the consequences of his actions, which adds more weight to the theory of Orlov being a desperate man and in over his head.'

‘Do you know who shadowed Orlov?’

‘Not yet. The voyeur, so to speak is well acquainted with the forensics involved and far more camera shy than Orlov. We’ve narrowed down the physical locations that were used to go online over a period of three months and came up with only a handful of useful images. We believe the suspect is somewhere in the mix and I need to work directly with Kris on this one. But I’m not sure if she’s up to the task and wanted to run it past you first.’

‘What are we talking for a workload?’

‘We have a substantial amount of footage from the street and public transportation along with the physical locations for both Orlov and whoever was stalking him.’

‘I don’t see a problem with bringing her into the loop but pace the flow of information or she’ll push too hard, and we need her as healthy as possible.’

When he called Kris, she was sitting with her back against a stonewall, out of the wind and bursts of hail coming off the sea. Earlier she had taken the lane leading away from the Church of Our Lady and St John, about a half mile from the cottage. This was the same church Anne and Tom Shepard were married, an event Kris found difficult to visualize after she entered the church and climbed the stairs to the choir loft and sat looking down over the empty seats to the altar where they took their vows and decided to never go back again.

The lane wound through a maze of interconnected, small plots of land with borders marked by stonewalls that eventually came to an abrupt halt at the edge of the sea. The stark and desolate beauty of the landscape was matched only by the purity of the silence that lay within the walls of stone. In another time the fields and lanes would have carried the sounds of children running with dogs at their heels, and the men and women of the island going about the business of sustaining life within a landscape as harsh and unforgiving as it was beautiful. In many ways those struggles, and hardships endure within the relentless winds and raging seas that define and set the islanders apart from their countrymen, if not the rest of humanity, and in this lay their strength.

A slate grey sky began at sea level, arced wildly upwards and folded into itself over and over like the smoke of a high plains campfire. Kris watched the Cliffs of Moher appear to rise and fall from across a wild expanse of open sea, anchored in place by O'Brien's Tower, a pinnacle of calm above the thunderous rage of the storm driven swells crashing against the cliffs below.

A stone's throw from her cliffside niche, the fierce winds sheared the tops off towering breakers that bore down on the island, and rose and slammed headlong into the fractured coastline in a sudden burst of cold, white sea foam, the strands hurling through the air, and still there was peace to be found amidst the chaos, and Kris pulled her legs in and pressed her back tight against the stonewall and nothing lay between her, the sea and the fury she embraced.

The ground shuddered with each new wave and Kris became absorbed by the rhythms of the sea, the wind and the solitude and remained tucked against the wall for more than an hour, as the sea rampaged and moved steadily closer on the rising tide. It was impossible to hear the quad barreling seaward down the lane, and when it came to a halt a few yards away, she assumed it was a summons for another session of scanning images from Boston, but the intrusion was out of character for the crew, and they rarely disturbed her on a walkabout or in the studio and her pulse started to race when told that Jack needed to speak with her immediately, as the agent handed off a cell phone.

'What's going on, Jack?'

'A few things have come up. The first you should be aware of and the second needs your personal attention.' There was a long silence. 'You still there?'

'The gale is raising hell over here. I can hardly hear you over the wind.'

'Alright, I'll make it short. An undercover agent from the Brighton Beach operation has come forward. Erik Petrov spoke to him about our inquiries before he disappeared and mentioned that the Taliban and Russian's had formed a special alliance within the drug trade after the runner eliminated their sleeper cells. As an act of good faith, the Russians offered to kill John Davis along with you and me. The runner is currently in the process of fulfilling a standing contract funded by the Odessa Mafia.'

'Cute.'

'Yeah.' O'Malley continued. 'Listen, the tech crew is sending you a series of images from cyber cafes and coffee shops. We have another person of interest and need you to sort out whoever appears most often or takes unusual measures to conceal their identity.'

Kris climbed on the back of the quad and returned to cottage. She felt the need for a shower to clear her head before getting into the images the tech crew was downloading. The shower room was in the oldest section of the cottage and although enlarged and updated, the act of taking a shower remained a cold, bracing experience, and she wouldn't have it any other way. The oversized upper window opened inwards and hooked to eye bolts in the ceiling. Kris stood with the hot, steaming water running over her head and down her back while the cold air blew in through the open window, and she could look out across the nearly deserted landscape towards Inis Oirr, and beyond to the tiny enclave of Doolin nestled into the rugged coastline of Co. Clare.

A ray of sunlight broke through the cloud cover and lay atop the angry sea in a shimmering patch of florescent green, which began to float casually along the surface, as though all was calm and as it should be. The tiny, steel grey island of Inis Oirr appeared much closer than it was and reminded her of the work awaiting her return. She had started carving a large block of sea tumbled limestone for the Art Centre before O'Malley hustled her away.

The stone remained lashed to a pillar outside the Art Centre at the top of the island with just the hint of a man's face emerging through the smooth, sun bleached surface of the stone. Kris knew when she returned to the work, the image she previously held in her mind would be gone and replaced by another. Her creativity had always demanded the same degree of continuity, as everything else in her life, and at the moment, not hers to control. She turned off the shower.

A baseball cap, hooded sweatshirt or at times a knit hat with sunglasses. The guy was no master of disguise but performed well enough to escape the scrutiny of the Boston crew. Within twenty minutes Kris had him sorted, and then got lucky with an exceptionally clear frontal image when he checked himself out in the window of Starbuck's, a block from the public library, where his time was spent in an alcove beyond the reach of the surveillance cameras. Kris tagged the guy and forwarded the image to Jack and the response was immediate.

'Pack a bag.'

Eighteen

Boston

Kris found it harder to leave Inis Meain, each time she was forced to do so, and realized how much the island had become a central part of her life, a place where she could exist on her own terms, a sanctuary that holds silent witness to an unfettered way of being. Dan Walker had once described the ability to be at peace with oneself, as a gift, and to Kris the stark, windswept Aran Islands were the physical manifestation of that gift. A bold validation of the solitude she longed to embrace.

The long flight from Galway to Boston and the rapid changes in elevation rattled her equilibrium once again, and at four in the morning, Kris crawled into bed on Ridgeway Lane and passed out for eight hours. It would have been longer, if not for the irrepressible hunger that drove her to the kitchen in a state somewhere between sleep and not, only to be immediately confronted by another presence and felt suddenly naked.

'Jesus, Sarah!' Kris cinched the robe around her waist.

'Sorry Kris, Jack asked me to come over and let him know when you're up and about.'

'I'm nether, if you don't mind.'

'Would you like me to leave?'

‘Of course.’ Kris started looking through the cabinet where the coffee had been the last time she was there and even the cups were missing. ‘But he’ll just send someone else.’

‘I believe so.’

‘Well then help me find the coffee.’

An hour later Kris was showered, and O’Malley was sitting in the living room in the usual spot next to the fireplace and had drawn the curtains against the harsh effects of mixing sunlight and vertigo. Sarah was working on a laptop at a desk in the corner of the living room, organizing a collection of images the crew gathered the previous day and needed to be cleared by Kris.

‘What is the source of the images?’ Kris walked into the room and over to where Sarah was working.

‘They came out of Quantico archives along with some of the older intelligence gathered by the New York Bureau.’ Jack answered. ‘The files are mainly of Russian Military personnel with a scattering of images taken of the Odessa Mafia. With any luck the suspect you identified following the hacker is somewhere to be found in these files.’

‘Sounds like we’re working from here.’ Kris looked back to O’Malley.

‘For the time being. It’ll be easier all around and less of a security risk than traveling back and forth to headquarters.’

‘Where does the CIA stand on all this?’ Kris continued.

'Good question, and I intend to get answers this afternoon when I meet with the field supervisor who was running the undercover operation when Erik Petrov washed up at Sheepshead Bay.'

'Any chance we'll get more cooperation this time around.'

'Perhaps. Even though I didn't notice any tears being shed over Petrov, I would find it hard to believe they don't intend to bring the house down on the comrades from Odessa.' Jack stood and put on his coat and started for the door. 'Hopefully, we get to our man before that happens, and I'll leave you to it.'

After Jack departed, Kris pulled up a chair next to Sarah. 'I think we should start with the current Russian Military personnel and work back as far as we can before getting into the Odessa group. How does that work for you?'

'Fine. I just need a few minutes.' Sarah inserted a flash drive and began scanning through the files.

'O'Sullivan. That would be County Kerry?'

Sarah looked pleased to be asked. 'Yes, my grandfather was from Killah West.'

'Have you been there yourself?

'Not recently. I have some family still living there, an uncle on my father's side and a few cousins. When I was young, I spent summer vacations at their sheep farm on the edge of Killah West.'

'When was the last time you visited?'

'Two years ago.'

'Was it as you remembered?'

'The buildings were more colourful than I recalled, and the atmosphere had transformed from a sleepy market town into an upscale tourist destination on the Ring of Kerry.'

'Big change. Did it still feel good to be there?'

'It really did in many ways, and I know the change has been good for the village, but I couldn't help but miss the way things were before.'

'Have you ever thought about moving there?'

'I've been tempted at times.'

'Too quiet for you?'

'Not really.'

'Work?'

'No, finding work wouldn't be an issue, but the culture would be.'

'Not what I was expecting to hear.'

'I've never said it out loud before, and I'm sure it sounds odd.'

'Not really. But I'm curious about what part of the culture you don't find so appealing?'

'The part where I become totally absorbed by it.'

'You consider that a bad thing?'

‘Not if you’re ready for it, which I’m not and might never be.’

‘That I can understand.’

‘Really. You seem to have adapted so well to Galway?’

‘I suppose, but not in the way you’re thinking.’

‘How then?’

‘Well, for one thing life on the Aran Islands has a rhythm of its own, which has more to do with survival than culture and you either adapt or not. But you certainly don’t get to choose.’

‘Sounds harsh.’

‘It can be, if you view that way.’

‘And you don’t?’

‘No.’

‘The islands are in the Gaeltacht, aren’t they?’

‘Yeah.’

‘And you speak Irish?’

‘No, I don’t.’ Kris hesitated. ‘Nor do I interact with the Irish to any real extent, and even then, it’s usually related to the essentials of getting by on the island.’

‘Sounds lonely.’

‘I’m sure it does.’

‘And you don’t mind being alone?’

‘I don’t.’

‘Can you teach me how to do that?’

‘Hardly. But you’re welcome to join me sometime if you’d like. I believe you might find being surrounded by the sea has a way of filling a lot of voids. Even ones you didn’t know existed.’

‘You wouldn’t be alone then.’

‘I think I could make an exception in your case.’

‘I’m flattered.’

‘You should be.’ Kris smiled. ‘How are we doing with the images?’

‘We’re ready.’

Kris liked this tall, dark haired woman with the striking green eyes, soft voice and easy manner, which were attributes she hadn’t noticed before. Her past interactions with Sarah were minimal, although Sam thought highly of her, and the woman was obviously a brilliant technician.

Their search became a tedious image by image progression through known Russian Military personnel going back as far as the cold war. The chronology of the files was hopelessly scattered, and the paranoia that existed on both sides of the Iron Curtain created reams of images gathered in haste, using all manner of equipment to less than desired results. The degraded images added an extra layer to the already daunting task. Sarah somehow made the process feel easier and brought a sense of order to the chaos, or at least this was how Kris perceived their time spent working side by side.

There was an element of angst in knowing that the portfolio from the Russian Mafia surveillance still awaited their attention. A rough estimate placed over six thousand groups worldwide as having links to Russian organized crime, and the Odessa branch of Brighton Beach had achieved an especially ruthless reputation as drug traffickers, extortionists and enforcers before entering the military arms trade.

The operation would have been much simpler if the voyeur had simply maintained his routine. The crew did manage to triangulate his movements with a fair amount of precision before he broke off and went dark. Another day or two and it would have been possible to rip him off the seat of whatever coffee shop, library or hotel bar stool he chose on that day.

Sarah and Kris worked five hours straight before Kris called for a break. One of the agents from the security detail chased down a pair of tuna sandwiches from Subway, and a huge bag of Cape Cod chips. Afterwards, they swapped seats, which made it easier for Kris to scan through the files at her own pace and much faster than Sarah thought possible.

At six thirty that evening, Jack showed up with two large pizzas and three bottles of wine that he later decided were of dubious vintage. Kris never knew what he was talking about when it came to the subject of wine, but Sarah held up her end of the conversation much to his delight. Kris listened to the back and forth and enjoyed the reprieve from participating.

Jack spent the weekend on the couch and Sarah slept in the second master bedroom. The vertigo eased ever so slightly and allowed Kris a glimmer of hope. The information stream out of Quantico slowed to a trickle, and they turned their attention to the cache of surveillance images that came from Jack's meeting with the CIA supervisor. The bulk of which focused on the Odessa roster, and included the rare capture of members with their families in what appeared to be a mafia style clambake, complete with kegs of beer, cases of vodka and a pair of orthodox priests thrown in for good measure.

The weekend disappeared under the cascade of images, with the only relief being the Sunday evening delivery of an enormous order of Chinese food by the security crew. The smell of food awakened long suppressed hungers and they regrouped at the island in the kitchen. Sarah brought along the laptop, so as not to break the momentum, while Kris took a much needed break to wash her hands and splash cold water on her face. When she returned Sarah had an image open, which appeared to be a family photo from the mafia clambake. The image stopped her cold. 'There he is.'

Her words hung in the air and Sarah sat starring at the image, while Jack jumped up and moved around the island. 'The young guy, two from the right is the voyeur.' Kris moved in closer to the laptop. 'Jack.'

'Yeah.'

'See the little girl peeking out between the two older girls on the left.'

‘I do.’

‘She’s the runner.’ Kris felt her heart skip a beat, as she spoke the words.

It was O’Malley’s turn to stare at the screen and finally he broke the stunned silence. ‘Nice work. Let’s get the image out to the crew.’

‘I need a shower.’ Kris started walking away.

‘I’m out of here.’ Jack stood and started for his coat. ‘Your ride will be at the curb at nine tomorrow morning and your welcome to stay another night, Sarah, if it works for both of you.’

Sarah looked to Kris who had stopped in the hallway leading to the bedrooms. ‘It’s fine with me, Sarah.’ Then she turned and continued toward the bedroom. ‘Just make sure O’Malley finds his way out.’

‘No worries.’

‘Don’t encourage her, Sarah.’

‘Who says I’m doing it for her.’

‘That’s it. I’m gone.’ Jack put on his tweed overcoat and scruffy brown leather cap. ‘Get some rest we have a long day tomorrow.’ He went towards the door looking like a well-dressed longshoreman going out for a pint. ‘You did well here today, Sarah.’ A moment later there were three knocks on the front door and O’Malley was gone.

At nine fifteen the next morning the entire crew began assembling in the conference room. Kris and Sarah were the last to make an appearance, and Kris hadn't looked so well since before the near miss in New Hampshire.

He opened the meeting. 'This moment has been a long time coming, and I thank everyone involved for the time and effort it took to get us to this point. That said, the first order of business when you leave this meeting is to make your apologies wherever necessary, because you're with me until this thing is finished. If this is a problem for anyone now is the time to speak up.'

Jack paused for a response, which was met with silence. Having never worked with nearly half the people in the room begged the question and he was pleased with the uniform response. 'I also want the entire crew to spend an hour on the firing range before the end of the day.'

O'Malley turned the meeting over to Anthony Russo who stood next to the image of the Mafia clam bake displayed on the big screen. 'I had a conversation this morning with our CIA contact at Langley who was able to put names to this entire gathering.' Russo pointed to a large man standing at the center of the group. 'This is Petr Volkov. As in General Petr Volkov of the Russian Federation. A man we believe to be a central figure in the Russian arms trafficking following the collapse of the Soviet Union in 1991. What we're discussing here is the wholesale sacking of Russian military stockpiles up to and including high grade nuclear materials.

Russo turned to face the crew. 'Prior to the disintegration of the Soviet Union, the mafia was virtually non-existent within the military. The changes that followed were swift and extensive. General Petr Volkov is now the single most influential member of the Russian mafia in Brighton

Beach, a Pakhan or boss, if you will, and a ruthless son of a bitch who happens to have diplomatic immunity. Keep in mind he's not our target.'

'This sweet looking child right here is our primary objective.' Russo held the red dot of the laser between the eyes of the little girl crowded in between two older girls. Her name is Anna Volkov, the only child of Petr and his former mistress who became wife number four. Her predecessor having been relegated to raising the remainder of Petr's brood in Brighton Beach. Anna and her mother returned to Russia with Petr, and she spent most of her early life there with only sporadic visits to Brighton Beach for special occasions, such as the one on the screen.'

'How much do we know about her?' Kris posed the first question.

'We know she was born in Brighton Beach, which makes her an American citizen.'

'And the half-brother she's been working with?'

'The half-brother is Anton Volkov who is Petr's only son and seven years older than Anna. He was born in Brooklyn and also spent a portion of his childhood in Russia. He returned to America to attend private schools in New York City and eventually earned a PhD in computer science from New York University.' Russo looked around the room for more questions, then continued.
'According to my source at Langley, the brother has been a fixture in two separate investigations concerning the cyber activities of the Russian mafia and their links to the Russian Government. There is little doubt concerning his role in raising the online presence of the Odessa Mafia to unprecedented

levels. Anton Volkov is a brilliant and well positioned member of the Odessa Mafia and most emphatically his father's son, which also extends to the ruthless part of the equation.'

'His sister, Anna.' Russo took a drink of water, 'is quite obviously, in the enforcement end of the business. At this moment we have absolutely nothing on her. Nor does anyone else. We have no idea concerning the level of formal education she received or where she acquired the obvious military training. The leading theory is that she was educated right here in America under another name and far removed from Brighton Beach.'

'And the military training.' Sarah asked.

'The military aspect is an opportunity that needs to be explored, and I will be assigning personnel to look at domestic paramilitary groups along with international organizations known to work with the Russian military.'

'Where does this leave us with the brother? Sarah followed up.

'This leaves us in a better place. We know where he lives, shops and spends his time online. We're going to collaborate with a team led by Marc Talbot, a CIA tech specialist from Langley.'

'Who's in charge?' Kris pointed the question towards O'Malley.

'For all things concerning the brother, Marc Talbot, will have the final word, and his team will handle the digital surveillance. Both you and Sarah will be joining them to protect our interests. Anna Volkov is ours and Talbot knows enough to stay out of the way.' Jack closed his folder. 'We believe Anton Volkov is going to lead us directly to his sister and in the process, implicate himself in the death of Sam Bordeaux, which will give Talbot's team the opportunity to leverage him against the Odessa Mafia. They need Anton taken alive and could care less about his sister and this is fine with me.'

O'Malley looked around the room. 'Anyone else?' There was no response and he continued. 'Kris, I want you and Sarah in Brooklyn tomorrow morning to meet Marc Talbot and the Langley team. I'll be coordinating our end of the operation from the New York office and the rest of the crew will be working from a safe house on the outskirts of Brighton Beach.' Jack picked up his folder. 'I also want everything coming out Langley verified to the extent possible. Nothing gets a pass on face value. Let's get to work.'

The next morning, Kris and Sarah left Ridgeway Lane in the dark. A small caravan of Suburban's transported the entire crew except for O'Malley, who flew out the previous evening. Three hours after pulling away from the townhouse, the Suburban carrying Kris and Sarah broke away from the caravan and was followed by the security detail assigned to Kris. Twenty minutes later both Suburban's were parked under the Manhattan Bridge.

A few minutes after they shut the headlights off, a panel van moved quickly in their direction, and came to a halt just shy of a very grave mistake. The passenger door of the van opened, and a man dressed like a construction worker in a faded, orange jump suit got out and walked towards the Suburban's. Two of Kris's security crew exited on the opposite side of the vehicle from the man and walked clear with their weapons levelled in his direction, which drew an immediate response.

'Whoa! The guy threw his arms in the air. 'Take it easy gentleman. We're here for Kris Shepard and Sarah O'Sullivan.'

The passenger window of the lead Suburban came down. 'Check the van.' The head of Kris's security detail held little patience for drama, and after a few intense moments, the van along with the three occupants in faded orange jump suits were cleared and the back door of the Suburban opened. 'Good to go, Kris. You know how to reach us.'

The van pulled away and the two Suburban's followed for a few blocks then broke off and headed back across the bridge for Brighton Beach. After Kris and Sarah were settled, the Langley team leader introduced himself as Bart Kennedy, and it was apparent her security team had inflicted some damage upon his ego.

'Your guys are intense.' Kris and Sarah let the comment hang in the air, and the remainder of the trip through Lower Manhattan and to Brooklyn passed in silence.

They moved swiftly through the predawn, and after a rapid series of turns they drove alongside a tall, chain link fence topped with barbwire. A wide metal gate began to open as they approached, and minutes later they drove into a dimly lit area dominated by a loading dock spanning the entire width of a recessed courtyard. Four similar panel vans were backed up to the loading dock. A long, pale grey sign bearing the name, 'Shannon Construction Inc.,' was above the dock. The van backed in under the sign while the gates closed behind them. When Kris and Sarah emerged from the van they were met by a tall, slim agent who appeared to be in his mid-thirties and extended his hand. 'I'm Marc Talbot.'

Kris shook his hand and introduced Sarah as they moved off the loading dock and into the CIA control room.

'Who's your lead on the tech crew?' Kris inquired.

'Susan Bryant from the Silicon Valley headquarters is leading the tech operation at the moment.

'Perhaps you wouldn't mind introducing Sarah to her, so she can orientate herself with the program while you bring me up to speed with the surveillance operation.'

'I can introduce both of you.'

'That won't be necessary at this time.'

Kris waited while Talbot performed a hasty introduction of Sarah to Bryant and her team. A few minutes later he returned, and Kris followed him down a corridor with a series of empty rooms on both sides. The walls of the corridor were glass from waist height to the ceiling and the oversized rooms reflected their age. One room contained a handful of cots with sleeping bags and makeshift nightstands at their side.

Talbot's office was at the end of the corridor. A large, well lit room with two battered oak desks of nineteen forties vintage facing each other in the center of the room. A desktop computer was on one and a laptop the other. Rows of security monitors were lined up side by side above the only entrance to the room. The monitors provided live images of the front gate and other possible entryways into the building. Kris's eyes were drawn to two monitors focused on the tech crew and she watched a woman assumed to be Susan Bryant standing with Sarah behind a line of technicians. 'Everyone bears watching.' Talbot had registered her interest.

'Whatever works for you. Right now, I'm interested in how much information you've gathered about Anton Volkov, and how long you've known about the runner.'

'You sound like you're wearing a wire.'

'And you sound defensive.'

'Should I be?'

'Only if your holding back information.'

'To be perfectly honest we didn't make the connection between the runner, and her brother until O'Malley approached me with a request to search our archives of the Brighton Beach Mafia. The brother jumped out at us because we were working him for over six months in connection with the mafia. Anton Volkov has been tying our technical team in knots whenever they attempt to trace his movements across the web.'

'Do you have enough to bring him in?'

'No, and it wouldn't be in our best interest. We know the Odessa group is dealing weapons, heroin and it appears they also have a rising interest in cybercrime. Anton Volkov doesn't work in a vacuum, and common sense dictates an entire network is out there somewhere with possible access to nuclear material, a thought we should all be losing sleep over.'

'Of course. But you do realize that Anna Volkov killed my former partner, Sam Bordeaux.' Kris paused for a few seconds 'She also killed an FBI research associate in Paris by the name of John Davis, and recently made another attempt on Jack O'Malley and me in New Hampshire.'

'I heard about Sam Bordeaux. But there was no chance I would have connected Anton to the Bordeaux shooting. Actually, for quite a while I wondered if he really belonged in this scenario or maybe it was just a matter of being in the right place at the wrong time.'

'What changed your mind?'

'This.' Talbot pulled up an image on the laptop and turned it towards Kris. The setting was in a restaurant and the runner was sitting in a booth across from her brother. She was reaching out touching his hand and it was the best profile of Anna Volkov that Kris had seen so far.

'Where was this taken?'

'The Skovorodka Restaurant in Brighton Beach not far from the train station.' Talbot answered. 'The place isn't as important as when it was taken.'

'And that was?'

'A half hour after Alexi Orlov was killed, and that point we began to question whether the meeting was a coincidence, or that Anton was involved on some level with your suspect. Had we been aware of

Orlov's existence, we could have done more to protect our mutual interests.'

Kris was absorbing the image of the Volkov siblings as Talbot spoke. 'As it stands we want the brother and you need to get to the sister. Strictly speaking, I don't care what transpires between the FBI and the sister, but we have every intention of taking Anton alive, and he will give up what he knows about the acquisition and sales of nuclear material by the Odessa Mafia, and his father in particular.'

'We have no problem with that, Marc. But I would suggest you send the image from the restaurant over to O'Malley with your apologies. That is, if you actually want to proceed in good faith.'

'I'll deliver it personally when we meet later today.'

'Not something I would recommend.'

Talbot reconsidered. 'Maybe you have a point, I'll get it off shortly.'

'I don't mind waiting.' She encouraged him. 'Everyone bears watching at some point.' Kris offered with no expression. A few minutes after Talbot sent the image, she received a text message from O'Malley. 'I want you at the meeting with Talbot this afternoon. Leave Sarah in place to cover our backs.'

Talbot was next to receive a text from O'Malley and turned to Kris. 'I'm going to open my image file from the surveillance of Anton Volkov from day one of my operation. I'll let you spend as much time with the file as you need.' He handed Kris a flash drive. 'But listen carefully. No images leave the file without my authorization. If you see something you need I'm willing to discuss the issue, but I wouldn't recommend trying to cut one from the pack. Are we clear on that point?'

'Not a problem. I'm quite aware that every key stroke I make will be monitored, and that someone is watching us as we speak.' Kris responded without looking up. 'Now, if you don't mind, I have work to do.' She inserted the flash drive and began the process of mentally lifting every face in the file, and when she walked out the door an hour later they left with her.

Kris and Talbot were accompanied to the meeting with O'Malley by Susan Bryant, whom he later suspected was running the CIA operation. The meeting took place at a former tire repair facility for tractor trailers, which O'Malley had chosen to set up as a control center. The deserted factory was three blocks within the Brighton Beach border at the heart of a rundown commercial zone.

Talbot and Bryant were escorted to a makeshift conference room while Kris met privately with O'Malley. Later, Jack opened the meeting without so much as a handshake. 'One thing needs to be said before we go any further.' He directed his words towards Talbot. 'If at any time, I sense you're moving on Anton Volkov without us involved, I will bring him down by any means possible.' Jack looked across the table and waited for a response, which was slow in coming.

'Understood.' Talbot finally spoke through a clenched jaw while Bryant remained mute. 'I'll pass your concerns along to our officer in charge.'

'Don't confuse the reality of the situation as some form of proposal. I won't be engaging in any further discussion on the matter and secondly, your superior officer has been sitting at your left shoulder since this discussion began.' Jack turned his attention to the assistant. 'Are we in agreement, Ms. Bryant?'

'Agreement may be too strong of a word, Mr. O'Malley, but we'll go with that for now.' She finally had something to say. 'Although, if you attempt to intimidate my team or its leadership again, I'll have your operation shut down in a heartbeat.'

'Alright then.' O'Malley sat down. 'Let's get down to what we're here for.'

Kris could tell Bryant had more on her mind that went unsaid, and this couldn't be a good thing. Two hours later, they were all on the way back to Brighton Beach in the back of a panel van.

The two weeks which followed, were long and tedious for both crews. Anton Volkov remained sequestered in his apartment the entire time and only showed up online to read the New York Times and the son of bitch even found his way past the subscription service.

Sarah on the other hand was enthralled by the cyber capacity of the CIA and enjoyed the access her new security clearance allowed. The nuances of the CIA cyber surveillance operation were subtle and finely layered and appealed to her endless fascination for detail, and Jack loved that about her.

In the middle of the third week of the surveillance operation, the moment both factions so patiently

awaited arrived along with a now familiar challenge
to keep up with what was happening in real time.

Nineteen

Brooklyn

When Anton Volkov decided to make a move, he didn't telegraph his actions or provide a window of opportunity for either crew to react, and it was Sarah who first noticed that the CCTV coverage at the Atlantic Chip House on 110 Atlantic Avenue in Brooklyn went down at exactly one o'clock on Wednesday, December 23, 2014. The restaurant was the farthest point Anton was known to wander away from the Brighton Beach neighborhood and considered a long shot as a possible location to meet with his sister.

Sarah set the wheels in motion with a call to O'Malley, who along with Kris and Marc Talbot were sequestered in a surveillance van a block from the Tatiana Restaurant in Brighton Beach. The CIA team was scattered along the boardwalk while the remainder of O'Malley's crew were stationed in the former tire factory six blocks away.

The call from Sarah immediately sent both crews scrabbling to get in position on Atlantic Avenue ahead of Anton's anticipated arrival, and those hopes were immediately jeopardised when he flagged down a taxi a block from his apartment. The insertion of an experienced Brooklyn cab driver into the mix wasn't going to help matters.

Both crews were broken down into teams with designated positions for the targeted locations. Once on site, they would await further instructions from O'Malley who was calling the shots now that the operation was a live event, and he wouldn't have been disappointed, if the brother was only out for fish and chips. The abrupt outing by Anton was the sort of action O'Malley had come to associate with the runner, and his gut reaction made the distance feel that much further.

Guy Wilson, the FBI sniper was the first to log in from the site and had moved into position on the third level of the parking garage across from the Atlantic Chip House. As feared, the cab driver made the trip from Brighton Beach to Atlantic Avenue in record time, and both crews had barely stopped rolling when the cab pulled up to the curb short of the Chip House. Anton paid the driver and stepped out of the cab and didn't bother to look around as he started walking towards the restaurant about thirty yards away. Once he made it inside, the crews would wait for the runner to show, and if not, they would track Anton back to Brighton Beach for yet another round of surveillance.

Anton was about halfway to the front door of the chip house when a motorcycle with two helmeted riders coasted to the curb about ten feet behind him, and what followed appeared to finely choregraphed, as the passenger dismounted from the motorcycle in one motion and fell in step behind Anton. The motorcycle continued to drift silently past Anton as the front of his head exploded, the shooter put two more rounds in his back while he lay face down and motionless on the sidewalk. In a matter of seconds, the shooter was once again on the back of the motorcycle.

The initial reaction was a stunned silence that ceased when the motorcycle burst away from the curb in the direction of the surveillance team. Talbot was first out of the van and the driver reacted instinctively to his presence and spun the motorcycle in the opposite direction while the shooter opened fire towards the van.

At precisely the same moment, Guy Wilson, the FBI sniper on the third level of the parking garage received a bullet to the back of his head. Then in rapid succession, the motorcycle spilled over in the middle of Atlantic Avenue with the driver dead before the motorcycle hit the ground and the shooter struggling to get out from beneath it. He had barely managed to get his leg free when the first bullet slammed him back against the pavement, the second one made sure he stayed there.

O'Malley and Kris had been barely out of the van when the motorcycle went down in the street, and neither they nor Talbot had fired a shot. Jack stood, looking up towards his sniper's position, while Kris moved forward with Talbot, toward the lifeless assassins, and he could see the barrel of the sniper's rifle protruding beyond the deck of the parking garage. The rifle pointed down in the direction of Kris and Talbot appeared to be following their movement, and the realization that the barrel was too short was both spontaneous and too late. And before Jack could utter a sound, the barrel jerked silently, and Talbot was hurled into Kris. The rifle barrel jerked a second time, and Jack began to fire at the only target that was available and the rifle barrel disappeared from sight.

Kris struggled to free herself from beneath Talbot, whose weight and momentum had sent them both to the ground. The second bullet out of the sniper's rifle had passed through Talbot and tore into the pavement a fraction of an inch from her head. Talbot's crew never got a shot off, and by the time they broke cover, Jack was loading his second clip into the Glock and moving toward the parking garage. He pointed to where the sniper had been stationed and Talbot's crew responded to his lead and spread out as they crossed the street. Jack passed through the entrance a few moments ahead of his backup crew who crashed the gate and piled out of the second van.

There was no response from Guy Wilson on the third level, and fifteen excruciating minutes later, Jack and Kris stood over his body as Talbot's crew continued towards the top level of the garage, a vast open space with only a handful of cars, and a white panel van off to one corner.

'Stay away from the van.' Jack responded to the information, and his words were no sooner spoken into the headset when a massive explosion shook the building. They rushed to the upper deck, which was covered with smoldering debris. Talbot's crew was stunned by the blast but saved by the distance and small amount of cover provided by the parked cars.

'There's no chance she was in there?' Jack thought out loud while staring at the burning remnants of the white van and then walked to the edge of the garage and looked down onto the street to where Talbot lay in the middle of Atlantic Avenue covered by a tarp. The entire area was overrun with police and more sirens could be heard approaching in the distance. A NYPD helicopter was closing in and Jack needed to gain control of the situation and started back down to street level.

Kris remained on the upper deck trying to sort out exactly what transpired. She knew the runner had remained close enough to detonate the bomb without being seen, but there was no place to hide on the upper deck and no way she was on a suicide mission. A few minutes later she heard one of the crew tell O'Malley he was needed at the utility room on ground level, at the rear of the garage.

'Did you copy that, Kris?'

'I'm on my way.' By the time she made it down, Jack was already standing near the doorway of the utility room with a captain from the NYPD. The utility room was short and narrow and one of the guys from Talbot's crew was standing halfway out of an open hatchway in the corner of the room.

'You'll want to see this O'Malley.' The agent descended out of view. Jack and Kris went into the room and followed him down the metal ladder. At the bottom, a narrow walkway opened into a wide tunnel with an extremely high, arched roof. The tunnel extended well beyond the reach of their flashlights in both directions.

'What are we looking at here?' O'Malley asked.

'The Cobble Hill Tunnel.' The voice of the police captain came from behind. 'It's an abandoned tunnel of the Long Island Railroad and runs below Atlantic Avenue. The buildings along the route still use it to run their utility lines.'

'We need the bomb squad down here.' O'Malley started back towards the ladder. 'And the specs for this tunnel with the layout for the exits in both directions.' His orders directed at the police captain and then he turned to Kris. 'I believe the runner just killed the last guy keeping her invisible, and we need to find out how she made her way to the parking garage, and where she exits this tunnel.'

Kris was the first one up the ladder. The NYPD had shut down Atlantic Avenue in both directions and no one was allowed to enter or leave the parking garage. The few people who were swept up in the search were detained and questioned. Kris sat on the back of an ambulance and attempted to clean Marc Talbot's blood off her face, and out of her hair with the help of an EMT. Although, her jacket and pants were still blood stained when she joined Jack in the back of the surveillance van. He was speaking to Sarah O'Sullivan who had remained stationed at the CIA headquarters.

'The Cobble Hill Tunnel has a limited number of exits according to the schematic from the city planning office.' Sarah was explaining to Jack. 'Seven to be exact including the parking garage and we're in the process of gathering the CCTV logs for the other six.'

'Alright then. Make sure Kris is kept in the loop.' Jack said as he acknowledged her presence in the van. Outside, the street remained crowded with FBI, CIA and NYPD personnel. As Kris sat down next to Sarah, a knock came to the door of the van and she opened it to find Susan Bryant standing there and looking as though every drop of blood had been drained out of her. 'We need to speak O'Malley,' the words appeared to take all of her energy to mouth.

'Come in Susan.'

'Alone. I need to speak to you alone.'

'Not going to happen' Jack responded.

Bryant looked over to Kris as though she would intervene on her behalf. 'Don't look at me that way.' Kris responded to her unspoken request. 'You had nothing to say to us earlier.'

Bryant stood at the door of the van, not quite sure what direction to take, then stepped inside and sat down in Talbot's empty seat. 'Petr Volkov was killed at a restaurant in St. Petersburg about an hour ago.'

'And why should I be interested in whether Petr Volkov is alive or dead?' Jack responded.

'We have reason to believe the same organization behind the assassination of Petr is also responsible for what happened here today.'

O'Malley and Kris sat looking at each other, trying to make sense of what they just heard. Kris managed to get there first. 'Are you saying Anna Volkov is involved with a group in Russia who killed her father while she watched her brother get shot in his head out there on the street?'

'Quite possibly.' Bryant didn't hesitate.

Kris's entire body tensed. 'And how long have you held onto this information, Susan?'

'I wasn't sure of the connection until this happened today.'

'That's not what she asked.' Jack's voice was tight and low. 'We followed her brother into an ambush, by an organization you suspected was involved with our subject. People died here today, and you can't walk that back, Susan.'

His eyes bore into Bryant. 'Was Talbot aware of the threat from this other organization?' She held his gaze, and not a word passed through her lips. 'I didn't think so,' he continued. 'Trust me, Susan, you'll never have another opportunity to put my crew on the firing line. Now get out of my van.'

Bryant sat riveted to her seat with eyes locked on O'Malley, then without a word she stood up and left. 'Lock the door,' O'Malley ordered the tech guy and turned to Kris. 'Get a hold of Sarah and tell her to collect everything relating to the Volkov clan that she can lay her hands on before Bryant shuts down our access, and also that a car is on the way to pick her up.'

A half hour later, O'Malley and crew were back at the former tire repair factory. Sarah was fifteen minutes behind them and came bearing two flash drives, which contained everything to date the CIA managed to gather from their surveillance of the Odessa Mafia. Sarah joined Kris in front of a solid wall of monitors and they systematically began sorting through both public and private CCTV coverage in the vicinity of the Cobble Hill Tunnel exits.

In all matters related to technology, there was no limit to what O'Malley didn't care to know. Over the years, some viewed his mindset as either ignorance, arrogance or some combination of both. He neither acknowledged or denied the unspoken accusation, and simply went about his business leaving the technicians to do the same. But this time was different, and he sat down beside Kris and Sarah at the monitors, and in a way his presence kept things calm and focused.

'Why do you think she did it?' Sarah put the question out there.

'You mean watching her brother being killed?' Jack answered.

'Yeah.'

'The short answer comes down to the money, but it's obvious a grudge also existed within the family. That said, a drug cartel on the magnitude of the Russian Mafia, has unlimited funds at their disposal for someone bold enough to kill FBI and CIA agents. I don't imagine there's an upper limit to what they would offer someone with Anna Volkov's skills, and she could write her own ticket.'

Two hours later they had managed to eliminate three exits out of the Cobble Hill Tunnel east of the garage. All three came to the surface through manholes in intersections with good CCTV coverage and were eliminated by scrolling back to one hour before and after the shooting. Afterwards, Sarah started loading up the exits west of the parking garage. A group that would prove trickier in the way they came up within utility rooms of recently erected buildings along Atlantic Avenue, as was the case with the garage.

The search efforts required a three sixty scan of each area to include all pedestrian exits of the buildings that connected to the tunnel, as well as every vehicle that entered or left the adjoining parking garages. Having no idea of the direction Anna Volkov took after entering the tunnel they alternated the search, and slowly expanded away from the garage. Kris worked best with as few people involved as possible, but after a couple hours of working with Sarah, Will Jenkins and O'Malley, a rhythm of sorts emerged within the process and they began to move at a rapid pace through the volumes of material.

Sarah rooted out the cameras available in each location, and Jenkins isolated the footage to an hour either side of the shootings, with the results queued for Kris to clear. The further west they traveled along Atlantic Avenue, the more labor intensive the search became due to the increasing density of exits from the buildings, especially where the tunnel served as a conduit for utility services.

A disturbing development arose when the bomb squad searching the tunnel, relayed the news to O'Malley that the information obtained from the City Engineers office was out of date, and they found more exits than existed on the schematic. The good news was the presence of a cinder block wall spanning the entire width of the tunnel. The wall sealed off access beyond the second exit east of the garage, which Kris had already cleared.

'We have to assume the same thing is happening west of the parking garage, and that we're going to encounter more undocumented exits.' Jack pushed his chair away from the console. 'I want to change our focus to include only the camera's mounted at intersections running west along Atlantic Avenue and away from the garage. Then scan the adjoining streets for one block either side of the intersections.'

'Why narrow the focus?' Jenkins was sceptical

'At this point there could be any number of exits that never made it onto the schematic, and it's plausible that Anna Volkov's association with the Russian Mafia introduced her to the Cobble Hill Tunnel, which would be a perfect drop zone for the Taliban heroin coming out of Afghanistan.'

'Makes sense.' Sarah followed up. 'They could off load a drug shipment in the garage and transport it through the tunnel to a secure location, where it could be processed and sent out for distribution the same way it arrived.'

'So, you're saying in one move, the brother is eliminated and the heroin supply line that her father controlled for the Odessa Mafia is exposed, which sounds like a dangerous a proposition for Anna Volkov to take on by herself.' Kris joined the conversation.

'Only if it was unsanctioned.' Jack continued. 'Which brings us full circle, and we may have just witnessed a major coup within the Russian military.'

'How will this impact us?' Sarah asked.

'It could mean that Anna Volkov has more support than we thought, as well as access to the Russian intelligence network on some level.'

'She still had to leave that tunnel.' Kris added. 'No matter who she's working for.' The pace at which Kris could scan a crowd had rapidly accelerated as time went on and the pace was surprising even to Jack. He recalled when John Davis first presented him with the results of his research during their first meeting in Boston. At that time, Davis had devoted most of his time and research budget into designing a series of tests to single out the truly elite among the super recognizers and was only interested in those who belonged to the less than one percent of people with advanced facial recognition skills. His tests were solely designed to identify individuals who performed with flawless precision and speed. Kris was the best Davis had ever encountered before he was gunned down, and the exceptional results of her efforts only served to validate those early findings.

Sarah began a slow, virtual march down Atlantic Avenue, an intersection at a time scanning in both directions for one block down the crossover streets. Kris was at her side and focused on everyone who walked, drove or rode a bike across the monitor. Two hours later, and six blocks west of the garage, as they were working a crossover street, Kris put her hand on Sarah's arm. 'Stop!' She ordered. 'Give me a close up of the crowd leaving the theater.'

Sarah enhanced the image of a large group of people leaving a theater complex on Court Street. The images were captured from a camera mounted on the intersection of Court and State Streets, and only a block away from Atlantic Avenue.

'Right there.' Kris was pointing at a woman wearing a black sweat suit with a red stripe down the legs and sleeves of an oversized hooded sweatshirt. The hood was up, allowing only a partial image of the woman, which was enough for Kris to spot Anna Volkov before she entered a black BMW with windows to match.

The BMW pulled away from the theater and traveled down Atlantic Avenue with no obvious sense of urgency, and even stopped on a yellow light, then meandered away on the green. The reason for the nonchalance became apparent when the BMW turned off Ocean Parkway onto Brighton Beach Avenue and promptly disappeared.

'What just happened?' Jack looked to Sarah.

'We lost the CCTV.'

'All of it.'

'Yeah. Looks that way.' Sarah was searching for any available cameras. 'Nothing Jack. The entire section of Brighton Beach from Ocean Parkway to Coney Island Avenue is down.'

'Russian's.' Jenkins added with nothing more needed in way of an explanation.

Jack sat starring up at the empty monitors void of expression. Nobody spoke. A few moments later he took his flat cap off the desk in front of him and turned to Jenkins. 'Get NYPD over there to find the BMW.'

'Do you want to put out a bulletin to Homeland Security?' Sarah asked.

'Go ahead. But I don't expect Anna Volkov to be going anywhere soon.' Jack replied. 'When the BMW turned off Ocean Parkway it drove straight into Russian territory. The motherland itself couldn't be any safer, and she'll have no reason to leave Brighton Beach. At the moment in time, I'm more interested in tracking Susan Bryant's crew, and if they make any moves within Brighton Beach, I want to know about it.'

'Is there no way of overriding the hackers once they get control of the cameras?' Kris asked Jenkins.

'Not in a timely manner. It's much easier to shut down a series of cameras, than it is to regain control. We would need to dedicate a team, and still they could come right back at us. The Russian's are known to treat this type of cyber interference like a chess game, and they get off on the challenge.'

‘Can we prevent them from turning the cameras on again?’ Kris persisted.

‘Interesting question.’

‘What are you thinking, Kris?’ She had Jack’s attention.

‘Anna Volkov has an obvious need to be in control at all times, and if there’s any way possible to take that away and leave her sitting in the dark, then we might force her to make a move.’

‘Can you do it, Will?’ Jack asked.

‘We could build a firewall around the area that the Russians shut down and possibly take possession of the cameras the moment they allow them to boot up again.’

‘How long could you hold them off?’

‘Hard to predict. They would need to make a massive effort to regain possession and would in effect be knocking on our front door, which creates the risk of exposing their location within the firewalled area.’

‘Alright. Do whatever it takes, and if you need more help, let me know.’

‘We can handle it.’ Jenkins was looking to Sarah who was already in motion on her keyboard and nodded confirmation.

‘Any chance Bryant can force us out of here?’ Kris asked.

‘Depends on how much pressure she can bring to bear on Max. She’ll work the national security angle, which never fails to send the oversight committees running for political cover.’

‘How much time?’

‘A week. Two at the most.’

‘What do you think?’ Kris was looking at Jenkins again.

‘If they underestimate us, we stand a chance. But they’ll only make that mistake once.’

Twenty

Brighton Beach

NYPD located the BMW in front of the Anteka Pharmacy on Brighton Beach Avenue, a few blocks from where it turned off Ocean Parkway. It came as no surprise that the vehicle was stolen or not a single witness from the assortment of nearby businesses was able to recall anything concerning the occupants of the vehicle, although it had been abandoned in broad daylight. O'Malley ordered the vehicle impounded and quarantined until the FBI forensic crew could take possession.

The theater complex on Court Street in Brooklyn where Anna Volkov had emerged and entered the stolen BMW was built on the existing footprint of an office building destroyed by fire a decade earlier. In the basement of the complex, a passageway led into the Cobble Hill Tunnel, which forced the evacuation of three city blocks surrounding the theater while the bomb squad cleared both the complex and the passageway below.

It took Sarah and Jenkins nearly four hours to create a firewall around the cameras the Russian hackers had seized, and another three to work out the moves for taking back control when they released their grip on the CCTV network. O'Malley tried and failed to gather more help from a beleaguered Max Cooper who was locked in a bureaucratic power struggle with Susan Bryant, which they both knew he was destined to lose. The crew managed by working in tag teams around the clock, as the hours stretched into days.

Waiting for something to happen was the difficult part. Sarah and Kris turned their attentions to the passport captures coming out of LaGuardia and JFK Airports, along with CCTV footage from Grand Central Station with no expectations of finding Anna Volkov in the crowd. Jenkins in the meantime remained glued to the CCTV network for any signs of digital activity by the hackers.

Jenkins first instinct had been to make a run at asserting control over the cameras, but he resisted out of fear of revealing their surveillance. The tactic finally paid off on the afternoon of the third day when the Brighton Beach cameras flickered once and went instantly black again. Three minutes later, they came back online, and it took Jenkins all of eight seconds to capture and shut the cameras back down. It all happened so fast the rest of the crew were left staring up at the empty monitors.

'Now what?' Jack was the first to speak.

'We wait.' Sarah answered.

The words barely spoken when the monitors came alive again in short, pulsating bursts, that appeared to be random attempts to recapture individual cameras within the grid. This went on for two minutes and then nothing.

'Safe to say they know we're here.' Jenkins said to no one in particular.

An hour and a half later, a streak of images ran across the grid like a hand along the keys of a piano, and then everything went dark again. 'Son of a bitch!' Jenkins slid in closer with hands scrambling across the keyboard, and no one moved or spoke and all eyes were glued on the mesmerizing duel with whoever lay just beyond his fingertips, and when Jenkins hands suddenly froze above the keyboard nobody dared move a muscle until he flopped back into his chair, looked up at the ceiling and with a slow sideward glance gave Sarah a half smile.

'They'll be back.' She responded.

For the next twenty-four hours, the monitors remained dormant by way of the induced coma that Jenkins forced upon the network. The Russian hackers appeared to be making no further attempts to seize back control of the Brighton Beach cameras, and the crew settled into surveillance mode. Jack took the opportunity of a long overdue break by Sarah and Will Jenkins to check in with Kris. So much had transpired in the brief span of time since the ambush at the garage, and despite her acute reluctance to discuss her condition, the fact remained that without her presence on the crew, the entire effort would collapse.

'I'm fine, Jack. Really.'

'You seem to be moving around without any problem.'

'Yeah, the feeling of near normality is wonderful and odd at the same time.' Kris turned in her seat to face O'Malley. 'Where do we stand with the forensics?'

'The lab is still working on the DNA profiles of the two assassins, but even if they are successful in establishing their identities, the leads will likely come to a dead end at the border of Brighton Beach.'

'Has Quantico come up with any information about what transpired in Russia?'

'All we know is that Anna Volkov's father was on the losing end of a Mafia coup, and to some extent from within the Russian Military. Petr Volkov apparently fell out of favor with his comrades in arms, otherwise none of this would have been tolerated. From what they tell me, his replacement moved into the suite of offices he occupied at the Kremlin the day after he was killed, and according to DEA people on the ground in Afghanistan, it was business as usual for the American bound movement of heroin out of Russia.' He stopped talking and sat looking up at the blank monitors, as though they had something to offer and then continued. 'You know, even after all this time with the agency, I find the concept of murdering a brother at the same moment an associate kills your father, as nearly beyond comprehension, but then doesn't it becomes real enough when there's blood on the ground' They sat quietly for a few moments then Jack stood up. 'How about a coffee?'

'Sure.'

He walked over to the makeshift kitchen on the other side of the surveillance room. A few moments later, Sarah returned from break without Jenkins and took a seat at the console. Jack glanced towards the windows facing the loading dock where fifty years of accumulated grime allowed a vague outline of Jenkins pacing back and forth, fully engaged in a bout of chain smoking. Sarah was unusually quiet and restless, and when she eventually broke the silence, it was in a way Kris hadn't seen coming. 'I'm not going back to Boston when this is finished.'

‘Does Jack know?’

‘Not yet.’

How long have you been feeling this way?’

‘Since we left Boston, and I suppose in some ways much longer.’

‘What are your plans.’

‘I don’t have any.’

‘Will you remain in Boston?’

‘Perhaps. My mother has been wanting to return to Ireland for a visit since my father passed away, and I’m going along to keep her company, and hopefully sort things out afterwards.’

‘You’re aware that Jack won’t try to talk you out of it.’

‘I know, and it’s one of the things I love about him.’

They returned to silence, as Jack approached with a coffee in each hand, and wasn’t until he sat down that he realized Jenkins had stopped walking back and forth across the dock, and he always returned straight away when he finished his smoke. Jack swivelled his chair around to face the windows and gave him a few more minutes. ‘Have either of you seen Jenkins?’

‘He’s outside having a cigarette.’ Sarah offered.

‘Not anymore.’ Jack stood up and started towards the hallway with Kris following a few steps behind. Sarah remained at the console, and when they entered the empty hallway their sense of caution intensified. Jack drew his gun and looked over to Kris who was on his left and slightly behind with her Glock coming out of the holster. They moved slowly down the corridor, past the rooms on both sides of the hallway and as they approached the exit leading onto the dock, Kris waited while Jack put his back against the door that Jenkins had wedged open with a small block of wood. He forced the door open far enough to allow a view down the length of the dock, and still no Jenkins.

Jack stepped out of the hallway and stood alone on the loading dock. The shipping yard stretched away in a wide span of tarmac towards a series of ramshackle utility sheds that ran parallel to the tire factory, and were separated from the street by a tall, chain link fence topped by three strands of barbed wire. There was nothing moving and not a sound to be heard. On the far end of the dock, a massive overhead door provided access to the former shipping room, and alongside it a windowless emergency exit was missing the padlock Jenkins had placed there on the first day of surveillance.

Jack headed for the exit, staying close enough to the wall to feel the heat coming off the bricks, and from inside the surveillance room became a shadowy figure moving past the soot and grim covered windows. Anna Volkov took aim and carefully led her target, squeezed the trigger ever so slightly, and had Jack been a half step slower, she would have been as deadly as it appeared.

Jack went down in a hail of glass and stayed there with blood flowing from a cut above his right eye. The entire sequence seemed to unravel in slow motion from where Kris stood riveted in place, the glass scattering across the shipping yard, the deathly moment of silence with neither of them moving, and then Jack raising his hand to stop her forward motion, standing and using his sleeve to wipe the blood from his eye, as he started moving towards the shipping room, pointing Kris back in the direction of the hallway, and the sickening realization that Sarah was still inside.

Jack turned the handle and used his shoulder to open the door leading into the shipping room, keeping both hands on the Glock. The space was crowded with old tire building machines and assorted equipment lined up for a removal that had never occurred. Less than ten yards into the room he found Jenkins on the floor between two piles of wooden skids. He was shot twice in the back of the head. Jack wiped the blood from his eye once more and started towards the archway leading into the surveillance room, moving slowly past the discarded machinery, rows of metal lockers and wooden crates stacked one upon the other.

Kris had come off the dock and entered the corridor backlit from the open door and stayed close to the wall, her eyes struggling to adjust, a nauseating echo announcing each step through the absolute silence of the hallway. She pushed back against the dread of Sarah being alone and kept her focus riveted on the end of the hallway. Her legs felt heavy and each breath came quicker than the last and she closed her lips, forcing herself to slow down and when she finally reached the edge of the surveillance room, stood with her back against the wall, face pressed tight against the door jamb with the deafening sound of her heart ringing in her ears. Then in a move as unnerving as it was bold, she stepped away from the hallway into the open space expecting a vicious response, but in its place an eerie silence.

The abandoned factory of a half hour earlier was suddenly ominous, the derelict tire building machines, gutted electrical boxes and fragments of an overhead conveyor made the ceiling appear low, the space crowded and dangerous. Kris stood locked in the moment, the passage of time excruciating, and then she took three steps and waited, three more and waited longer, and again in the unnerving manner of one in search of prey.

The perception of time and place and motion were nearly lost to the fear that threatened to overwhelm her senses with each step, but still her hands remained steady, and it was through that thin veil of fear that Anna Volkov began to emerge. At first, a glimpse of a shoulder protruding from behind a steel pillar, and then a side profile with arms lowered in front of her. Kris kept moving until she had an unobstructed view of the tall figure in a black jump suit with Sarah at her feet, one hand entwined in her long, blond hair and the other holding a gun to the top of her head, and Kris felt the withering intensity of the steel grey eyes the moment they made contact with hers. The back of Sarah's neck and blouse were saturated in blood, and she appeared to be unconscious, and no way of knowing if she was dead or alive.

'I need you to let her go.' Kris moved a step closer, and there was no reaction from Anna Volkov. It was as though Kris wasn't even in the room, and it was brutally obvious from the dark, expressionless gaze that Anna Volkov held but one intention, and the cold, hard conviction to see it through.

'She's no threat to you.' Kris tried again.

‘I’ll decide who is a threat, Ms. Shepard.’ Her voice carried a surprisingly soft, melodic cadence and she shifted her weight and looked down at Sarah then back at Kris. ‘The time has arrived to place your weapon on the floor.’

Kris took a slow, easy breath in an attempt to control the rush of adrenaline coursing through her body, and remained still and silent, waiting for the slightest movement to telegraph the gun barrel moving away from Sarah’s head. ‘I won’t be asking again.’ Anna Volkov’s voice deeper, more direct and Kris felt her throat tighten, as she slowly began to release her grip on the Glock.

‘Neither will I.’ Jack’s voice pierced the void and Anna Volkov turned her entire focus in his direction, and if surprised to see him still standing, it didn’t show. The harsh, lingering silence that pursued was broken when Anna Volkov shifted her weight once again, and with eyes locked on Jack, adjusted the grip on Sarah’s hair and jerked her head violently upwards. Sarah gasped in pain, and what followed defied all sense of moral expectation, a moment when conscious thought ceased to exist, and all that remained was a tortuous attempt to rectify what the eyes observed, and the mind was willing to accept.

The bullet entered Sarah’s brain and fragmented through her body at precisely the same moment the sound of the gunshot echoed through the warehouse. Anna Volkov used the recoil to lift the gun in Jack’s direction. They both squeezed the trigger and neither missed. Jack went down on his back, hit high on the left side of the chest. Anna Volkov was nearly spun around but remained standing, regained her balance and stood facing Kris with arms limp at her side, the gun in one hand and fragments of blond hair in the other, the blank stare replaced by an aura of amusement.

The high-pitched scream of a diesel downshifting off the expressway gave voice to what was about to ensue in a dimly lit warehouse on the edge of Brighton Beach. From Anna Volkov's perspective, the bullets pierced her body in controlled and precise succession, and there was neither shock nor fear, as she was repelled backwards with each squeeze of the trigger, followed by the sound of an empty clip hitting the floor, the snap of another sliding into place and a sudden return to silence that defied the reality of all that came before, and lying on her back could hear footsteps moving behind her, the Shepard woman walking soft and slow, much as she would have herself under different circumstances. A warmth was spreading beneath her and soon became the only point of reference within the pulsating array of senseless images flooding her consciousness, stealing first her reason, and then her breath.

Epilogue

Jack O'Malley survived the bullet that smashed into his chest and continued out his back, the trajectory caused a lung to collapse, and the blood loss was immense. Although, it was the infection which followed that nearly accomplished what Anna Volkov failed to do. Kris remained at his bedside for three weeks and when he was released from the hospital they returned to Boston together.

Now, they haven't spoken in months, and only during the darkest moments does she miss his presence. O'Malley's official report of the events that transpired in the tire warehouse began and ended when he traded bullets with Anna Volkov. The exact point at which he lost consciousness remains ambiguous, the fertile grounds between truth and reality untrampled, and if questions lingered, he never gave them a voice beyond the moment the bullet slammed into his chest.

The body of Anna Volkov remained unclaimed and known family members in Russia refused to acknowledge their relationship or made any attempt to repatriate her remains. She was buried at taxpayer's expense on Hart Island, the New York equivalent of Potter's Field. Members of Susan Bryant's unit of the CIA observed the burial. This information came by way of Max Cooper, although the reasoning behind the post-mortem surveillance, or how it played out, was no longer a concern for O'Malley. His reason for being focused solely on gathering the strength and endurance for the resurrection of a waterfront cottage in the shadow of the White Mountains, a vow he was determined to keep.

Kris traveled to County Kerry in the company and at the request of Margaret O'Sullivan. The woman who remained in a perpetual state of mourning over the loss of her husband three years earlier returned to Ireland bearing the unfathomable weight of her daughter's ashes. Kris stood at her side on the bridge at Killah West, and together they watched Sarah's ashes carried away by the ebb tide on a final journey down Killah Bay to the open sea. Margaret said she felt closer to Sarah in Ireland, and to a god she needed more than ever.

Kris stayed with her throughout the afternoon and they shared a pot of tea at the Park Hotel, walked down through the village, sat on a bench in the enclosed garden at the square and the moments of tears and words and silence moved seamlessly, one upon the other and the image of the woman with her heart so thoroughly and inconceivably broken would remain with her always.

The following morning, she boarded the shuttle bus for the Aran Islands ferry in front of the Victoria Hotel on Queen Street in Galway. Kris was at the end of the queue behind a handful of islanders, and three American tourists still reeling from a night in the Queen Street Pub. The tourists congregated in the first few rows of seats near the driver while the islanders paired off with family or neighbors. Kris walked the length of the bus to the last row and sat by herself next to the window. Ten minutes later the bus pulled away from the curb and merged with traffic coming away from Eyre Square, moving slowly past the Galway Docks and across the Wolfe Tone Bridge to Father Griffin's Road towards Salthill.

They traveled parallel to the Seapoint Promenade, passing walkers with dogs, a scattering of runners, and empty benches facing out towards Galway Bay. A lone swimmer braved the frigid sea along the base of the Blackrock Beach diving tower, and thirty minutes into the journey the bus ventured beyond the outskirts of Galway into the wide open of Connemara, the driver whistling a delicate and vaguely familiar Irish melody.

Kris watched the boglands roll past, the stark and evocative landscape assuming a presence of its own under a dark, moody sky. Her thoughts turned to Sam and instantly retreated with a quiver and a single breathless moment, and there was never a time when the reaction would have been different, and she had learned to accept the flashes of memory for what they are and more importantly, for what they could never be. She pulled up the hood of her sweatshirt, leaned back in the seat and closed her eyes.

At Rossaveal, the Americans headed for the ferry bound for Inis Mor, and Kris walked down the ramp leading to the smaller vessel that services Inis Meain and Inis Oirr. The islanders from the bus had crossed the metal gangplank ahead of her and were soon joined by another group on their way back to Inis Oirr with boxes of canned goods and produce from a shopping excursion to Galway. Kris dropped her bag inside the cabin and went back out to the lower deck to sit on a wooden bench with her back against the bulkhead and remained there while the ferry made its way out of the harbor to the open sea.

The harsh sound of the diesel engine and the chaotic rise and fall of the ferry assured her of complete solitude for the crossing, and when Inis Meain was close enough to pick out familiar landmarks, she retrieved her bag from the passenger cabin and hauled it rung by rung up the metal ladder onto the upper deck of the ferry. The morning was clear and cool, her windswept hair everywhere at once and in the distance the silhouette of her grandmother's cottage stood at the edge of highest bluff on the island, and she couldn't take her eyes off it.

The ferry slowed as it approached Inis Meain and slipped cautiously between the sea wall and the imposing concrete pier to make a slow, careful turn within the narrow sanctuary that serves as a harbor. A controlled drift placed the ferry alongside the pier, and mooring lines were tossed to the island's beekeeper who tied them off to short, metal bollards and the gangplank was quickly positioned to bridge the gap between ferry and pier.

Kris recognized the ferry crew as residents of Inis Oirr, as well as Mic Conner, the young ferry captain who had fought so hard and succeeded in getting her ashore on that first stormy night, which now seemed so long ago. Mic stood in the doorway of the wheelhouse and while Kris disembarked, the beekeeper handed off a shipment of honey bound for Galway.

Within moments the gangplank was hauled aboard again, the mooring lines released by the beekeeper, and the ferry floated away from the pier with its deep throated diesel barely audible above the wind. Kris adjusted the straps on her bag and slung it over her shoulder. The beekeeper offered a lift to the upper island in his battered, yellow van, but she preferred to walk, needed to walk.

The road hugged the shoreline on one side and bordered a patchwork of small enclosed plots of land on the other. Some held the occasional goat, a donkey or a garden patch lying dormant under a blanket of fresh seaweed. A currach was perched above a sandy inlet within dragging distance of the high water mark, and a lone seagull worked the shoreline ahead of the rising tide.

The likelihood of meeting anyone between the pier and the cottage was slim, and one of the things she loved about the island, along with a lifestyle that offers safe haven for those willing to accept the terms and circumstance of living on the edge of the sea, the anglicized tongue and the tender mercy of solitude.

Kris turned away from the shoreline and lost the wind to the stonewalls of a lane she had walked many times and always with a sense of relief, a knowing that each step was an escape from the outside world. Although, this time was different with the illusion of escape forced to bear its own weight and the familiar offered little protection from what accompanied her ashore. It was warm between the stone walls, and the sound of breakers pounding the cliffs of the outer island resonated on the wind, and she moved up the lane at an ever increasing pace through the twists, turns and switchbacks until she was standing at a gap in the stonewall, the studio a few meters beyond and the thought of entering suddenly repulsive.

She stood as though stranded halfway between the pier and the cottage, halfway between who she was and who she had become, the one who creates and the one who kills, and the numbing sense of loss, at times vague, at times profound was everywhere at once. She remained motionless until the pain subsided, and the fog of guilt dispersed within the restless winds of Inis Meain and should redemption be a final destination, the only certainty was that she would arrive alone.

About the Author

Sam Montana is an expat American writer living on the Beara Peninsula in the West of Ireland.

Lightning Source UK Ltd.
Milton Keynes UK
UKHW012258220520
363742UK00008B/260

9 780989 461481